TIED
TO
DECEIT

NEENA H. BRAR

Penguide Books

Cover Design: Penguide Books

First Edition, 2018

ISBN: 978-1-7751580-3-5 | 978-1-7751580-3-5

Printed in United States of America

Registration Number: 1139167
Type: Copyright
Author: Brar, Neena.H
Registration Date: 2017-04-03

PENGUIDE BOOKS 2018

PUBLISHER'S NOTE:

For my parents,
who saw a dream for me and held fast to it.

There is a Smile of Love

And there is a Smile of Deceit

And there is a Smile of Smiles

In which these two Smiles meet

—*The Smile*, **William Blake**

BOOK 1

"God has given you one face, and you make yourselves another."

—*Hamlet,* William Shakespeare

Chapter 1

"Remembering is only a new form of suffering."

—Charles Baudelaire

On the evening of Monday, 4 August, nine days before the killing, Gayatri Bhardwaj had interrupted her philandering husband's secret rendezvous with a woman half his age. The murder was approaching its first anniversary, in four days' time, and now Gayatri regretfully understood that her seemingly accidental discovery of her husband's adultery had in fact been a calculated act – efficiently planned and effectively carried out. This event designed by the astute perpetrator, had set the stage for the murder.

That day had been an ordinary monsoon day in the hill town of Sanover, which is enclosed by the spectacular Himalayas and the dense forest of *deodar* and blue pine all around. The town, despite having all the comforts of the present day, still possessed the old-world charm; it was a place still largely unaffected by modern life, people's faith was simple, beliefs primitive, and traditions hard to comprehend. It stayed quiet for most of the time during the year, except for the winter months when its peace vanished and it was transformed into a bustling hub for tourists from all around the country and abroad.

On a clear summer night, one could see nearby cities' lights in the distance. The main market lay in the center of the town and was easily accessible from every part. There were paved streets with houses on both sides, where women sat behind their windows or on the front steps to watch neighbours and strangers. Stray dogs roamed around looking for food during the day and guarded the streets at nights. Children marched the narrow alleys in the mornings, their backs bent with heavy school bags, and played cricket in the evenings.

The night before, it had rained heavily. Gayatri Bhardwaj, unable to sleep, had spent the night tossing and turning in her bed, listening to torrents of rain, while the wild wind howled through the vast woods, and envying her husband of twenty-four years for sleeping unperturbedly throughout the storm. If she could have foreseen the future, she would have intertwined that night with the impending catastrophes in her life.

A heavy mist hung around the distant Himalayas in the early morning light. Occasionally, the clouds lifted sufficiently to expose the lush green peaks of the mountains in the distance.

Dr. Rajinder Bhardwaj's family had generations of aristocracy behind them and abundant money. Dr. Bhardwaj's great-grandfather had laid the foundations of his two-hundred-year-old house when he had bought the land and the surrounding forest. His successors had built a *haveli* there, which had been reconstructed by Dr. Bhardwaj's father, and later Dr. Bhardwaj had added one more storey to it. It stood in four acres on the outskirts of Sanover, overlooking lush mountains and surrounded on one side by the intimidating *deodars*, and on the other side by the sturdy pines which had a bluish hue from a distance, especially on a windy day when the breeze upturned their spines.

Dr. Rajinder Bhardwaj, the owner and the head physician at Lifeline Hospital, Sanover, had showered after his brisk morning walk and joined his wife for an early morning tea. Gayatri Bhardwaj sat with her second cup of ginger tea on her favourite old, worn, woven chair on the verandah which overlooked their front garden: a tapestry of blooming carnations, marigolds, roses, and chrysanthemums. She longed for a clear, bright day and the dazzling blue sky of summer.

It was her favourite spot to sit in the mornings; a place from where she could witness the brilliant dawn streaking half of the sky coral; raindrops soaking everything wet during the monsoon; specks of silvery snow falling from the sky during winter. She could take in everything from the serene mountain peaks and the forest to their house—its roof, windowpanes, and the pebbled driveway that snaked its way criss-cross toward the outside big iron gate. She would sit there until Dr. Bhardwaj joined her after his daily ritual of a brisk morning walk.

They had done this for years despite the changing seasons and the changing equation of their marital relationship. They had spent endless mornings of their initial married years there, when their hearts were still giddy with the feeling of young love, and they would talk about everything and nothing. She'd been a bride at barely twenty, young and naive. He'd been ten years her senior, already on the way to establishing himself as a successful physician, the younger son of a landlord aristocratic family with old wealth. He had swept her off her feet then, and was all charm and charisma but then the magic slowly diminished and finally died due to his secret betrayals over time. Thousands of little resentments had replaced the early warmth. But their hearts, although heavy with bitterness and anger at the failed expectations, had gotten used to the solace of each other's company that often comes with years of living together, and they never stopped performing this morning ritual of their married life.

Their morning on that day did not differ from their usual mornings. They had sat together in customary silence sipping their hot tea, marvelling at the brilliance of the monsoon foliage in the distance until the morning paper arrived. He started reading the news while she quietly watched his profile.

Now a year later, she remembered looking at him and thinking how he had shrunk an inch or two with age, but otherwise he looked the same as he always did except for the shock of his thick, close-cropped hair that had turned white, how his face was still handsome despite somewhat irregular features: a nose too big and thin lips getting thinner with age. She had marvelled at his vitality, his youthful appearance, and the fact that he had changed little despite the passing years. He looked forty-five, her age; a full ten years younger than his actual fifty-five. She remembered secretly envying him for that. He was one of those men who had the advantage of aging slowly.

At the time, of course, their morning chitchat was both ordinary and rather dull.

"You seem quiet today, and beat," he remarked sipping his lemon tea.

Like his fellow peers, he had little or no clue about what went on in his wife's mind most of the time and he mostly, if not entirely, put his faith in her verbal replies alone.

His voice brought her out of her thoughts. She replied, "I could not sleep well because of the storm."

"Hmmmm." Satisfied, he was lost in his newspaper again.

Sometimes, he suspected his wife of turning a blind eye to his infidelities, but mostly he assumed her to be blissfully ignorant of his consecutive casual affairs that had occurred during the last two decades.

His tea finished and his newspaper read, Dr. Bhardwaj, unaware of the impending catastrophe that would fall later that day, left for the hospital.

Gayatri Bhardwaj had a busy day ahead. She had a wedding to attend in two hours, and later in the evening one of her friends who had recently opened her designer-clothing store in Shimla had invited her for the store's inauguration ceremony. She had attended the wedding, which was a grand affair as it was the wedding of one of her close friends, Mrs. Tandon's only son, who had returned from London after finishing his business degree. She had spent only an hour at the venue, owing to her splitting headache, and had returned home. In the afternoon, she sat down to go through the day's mail. Among the usual envelopes, there was another anonymous letter. She remembered eyeing it with dread and reading it. She still had it in her hands when suddenly Rudra had approached her.

Now almost a year later, on Thursday, 31 July 1975, the memory of that morning lay buried in her mind after the crucial events that followed, but gradually the images resurfaced in her mind, bringing with them a terrible sense of foreboding and unease, and altering her perception of what had since happened.

The dim and blurred image of Rudra walking toward her became clear in her mind. She saw him striding toward her in his faded blue jeans and plain white shirt, silhouetted against the misty backdrop of that monsoon afternoon carrying a foreboding aura around him. With the smug face and insolent look he habitually wore when near her, he had asked for the keys to her and her husband's villa in New Kanauji which they had bought last year before *Diwali*. She went to the villa herself, the action that Rudra's arrogance had prompted and which she had regretted later. He had merely shrugged his shoulders and left then. The visual image of that event brought a sorry smile to her face.

It was an ordinary white envelope that arrived with the usual post on the afternoon of Monday, 4 August 1974. It had Mrs. Gayatri Bhardwaj written in plain black letters at the top right corner, under which the word 'urgent' was inscribed in large bold letters in red, clearly to generate curiosity, and it proved to be the case, as it caught Gayatri Bhardwaj's attention at once, when she saw it among the pile of junk letters. Eyeing it suspiciously, she sliced it open. Inside the envelope there was a pink piece of paper, neatly folded.

The note was sloppy with the writing all pouring into the right side of the page. The writing was childish, and the words badly spelled. The sender had written to say that at around six in the evening, Dr. Bhardwaj would meet someone at their villa in New Kanauji to have one of his usual relaxed evenings and, for a change, Mrs. Bhardwaj should surprise him by making an unannounced arrival there. The message was subtle, but in no way inconspicuous. She checked the time on her wristwatch, which was an exquisite affair of twenty-two-carat gold and tiny sparkling diamonds. It was a quarter to three in the afternoon.

She read the note a few times, wondering about the person who had written it. The sloppiness and the uneven childish scrawl seemed to be a conscious attempt to disguise the identity of the sender, but the infantile scribbles were at odds with the wording, which was anything but uneducated. The sender could've engineered the contrast on purpose, mused Gayatri, but for what purpose she couldn't fathom. Using illiterate phrasing would have been a simple way to cover the sender's tracks, if he or she was an educated, bright person, but the sender hadn't done that. It could be someone from the hospital, thought Gayatri. She scrutinized the envelope carefully. There was no stamp and no return address written anywhere to suggest the identity of the sender. One thing was for sure, she thought, the envelope had been hand delivered, and the sender knew what time the post was collected from the letter box on the main gate. The way the envelope had Gayatri's name written on it, instead of the full address, pointed to someone who knew the Bhardwaj household's usual routine well, and who was sure that the envelope would reach Gayatri's hands instead of Dr. Bhardwaj's.

Could the sender have assumed, thought Gayatri, that she had been living entirely in oblivion, unaware of her husband's philandering? But then she had always kept up the facade of being happily married. They both had kept up their own facades: Dr. Bhardwaj to suit his purposes, and her to get through life and to feel in control. She understood his need for disguise, as she hid behind a disguise too: the disguise of a cool, poised exterior. The woman underneath, she knew, was afraid of losing control. They both had worn their masks for so long that their veiled sides had mingled with the real ones. Did the sender know, and wanted to see their masks coming off, wondered Gayatri?

The note wasn't the first of its kind. She had received three other letters in the past two months. However, those notes had no such explicit information about Dr. Bhardwaj's clandestine meetings. This time, perhaps someone was eager to see Dr. Bhardwaj in a tight spot, or else it could be someone who wanted to see her in distress, she concluded. The thought that it could be a well-wisher didn't cross her mind. She was too cynical to expect kindness for free. For a moment, she felt tempted to check on her husband but then brushed the thought aside. Whoever the sender was, whatever purpose it served them, Gayatri had no intention of gratifying them, and giving them the satisfaction they had anticipated.

She never had any illusions about her husband's philandering. Having been his wife for over two decades, she knew him inside and out. After spending the first four years of their marriage in happy ignorance and bliss, when the first glow of romance had worn off, Gayatri had understood that the word 'loyalty' did not mean unswerving devotion in Dr. Bhardwaj's opinion. He had an undying aptitude for seducing the prettiest and the most gullible of the young female staff. Despite being a curious woman, she had purposely avoided prying on him. The realization was just a matter of awakening to the truth which the mind already knew. The realization that he had not been entirely faithful to her gradually dawned on her, but she had no intention of agonizing over it. She understood that the unbridled truth could be harsh and painful, and she wasn't a worshipper of it anyway.

She knew the women he cheated with were a mere relief for his boredom. They were just sexual objects in his eyes, a means to indulge his puffed-up male ego. He was not bothered about their individuality, as they were all the same for him. She knew at the end of the day he had no desire for burning passion. Instead, he needed to come home to that which was familiar and secure.

After spending the next ten years in constant hope and despair, she had learned she was not destined for motherhood. But Gayatri was a woman of great practicality and little emotion. The things that perturbed average women barely touched her. A child might have evoked underlying gentleness and sensitivity in her, but a child she could not conceive. Inwardly, she compensated for her barrenness by ignoring her husband's intermittent flings. Without comprehending the need for emotional depth in her marriage, she attended to her wifely duties.

She appreciated the power of money, for she had come from a family of lesser means. A thousand things kept her busy. She was engaged in activities that a woman of complex emotions and fragile feelings would have considered futile in her situation. She was actively involved in running NGOs, attended various charities, sat on the committees of prestigious family-administered schools and a college for girls, and attended administrative meetings at the Lifeline Hospital. She loved the power of her husband's money and the status it had given her.

During all those years, the thought of adopting a child never crossed their minds. They both belonged to a generation that found adopting outside their extended family obnoxious. Gayatri could not imagine herself loving and raising someone else's child as her own. As far as Dr. Bhardwaj was concerned, he considered Rudra Bhardwaj—son of his late elder brother—his heir, and knew he would carry their Bhardwaj family name ahead.

Rudra was already a grown man by the time he became part of his uncle's family. The affection that came easily to Dr. Bhardwaj, Gayatri could not develop. She knew her husband saw him as his heir, but then there was her own paternal family—her nephews and nieces—and she had no intention of letting everything they owned go to Rudra alone.

Gayatri still had the letter in her hand when Rudra approached her. It was unusual for him to come to see her alone. She folded the letter calmly and slid it back inside the envelope.

Without preamble, he said, "*Chachi*, I want the keys to the Kanauji villa for a few days."

"Why? Subhadra already getting on your nerves?" she couldn't help but taunt him. It didn't help that she was currently in a bad mood; she had never liked him.

A hint of anger flashed in his dark-brown eyes, but when he spoke his tone was unruffled. "Mothers tend to, although I get along fine with Mummy. You're not a mother, but you have a mother, so you know that."

The cruelty underneath his words hit her hard. He had touched a raw spot. She looked at him and saw in his eyes the persistent gleam of amused mockery.

"I need the place for myself. You have to wait until next week if you want the keys," she said in a rigid tone.

"How about just for tonight?"

"Next week," she said in a flat tone.

He shrugged. "Well, as you wish." He turned and left.

His coolness enraged Gayatri. She felt a strong urge to hurt someone. Still reeling with anger, she looked at the envelope in her hands and decided to go to the villa that evening.

This offhand decision of Gayatri had set things in motion for the murder and all the unfortunate happenings afterwards.

She had acted in rage prompted by her own hatred for him. Had she been a different person, more tolerant and kinder, things might have been different. She could have tried harder to accept Rudra as her own, stayed unaffected by his haughtiness, and chosen not to go to the villa that day—avoiding the embarrassing confrontation.

Chapter 2

"Doubt is an uncomfortable condition,
but certainty is a ridiculous one."

—Voltaire

Every time there was a woman, Gayatri had known instinctively—but that was a thing of the past; the time when she still cared. It was as much Gayatri's natural instinctiveness, as Dr. Bhardwaj's obvious guilt. At those times, he would look energetic, somehow more vigorous, and youthful. He would be charming, caring, and attentive to her needs. The pattern never varied, and would make her suspicious. She would look for signs of his deceits, instead of prying, which scared her as she could cause untold and grave hurt to herself. She would indulge in imaginary situations where she caught him red-handed, and he refused to let the other woman go. The fear she could lose everything to some unknown, insignificant rival would agonize her for months.

But all of that misery was a thing of the past. She only cared about their reputation, status, and family name. He could die tomorrow as far as she was concerned, provided he died respectfully.

On the way to the villa, she kept wondering about the woman with whom he was involved nowadays. She couldn't be from Sanover, Gayatri told herself, where one's business was everyone's business. She knew he had his reputation and his status to keep intact. He had always been careful in the past, but if he wasn't this time . . . the thought made her shudder.

Although she had somewhat expected it, finding her husband's car on the porch surprised her. It was past six in the evening. Despite being aware of her husband's nature, she had half convinced herself that the note was a lie. She tried to push the door open, but it was locked from inside. That was when she knew with absolute certainty what was awaiting her. She thought about turning back, but her hands already refused to take command from her brain and she fumbled inside her purse to find the keys. Without a thought, she impulsively turned the key in the lock, shut the door behind her, and scanned the pale-white gallery and rooms beyond. She walked toward the smaller bedroom on her right, the only room with the door closed, paused for a fraction of a second, and pushed the door open.

She saw him first, and their eyes met. She saw a look of incredulity pass over his face, followed by shock mingled with shame and fear.

Then she noticed the woman, a creamy-white face framed with black curls, from which a pair of heavy-lidded charcoal eyes lazily stared at her. The room smelled of raw, savage sex—the unmistakable smell of passion mingled with body sweat. Gayatri stood there taking in the sight of the wrinkled bed cover, their clothes lying in a pile on the adjacent chair, and one flowered pillow in winter grey on the floor—part of a set she remembered buying from the handloom khadi bhandar last spring. Next to the pillow was her husband's hastily discarded white shirt, one of many she had seen Leela kaki carefully iron each morning with precision and tenderness, instinctive to a servant who had lived and served long enough to become a part of the master's family. The orange glow of the fading evening sun seeped in from the thin partition of the drawn curtain. The air felt heavy with their collective breathing. Gayatri was aware of the silence that had fallen in the room. The woman looked so young, lying there, naked and uninhibited. Her husband had pushed himself out of the bed and started pulling on his pants. Gayatri was aware of him, shamefaced and embarrassed, as he clumsily put on his shirt.

Gayatri stood frozen, transfixed by the unsurprised stare of the woman's heavily kohl-lined eyes. There was something about her, in the shape of her face, that made Gayatri realize that she had seen her somewhere, but she couldn't remember where. As the woman sat there, her beauty—exotic and absolute—disgusted Gayatri. Aware of her husband, who had finished dressing, walking toward her, she felt a wave of nausea and dizziness pass over her. She stumbled forward but steadied herself in time to push her husband's approaching hand away weakly.

A sense of recognition rippled through Gayatri's mind; with her eyes closed she tried to remember the woman's name. She was sure she had met her somewhere, but she could not remember when and where. She tried to think. Could she have met her through her family-run NGO for women, Aasra? He could not have lowered himself to that level. Those women were all from the lower section of society, at the bottom of the social ladder. Could he have found one among them to take to his bed? She opened her eyes and stared at the girl's face again. It came to her then. She was Devika, Devika Singh, an employee at her husband's hospital. After realizing she wasn't from Aasra, Gayatri gave a sigh of relief and laughed inwardly at her prejudiced vanity which she still wasn't ready to give up.

Her husband mumbled something that she could not understand in her reverie; she saw the woman stirring in the bed, leaning sideways to pick up her *kurta* from the chair, her breasts as full and heavy as a new mother's. Instead of putting on her *kurta*, she got out of bed, stood there unembarrassed, her gaze still intent on Gayatri's face, her body slightly bent in a provocative position as if in exhibition. She lazily got her other clothes from the chair as well, and started putting them on, finally. Gayatri stood there in a trance, taking everything in as if something unreal was happening and was unfolding gradually.

Finally dressed in a yellow *churidar*, a short, fitted *kurta*, and double-died matching *dupatta*, she took a few steps toward Gayatri and stood facing her. A whiff of lavender blossoms mixed with something lemony caught Gayatri—her scent.

She spoke to Gayatri directly, "It is good you have seen us together. He was about to tell you anyways. Right, Rajinder?" With a hint of half-sarcasm and half-humour, she turned to face Dr. Bhardwaj.

Gayatri, still dazed with shock, looked at her husband, whose face had turned ashen white. She saw a look, familiar and long-forgotten, pass over his face: a look of pain, of agony, and of mournful acceptance of loss, from after she had lost their third and consecutively last unborn child in her womb. The memory, faded and buried long ago, brought back all the pain, agony, and misery of the past she had buried deep somewhere inside her heart. Her wound, old but raw underneath, throbbed with the pain of the resurfaced memories. She did not want to think about that now.

"There is nothing to tell, nothing important that she needs to know." She heard him addressing the woman, his voice formal, devoid of emotions, but his face still bore the same expression of pain.

"Really? Whatever we had was never important to you? You could not keep your hands away from me during all this time." A chilling harshness had crept into Devika's voice. "You thought I had no clue. I saw through your disguise long ago. Why do you think I accepted all the fineries? Not as gifts. You owed them to me. I am sure you are not dumb enough to believe I have been sharing your bed for the sake of my pleasure."

"I would like you to leave," he said in a firm voice.

The dark eyes burned with hate. When Devika spoke, her tone was threatening.

"As if I care to stay, but there is one thing left . . ."

She looked at Dr. Bhardwaj with such hatred he flinched instinctively.

"I am carrying your child. Let me know what to do about that." She almost whispered the last line. Without bothering to wait for his reply, she stormed out—slamming the door so hard that the tapestry fell off the wall.

Too numb to speak until now, Devika's last few words brought Gayatri out of her stupor. She looked at him and said, "I would have thought you'd have had more pride than to get involved with a woman like her."

"It was not important, Gayatri. It was nothing."

"Hasn't my life been burdened enough with past miseries, Raj? Why did you have to do this?"

"I know I made a mistake. I never wanted to hurt you, but she would not leave me alone."

He sat slumped in the chair, staring at the floor.

"Really, Raj? Were you born yesterday? For God's sake, she is nobody. Women like her come to Aasra every day. Let me spell it out for you, goddamnit, A-A-S-R-A. Do you have any idea what kind of homes these women come from? Don't try to defend your lies, Raj, not now."

"Don't be such a stuck-up, Gayatri. And she's not from Aasra. Don't talk like that. It doesn't suit you."

"Talk like what? What about you, Mr. Righteous? You dared to bring her here, in my home, in my bed, for God's sake." A note of hysteria had crept into her voice.

He stayed quiet, which angered her more. "You bought this villa so you could have a place to entertain yourself. How long has all this been going on? Tell me. Weeks? Months? Years? Is she the only one or are there others?" she shrieked.

"Gayatri, please calm down. Believe me. It happened a few times only. I must have been mad to fall into her trap."

"Don't you dare tell me that she trapped you—I never imagined you would stoop that low! An everyday tramp like her, and you brought her here in this house, in my bedroom." She paced around the room in a manic frenzy.

"Imagine a headline in tomorrow's paper: 'Doctor Rajinder Bhardwaj, a Doon School graduate, caught fornicating with a commonplace whore.' God! You would be a legend in the history of Sanover."

Dr. Bhardwaj tried to hold her hand, but she pushed him with such vehemence that he withdrew his hand on impulse.

"And what are you going to do now? You will be a father," she said, laughing bitterly. She kneeled on the floor. "I imagine my respected father-in-law will be brimming with happiness now, sitting there in heaven. He must be proud of his capable son, Doctor Rajinder Bhardwaj who will soon father a bastard, a bastard, with a whore. My father-in-law, who had disowned his other son for marrying a girl from another caste."

She slumped down on the floor and covered her face with her hands. The humiliation had brought out all her smouldering anger. She had stopped caring about other women in his life a long time ago, but the thought of another woman carrying his child enraged her. She had ignored his unfaithfulness. Today's confrontation brought out all the anger she had buried deep inside her heart. She always considered herself to be in control of her emotions, but she was wrong. She hated herself now for being so weak and helpless and for behaving like a petty lower-class woman.

He leaned toward her and tried to take her in his arms, but she pushed him away again.

Crying softly, she said, "Please go away. Leave me alone. I want to be alone."

She covered her face again and heard him close the door. She went across to the window, stood looking out onto the empty road, and watched him walk to his car. He looked diminished, beaten and old. Was he hurting as much as she was? Was he grieving the loss of their unborn children or the child that Devika was carrying, the child who could never become part of his life? Was he sorry that he had to let that woman go?

Time heals everything, that's what everyone says. Wounds heal and leave only scars behind. But some wounds run too deep to heal, and pierce the deepest layers of one's soul. They stay there unhealed and ready to ooze blood at the first sign of grief. The hurt she felt today unlocked old wounds. The memory of the morning when she had lost her last unborn child came to her. Strangely, the only thing she remembered was the hospital bed, the room, the distinctive hospital smell of that day. The vivid details of that morning, of those days, weeks, and months afterwards did not come to her. Her mind acknowledged there was a horrible pain, an agonizing affliction, an ache in her heart for months; throbbing and unbearable at the beginning, but dulling gradually with time— yet it never went away completely. Although she couldn't recall the exact intensity of her grief, the knowledge that this sorrow had shadowed her life at that time was sorted, documented, and locked up somewhere in her mind's registry with other memories. The mere fact she had suffered that immense loss intensified her existing anguish. She grieved for her past miseries, which seemed extensive compared to her present heartache. And when there were no tears left, she wondered how the sheer despair never failed to surprise her each time she encountered it, and how it felt so raw and shocking.

She could not get Devika's words out of her mind. Was she lying about the child? If not, what was her plan? Her heart thumped in her chest. She felt anguish thinking about what it could do to her life—their life, their reputation, their prestige. All she wanted was to lose herself in oblivion, forget everything, but she knew she couldn't afford to mull over his shame and her desolation when the timing was so crucial. Devika couldn't be allowed to give birth to her husband's bastard.

She knew something had to be done to stop Devika. She had to know how far along Devika was in her pregnancy. The desperate time called for desperate measures, she knew, and she also knew she had to get herself ready for that.

She walked outside, locking the door behind her, and strode out to her car with determined steps.

Chapter 3

*"The habits of life form the soul, and
the soul forms the countenance."*

—Honoré de Balzac

Dr. Rudra Bhardwaj had spent his childhood in poverty, unlike his father and his father's father who had the pleasure of being born into a privileged family of aristocrats. Unlike his predecessors, he had lost his inheritance before his birth owing to his father Rameshwar Bhardwaj's decision to marry Rudra's mother, a low-caste girl belonging to a Chamang family. Rameshwar Bhardwaj had met her in university during his Master of Arts in drama, the course which was an intended act of rebellion against his father's orthodox beliefs.

Being a high-class rigid Brahmin, at the pinnacle of the caste pyramid, Rameshwar's father refused to let his wife perform the *greh-pervesh* ceremony for the new bride whom his son had brought home after marrying in a small temple in the presence of their mutual university friends without the consent of the immediate family. He had disowned him on the spot.

Being a rebel and an idealist, Rameshwar Bhardwaj never set foot in his father's house again. He never mentioned his parents and brother in front of Rudra. He went to Bombay to try his luck in the theater but didn't succeed. He moved back to his wife's hometown near Guwahati, and gave private tuition with her, and together they made barely enough money to keep their small family, but he was too proud and vain to accept any financial help from his younger brother. Having been born into a privileged family, he was not used to the daily struggles of the common man, and lost his passion and dreams, went into major depression, and died as an undistinguished man.

After Rudra's father's death, his uncle, Rajinder Bhardwaj, came to attend the funeral. He had offered financial help that the proud widow of his brother refused. Rudra, who knew about his distinguished lineage was too young to understand these things. Later, when he was old enough to understand, the loss of his rightful inheritance pained him deeply.

Rudra had a sharp academic mind and was accepted into a medical college. His mother could barely afford his MBBS fees. He wanted to get financial help from his uncle, but Subhadra Bhardwaj was dead against the idea. She refused to hear about it. The issue became a bone of contention between mother and son. She sent him to the medical college, somehow, but Rudra stopped visiting her. Afterwards, he joined a small practice with two other doctors, but that lasted a year only. Prior to his move to that group practice, he worked for a year in a small rural hospital near Shimla, close to Sanover, hoping to join his uncle's hospital, but he was too proud to ask for a job. He visited his uncle a few times but never could accept him and his wife as one of the close family members. The future seemed dim to him. His hopes of establishing himself as a reputed doctor and running his own hospital had diminished.

Realizing that his uncle seemingly had no intention of ever asking him to join his hospital in Sanover, Rudra moved away from that part of the state. He knew he had to find his path. He stopped visiting his uncle. It was only after eight years, during his visit to Subhadra Bhardwaj, that Dr. Rajinder

Bhardwaj expressed his wish for Rudra to join his hospital in Sanover. Rudra had mostly stayed away from his mother. He would visit her once a year, but that was the extent of their interaction. She passed on Dr. Rajinder's message to Rudra when he came to visit her in July of that year. To her dismay, he wasted no time in accepting the offer.

He joined the Lifeline Hospital as a physician and could see his dreams turning into reality. However, that was just the first step toward his next goal—to open his own hospital in a big city. Rudra had high ambitions, and settling in a town was not part of the plan.

In a cramped, small bedroom that faced the backyard, Subhadra Bhardwaj had sat on her bed ready to unwind for the night. Rudra sat down beside his mother.

She looked at her son and thought she was looking at some stranger. She did not understand what kind of person he'd become in all these years living away from her. She didn't know him anymore. But then he had always been like that, she realized: unhappy, materialistic, and hardened. His dreams revolved around money. He aspired to nothing but wealth. They hadn't seen each other much during his stay at the medical college in Shimla. He had told her it was hard for him to visit because of the long distance between Guwahati and Shimla. She had hoped that he would do his residency in Guwahati or a nearby city, but he had opted to stay in the north. Afterwards, he didn't ask her to come and stay with him, and she had no desire to leave her hometown. This was the first time she had come to stay with him in Sanover.

It was Tuesday, 5 August and she was leaving for Guwahati the next morning, merely five days after her arrival. He had asked her insistently for this visit. For a time, she had taken secret pleasure in the thought he wanted his mother around, but soon he had revealed the real reason for his invitation. He wanted her to talk to his uncle Dr. Rajinder Bhardwaj and ask for money, so he could open his own hospital in Shimla. But Subhadra Bhardwaj had no intention of asking for any monetary favours from her brother-in-law, and she had made it clear to her son. He had tried to persuade her but to no avail. She had her return ticket booked within five days of her arrival and had no intention of prolonging her trip further.

"I already told you, I will not talk to Rajinder *bhai saab* about money. It does not feel right, Rudra. Your daddy was a proud person. We faced many hardships, but he took no one's help."

"Daddy was susceptible and impractical. Don't forget, he was born into money, Mummy. No wonder he did not understand what a privilege it was to be born in luxury. And that was the reason he rejected it altogether, damned it all. I am not Daddy. I never can be like him. How could I be like him?" He looked at his mother who sat staring at him in desperation. Knowing her, he expected no answer and continued, "I did not get things on a silver platter the way he did. The value that the glamour, the small luxuries of life hold for the destitute could not have any value in the eyes of the rich. Daddy had no value for it, but I appreciate the value of money."

"Rajinder *bhai saab* considers you as his son, Rudra. He would do no wrong with you. Why can't you have patience? You are working at the hospital and earning enough. Don't forget he wanted to pay for your MBBS as well. He is doing everything your daddy would have done."

"Why didn't you let him pay then? All you cared about was your damn pride. Even now you hate it that I work for Rajinder *chacha ji*. Gayatri *chachi* never leaves a chance to remind me of their favours."

He understood his mother was proud and sentimental, so much like her late husband. That was the reason she never could understand his ambitions and his dreams. It irritated him when she devalued the worth of money. He had done what he wanted, and his mother had accepted it, though unwillingly. He might have stayed in one of his earlier, less lucrative, group practices, and his mother would have been happier. But he saw nothing wrong with getting back his inheritance, which was his in the first place.

"I don't know why you keep thinking like that, Rudra. I don't think Gayatri has anything like that in mind," said Subhadra.

Rudra replied, "She thinks *Chacha Ji* is doing me a favour."

"She is fine, I would say. She is a little haughty but kind and considerate. You just don't like her, that's all," she said.

"I cannot pretend that I like her, and I suppose you don't either, not much. Honestly, I am merely reciprocating her feelings. She does not like us much either."

"Why do you think that? I find her to be very nice. You share blood relation with Rajinder *bhai saab*. It's wrong to expect things from Gayatri."

"She never misses a chance to remind me of the reason why *Dada Ji* disowned Daddy. I hate it when she mentions your caste."

"People have practised endogamy for centuries in our country, Rudra. It is just natural that being a part of this society, her views mirror majorities. You are just being oversensitive."

"Do you think I feel proud to see you struggling, trying to make ends meet, making small housekeeping economies—watching the electricity bill, doing all the cleaning and laundry yourself to save a few rupees, walking to market instead of taking a rickshaw? I hate to see you living in that hole like a pauper. I feel guilty. I feel suffocated for you, Mummy."

"I never knew it affected you that much." A note of sarcasm had crept into Subhadra's voice. She couldn't help it.

"I didn't want you to leave the house which Daddy had built for us. Moreover, I always thought you were happy living near *Mausi*." He rose and paced back and forth. "Mummy, please don't start all this sentimental melodrama. You know

Neena H. Brar

you can come to live with me, if that's what you want," he said half-heartedly.

Ignoring his uninterested invitation, Subhadra Bhardwaj said, "Let's not argue further. I already told you my decision. I will not ask Rajinder *bhai saab* for money. I'm leaving tomorrow morning." She looked at him, her glance devoid of any emotion. "And you're right. I don't want to leave Guwahati. I'll stay there only."

He stopped pacing. He stood there facing her, his hands spread open in desperation. "What is wrong with asking for what's mine anyways, Mummy? I'm the rightful heir of half of the Bhardwaj property."

"For God's sake, Rudra, stop thinking like that. It pains me more than anything else to see you like this—unhappy and measuring everything by its relative value. Money is not everything, *Beta*. I fear you would lose your soul in this calculating pursuit of wealth. Rajinder *bhai saab* will make you his heir someday. He has implied his wish to me, indirectly though. You're earning enough to start your family. Think about getting married now."

"Do you think Gayatri *chachi* would let him do that? I cannot marry until I open my clinic."

"You know best, Rudra. But don't you think you are better off than many and happier as you are?"

He said, "No I'm not happy. I'm frustrated with my life. I agree money cannot buy me happiness, but it can help me bear miseries better. Life is never perfect, Mummy. There are hardships we are destined to face. Some we cannot avoid, but I want to be free of financial worries. And I'm talking about my money. *Dada Ji* took a decision in anger when Daddy married you. *Chacha Ji* himself should understand that. And then, I'm not asking for my full share. I need a part of it to start my clinic in Shimla. Why don't you try to look at it from my perspective? Just stop being absurd."

"Absurd?" said Subhadra, raising her eyebrows. "What has happened to you, Rudra? I'm sorry, but you are the one who

is being absurd. I only want you to be happy and to be comfortable."

He rose and walked over to the window. "I cannot be happy unless I lead a different life from the life of struggles and hardships I lead now; the life I was meant to have as heir of the Bhardwaj family."

"That's a pity, Rudra," said Subhadra, shaking her head with a regretful air. "I have to leave early tomorrow. I want to sleep now. It's a long journey. Don't forget to turn off the lights before you leave." She lay down on the bed and turned her back to him.

Seething with rage, Rudra turned off the lights and walked out, slamming the door behind him.

Chapter 4

*"To God all things are fair and good
and right, but men hold some things
wrong and some right."*

—Heraclitus

Looking at the empty chair at the head of the fine-grained oak plank which made up the eighteen-foot-long boardroom table at the Lifeline Hospital, new secretary Vineeta Dhirwan, a competent-looking girl with a plain face and a slight body who'd been employed a week ago, had been quietly listening to the conversation which was partially amusing and spiteful. The frantic chitchat came to an abrupt end as Dr. Bhardwaj entered the boardroom with his wife Gayatri Bhardwaj at twelve forty-five. They were fifteen minutes late; the emergency meeting had had to be started fifteen minutes early at half past twelve as scheduled in the morning. It had been called in the wake of a recent unfortunate incident where a young girl of seventeen had committed suicide after hospital receptionist Devika Singh made news of her unmarried pregnancy public.

Devika, who was in the dark about the objective of the meeting an hour before it, was infuriated to learn the meeting had been called to discuss a disciplinary action against her because of the role she had played in the suicidal death of the young patient. Vineeta asked her to wait outside. Devika was furious to see Gayatri Bhardwaj arrive with Dr. Bhardwaj for the meeting. Although it was not the first time she had attended an administrative meeting at the hospital, her arrival today seemed to Devika to be a calculated and clever tactic. Devika had been expecting a drastic step on Gayatri's side after the exposure of Dr. Bhardwaj's infidelity last week, but they were still together. With thunder in her eyes, she had looked at Dr. Bhardwaj, who had walked by unperturbed with a stony face. She was furious to see him oblivious to her presence as she had not seen him for over three days after that day's incident.

Deputy Medical Administrator, Dr. Sanjeev Kaundal, had difficulty concealing his annoyance that the lunch-hour break of his hectic day should have coincided with this emergency meeting. As an experienced and old doctor, he had seen many patients lose their lives. As a firm moralist, the death of the patient was less bothersome to him in the wake of another bigger sin—her unmarried pregnancy.

Mrs. Saroj Rani Jaiswal, one of the oldest, sternest, and experienced of the employees of Lifeline Hospital, was the head of the nursing staff, and today's meeting in her eyes was an apt act by the hospital management. She was a conventional person who believed in living up to her principles and had a reputation for integrity and fastidiousness at work. The slightest offence against those principles angered her. She was a kind soul, but her stern behaviour and lack of empathy for those who didn't live up to her pre-defined set of principles had earned her a reputation of being insensitive. Like many honest and straightforward people, she had a brutal way of stating facts, a quality which had earned her an additional unwarranted reputation for callousness.

She was a stern-looking, confident woman of around fifty-five. Those whom she favoured among the staff, the hard-working ones, she did so with complete, wholehearted devotion, and the ones she deemed unfit for their job, owing to their laziness or inefficiency, she would set to work with a vengeance to oust them. Devika Singh had scored the top position on her list of unworthy employees owing to her rudeness and lack of work ethic. Saroj Rani Jaiswal had reported Devika in the first place.

To Dr. Anju Trivedi, this meeting meant another episode of extreme emotional exhaustion. She was a young woman of twenty-six and a newer addition to the staff. Inexperienced and idealistic, she had a romantic notion of her job and held high and unrealistic hopes of altering the medical profession. She had been on duty when the family brought in the patient. She blamed herself for being intimidated by Devika who had insisted on calling the police first. Had she possessed more courage, she could have started treatment of the girl at once and saved her life. Now she sat guilt-ridden in the meeting, red-eyed and puffy-faced, with a nervous and rather abject air. It was awful to think she had played a part in the girl's death, however unintentionally, but she couldn't think otherwise. When a life had been at stake, she had failed in performing her duty as a doctor.

Dr. Namita Kaushik, who had been on duty the night before, had been called from home to attend the meeting and had been the last one to arrive. She was Gayatri Bhardwaj's close friend's daughter and held a soft spot in Gayatri's heart. There was talk about her possible marriage with Dr. Bhardwaj's nephew, Dr. Rudra Bhardwaj, whom Namita secretly held in awe.

There were others: Dr. Naresh, Anandmoorti Babu, Shobha Mangal, who were never part of any administrative meeting but had been asked to attend this one on instructions from Gayatri Bhardwaj.

Dr. Bhardwaj asked Vineeta to hand out the agenda of the meeting to everyone. The head nurse, who considered any formality a waste of time, stated the bare facts. For such a big woman, her voice was unusually soft.

"The patient, Kavita Asthana, was in a critical condition when the family brought her in. Miss Devika insisted on calling the police first before Dr. Anju could start treatment. By the time I arrived, she had already called the police from the front-desk telephone. We had no choice other than to wait for the police to carry out legal formalities first. When the police arrived, it was too late to do anything for the patient. Moreover, the police's involvement revealed the patient's unmarried pregnancy status and left the family to face the social stigma."

The head nurse then looked expectantly at Dr. Anju sitting right next to her. Taking a cue from her, Dr. Anju continued, "The patient was suffering from convulsions by the time I saw her. The family knew she had consumed rat poison and they informed us. I wanted to start treatment instantly, but Miss Devika insisted on calling the police first. The patient went into a coma. I could not do a single thing by the time the police arrived. I watched her die in front of my eyes," she said in a soft voice.

"Miss Devika should have known that the first and foremost duty of any health practitioner is to attend to the sick first. The life of a person is more important than the legal formalities," Gayatri Bhardwaj said dryly.

"As a matter of fact," stated the head nurse, true to her reputation of being meticulous, "only in the case of death by suicide, we must report the matter to the police for further investigation. If the patient is alive and suicide is suspected, we are not obligated to bring the matter to the police's notice."

"I don't see how Miss Devika could have broken any rule here. She was trying to abide by the law. Whatever happened was extremely unfortunate, but we all are aware the girl made her bed, and she had to lie in it." Dr. Sanjeev possessed the moral scruples of an average conventional person of the society. His antagonistic views about the whole situation infuriated all the women in the room, and they received his statement with downright hostility.

Gayatri Bhardwaj was the first one to protest. "So according to you, Dr. Sanjeev Kaundal, the bigger crime was the girl's unchastity rather than Miss Devika's inhuman approach?" The emphasis on a full name with prefix wasn't lost on Dr. Sanjeev, whom Gayatri had always called "Sanjeev *bhai saab.*"

"The notion of female chastity and virtue is not something new in our society. For centuries, we have associated this feminine virtue with the ideal female identity," said Dr. Sanjeev.

Trying to control her mounting anger, Dr. Namita, who strongly believed in female empowerment said, "Let's not forget the role of a man in this tragedy. The so-called divine goddess—the virtuous woman notion—has taken away women's most basic right of humanity, the right to equality. When unchastity is revealed, we people in this society reserve our apathy for the man and set about condemning the woman alone. How's that fair, Dr. Sanjeev?"

Dr. Sanjeev obstinately defended his opinion. "It's the moral obligation of a woman to protect her dignity. Besides, I am merely depicting the rules of our society."

Mrs. Shobha Mangal, who was very conservative in her approach, sided with Dr. Sanjeev. She said, "Dr. Sanjeev isn't wrong. To live in society, one must follow and abide by its social rules. There are certain norms that women practise in our society—observing modesty is the first and foremost of those. I was raised in strict discipline. I still remember my college days when we walked outside with lowered eyes. My mother would tell me to speak or laugh softly in the presence of strangers. But girls nowadays have forsaken those values. If that continues, then our society will go to pieces."

Gayatri Bhardwaj answered this time. "The rules of society are not written by God and can be changed. Things change with time eventually. We educated people at least should not fall into the category of those so-called advocates of traditional values who condemn women alone for unchastity." Turning to Shobha Mangal, she said, "The old-fashioned customs you're talking about which require us women to remain ever vigilant, and hinder our freedom of expression and thought, should not be encouraged while men go scot-free for actual debaucheries." She glanced at her husband, whose expression was hard to read as he sat there impassively, and went on, "We have come a long way from observing *sati partha* and the widow remarriage prohibition. These so-called rules have done nothing other than drive our society to delimit the worth of a woman."

"We live in a traditional country, ladies. Once pleasure is gone, the sting of the sin is that it leaves remnants behind here," said Dr. Sanjeev, who had no intention of yielding in an argument which in his eyes was pointless and wrong.

A heated discussion can kindle a bad temper, and Dr. Sanjeev's statement had provoked Dr. Anju's ill humour, who answered in a harsh voice, "We do not know what intolerable strain that poor child went through, which forced her to take that terrible decision. Dr. Sanjeev, let's not forget that Kavita was a mere child—barely seventeen. Now that she is not here, let's not gauge her conduct sitting here."

If the child had lived, she could have evoked contempt from many, but in death, she had found supporters who wanted to fight and win her battle. Her death had made all the difference. It had gained her the sympathy of strangers instead of their scorn.

Gayatri broke in, "I'm inclined to agree with you, Dr. Anju. But, even if we overlook Miss Devika's conduct here, you all would agree that the girl's death has brought out many supporters into the open. Miss Devika's callous disregard for the patient's condition has complicated the whole situation. People are questioning the hospital's role in the girl's death. They are planning to conduct protests outside the hospital. It will give the hospital a bad name. You must agree that the situation is rather delicate at the current moment."

Dr. Naresh, who had been a quiet spectator in the heated discussion, found an opportunity to contribute a few words offending no one. He said, "Our priority right now should be to save the hospital's name. For that, we need to calm down the protestors first."

Dr. Bhardwaj stepped in to stop the heated discussion that had irked everybody's mood in the room. Avoiding Gayatri's intent gaze at his face, he said, "Let's just stop here, ladies and gentlemen. We are not here to debate the societal rules of virtue. We are here to discuss the course of action against Miss Devika Singh." He looked at everyone before continuing. "Let's stick with that. We all agree that a doctor's—and any other medical staff's—duty is to attend to the injuries of the person first. The primary effort should be to save the life of the patient, and then inform the police. That's the rule we have always followed in our hospital. Miss Devika Singh failed to comply with that simple and basic rule. I suggest she be dismissed with one month's pay, according to our policy. I would like to know everyone's opinion about that."

Gayatri Bhardwaj was first to reply. "We know that Miss Devika Singh was unprofessional and ethically wrong. Not only did she hinder the treatment, but she also spread the news of the girl's unmarried pregnancy without reserve. The family is left to face the social stigma for life. I agree with Rajinder's proposal."

The head nurse, Dr. Rudra, and Dr. Namita were the first ones to nod in agreement. The others followed their lead. Dr. Sanjeev, who had defended Devika's actions, surprised everyone by agreeing with Dr. Bhardwaj's proposal. Vineeta was asked to prepare a letter of dismissal for Miss Devika Singh.

Anandmoorti Babu, who like a few others had suspicions about Dr. Bhardwaj's affair, was disappointed that Devika hadn't been invited to sit in on the meeting. Knowing

Devika's discourteous nature, he had hoped to witness a scandalous ruckus.

Dr. Rudra Bhardwaj, who was sitting next to his uncle, had said nothing during the meeting. Being a tactful person, he decided it was better to avoid any confrontation by staying quiet. Now, as he looked around, he could smell tension brewing in the air. The gradual unfolding of the affairs over the meeting, and the mutual feeling of enmity among the female staff toward Devika, had aroused his interest, and he found himself keenly interested in the upcoming events.

The uncomfortable silence that hung in the air was shattered a minute later by the entry of Devika, who stormed in with a blind fury. For such an outwardly beautiful woman, they were shocked to see the ugliness on her face.

She looked straight at Gayatri Bhardwaj. Her words were jeering. "Do you think I have no idea what this meeting was about? Don't consider my dismissal your victory. Don't even think for a moment I have lost. I take my dismissal as your husband's answer. I believe everyone deserves a second chance. Here, you take this." She took out a paper from her purse and handed it to Gayatri. "Remember the day when I asked your husband to think something over? I think the pair of you considered it an empty threat. I will give you twenty-four hours to respond. This is your second and last warning. In case you do not bother to reply, do not forget to read the Dainik Jagran the day after tomorrow."

She scrutinized everyone's stunned faces.

"All of you look scandalized. Had I known it was this easy to shock you, I would have done it more often." With a malicious smile, Devika continued, "You must be wondering what I am talking about? I am sure you know half of it already. It all depends on Mr. and Mrs. Bhardwaj now. Let's see if they will reveal it to the world or not. You shall know soon."

She observed the look on the faces of Dr. Rajinder and Gayatri Bhardwaj, whom she had just robbed of dignity. It was ugly. She felt the swell of cruel pleasure rising inside her chest.

Dr. Rudra Bhardwaj, who was sitting with his elbows on the table, eyeing the whole scene unfolding until now with a cool demeanour and slight boredom, got up, held Devika's wrist, and said, "It would be better if you leave right now."

She looked at him with a menacing delight. "Don't let me start on you, Doctor Sahib. I could say a thing or two about you that would give your honourable staff here something more to talk about. My God! It would be fun." She stared Rudra in the eyes, and he looked at her with a cool disinterest. She patted his cheek. "You're so dear. You know I would never hurt you."

With that, she took a few steps towards the door but spun and came to stand behind the head nurse's chair. She placed her hands on her shoulders, leaned closer to her face. Devika's eyes were big and dark, her mouth scarlet, full and perfect as an artist's painting, but the words her lips uttered were ugly. They spat venom.

"Look at you, the paragon of virtue, sitting here and feeling noble like a liberator. You act as if you are here to protect and save the fallen ones. You pretend to fight their battles as if you really care. I know what is hidden behind your disguise of goodness."

Saroj Rani Jaiswal wasn't a person to get intimidated. She said in a hard voice, "You might be fond of playing games but, I am sorry, I am not playing your game. You'd better say what you have in mind, Devika."

"You are in a rush to hear the truth about yourself. You are courageous, I would give you that much," Devika sneered. "You pretend to act virtuous when in reality any man would think twice before looking at you. I know who you give a damn about even more than yourself. You think others cannot see behind your fake decency. Everyone knows how you lust over your precious Doctor Sahib." Smiling at Dr.

Rajinder Bhardwaj, she continued, "A second-rate person like Rajinder Bhardwaj has some class, at least."

She surveyed everyone's faces. All eyes were on her. With a smudge of satisfaction, she left the room, leaving behind hearts clouded with dark, vicious hatred.

Saroj Rani was seized with anger so intense her whole body shook. She fumbled with the files in front of her. They fell with a thud on the floor. She took a deep breath. She could not let herself lose control like that. She knew she had to get out of the room. She couldn't bear everyone's eyes on her. She mumbled something about the inventory recordkeeping and left hurriedly. She walked straight to her small office, her body rigid, her head held high. Once inside, she stood there trembling, pressing her hands against her face. She felt anger rising in her heart, but she knew she had to preserve that anger and nurse it until it turned into a pure blind hatred which would destroy that disgusting woman.

The silence that had fallen in the boardroom seemed to last for eternity. Dr. Sanjeev was the first one to break the silence. He left on the pretext of the hectic schedule ahead. Dr. Namita looked at Dr. Rudra who then muttered something about leaving for home because he was feeling unwell. She followed him out of the door. The others followed her lead, leaving the Bhardwajs behind.

Gayatri leaned forward on her chair and looked up at her husband, still sitting back in his chair. She said, her voice steady with a trace of sarcasm, "You have dug yourself into a hole."

She threw the paper that Devika had handed her across the table. "She has planned it well."

Dr. Bhardwaj read the paper. It was Devika's pregnancy report. His face flushed. He replied, "I'm sorry, Gayatri. I wish I could undo it all."

"What can your bloody 'sorry' do now, Raj? For God's sake, stop wasting your time on this bloody remorse. Your apology will set nothing right. If you want to ease your conscience, and feel better about yourself, you can tell me sorry later, but now we need to focus on fixing the situation." She pushed her chair backward and got up. "Now, think of a way out of this. That woman is brazen. She has no regard for her reputation, but I have for mine. Just imagine the consequences if she goes to the newspaper. People will ridicule us. They will relish this scandal for months."

Dr. Bhardwaj opened his mouth to speak, but before he could say anything, Gayatri said, "Let's not talk here. All the staff outside must be wondering what is going on now. We should go home."

She stood up. Dr. Bhardwaj nodded in agreement, and they left together for home.

He was miserable and silent in the car. He said with a note of guilt, "What do you suggest now?"

"We can't let her do this. You know that, don't you?"

She leaned back against the car seat, closed her eyes as if nothing significant had happened. She kept her eyes closed for the rest of the drive. Dr. Bhardwaj stayed silent too.

Chapter 5

*"Ultimate horror often paralyzes
memory in a merciful way."*

—H.P. Lovecraft

It was the sight of her mistress's white, made-up face between the rumpled deep-blue sheet of comforting cotton on the canopy bed, that would stay in the dreams of Kammo for the coming few months.

It was eight-thirty on Wednesday, 13 August, when Kammo reached the Satyalok Society, smiled at the watchman, climbed the stairwells, and rang the doorbell of number sixty-six. She rang it twice. That's what she did every morning if madam was to go to the hospital, and Kammo would open the door herself. In the past, Kammo used to go with her mother to work only occasionally, but now she came every day, as her impending wedding was approaching fast. She had turned nineteen two months ago, and her wedding date was fixed now. Sumitra Dayal from number fifty-four had suggested the groom. The boy's father worked as a *peon* in Mr. Dayal's office, and the boy himself worked as a junior typist in a factory. They wanted Kammo to prepare for her private tenth-class exams and then enrol on a typing course. Shantabai, Kammo's mother, was beyond happy. All six occupants of the flats where her mother worked had promised to contribute enough to pay for her wedding, so she didn't have to worry about anything. They had split the wedding expenses among themselves. Although the groom's family had assured Shantabai they were not the dowry type, her mistresses from the building had promised to arrange for a mini fridge, a television set, a Godrej *almirah*, a boxed double bed, a wooden *peera* set, Kammo's wedding clothes, and all the kitchen utensils. Shantabai only had to arrange the food for the guests, and there were only twenty people coming in the *baraat*. Shantabai had three brothers, and they were bringing a light gold chain with a matching pair of gold *bali* for Kammo, a gold ring for the groom, and clothes for all the family members of her *sasural*.

Kammo liked working in number sixty-six, as madam never ordered her around the way the other flat-owners did. She would ring the doorbell twice, wait for madam to open the door if she was home or, otherwise, open the lock with an extra key that madam had given to her mother.

She waited to see if madam answered the doorbell, and when there was no answer, as she had expected, she put the key in the lock and turned it. But, as always happened with this door, the key wouldn't turn at first. She pulled the door toward her and tried turning the key again. But, as she tried to turn the key all the way round, the pressure of her hand moved the handle down, and she found it was unlocked. That was very unusual. She had never known her mistress to leave the door unlocked.

She pushed the door open and stepped inside. "Madam *Ji*," she called, "*Madam Ji kahan ho aap?*" She stood and listened, but there was no reply. Timidly, she walked toward the gallery. She realized the light in the gallery was still on, and the curtains in the drawing room were all closed. She knew the curtains in the drawing room were kept open all the time despite the weather. That should have warned Kammo that something was amiss and stopped her from going further toward the bedroom door, but curiosity took over. She opted to set aside her apprehension and moved forward, a step at a time, and took a deep breath.

The bedroom door was closed. She pushed it open and saw the body. At the threshold, she stood rooted in terror, unable to move. A peculiar little sound between a cry and a moan escaped her throat while her eyes refused to look anywhere else but at her mistress's listless face staring at the ceiling, until finally a loud scream escaped her mouth. She had no memory of running back to the gallery or going down the stairs. *Chowkidar* Narayan Das was at the front-counter desk. She tried to tell him about the incident with chattering teeth, but the words wouldn't come out at first. Later, she remembered jabbering something about the murder in number sixty-six. Narayan Das said something that she couldn't understand, made her sit on one of the empty plastic chairs against the wall, and raced upstairs.

She sat there, staggered, in the chair, unsure of her surroundings as if she was sitting in a cinema watching actors playing their roles to perfection. In her dazed state, she watched a man walking to the front desk, saw him dialling the telephone, and heard him talking about the murder in a slow, deliberate tone. Then the front door was opened, and the hall was full of people talking simultaneously in loud voices. Someone patted her back, handed her a glass of water, and urged her to drink it in a hushed, consoling voice. Kammo gave a little gasp as she came out of her stupor and looked at the face of the visitor. It was Mrs. Mukand, who lived at number fifteen on the first floor, right below Devika madam's flat. Kammo pushed the glass away and, instead, threw herself in the soft motherly bosom of Mrs. Mukand and started to cry.

Chapter 6

*"For I have sworn thee fair, and
thought thee bright,*

*Who art as black as hell, as dark as
night."*

—William Shakespeare

Like many other small cities, Sanover had been experiencing an immense population surge as people relocated there from the surrounding villages. This urban sprawl meant low-rise residential complexes had become a necessity. Built opposite a small hill, the Satyalok Society was a residential complex of several one-, two-, and three-bedroom units with separate balconies. The predominant and almost ornamental use of bricks and its sloping roof gave the building an impressive facade.

It took some time for the Superintendent of Police, Vishwanath Sharma, to arrive at Satyalok Society after he received the news of the woman's murder, as he had taken a day off from work to attend the funeral of Banarsi Das, his neighbour. The man must have been at least one hundred and ten, as far as Sharma could make out, and his funeral had been due long enough—he had conveyed this same thought to Nandini, his wife. She hadn't responded kindly to his callous remark, and had asked him in clear terms to take a day off to attend the funeral or face the consequences. Sharma had had enough of hunched men in white *kurta pajamas, dhoti kurtas,* talking in hushed tones, and wailing women in white *sarees, salwar suits,* when ASI Jigesh Diwakar telephoned his house. Savitri, their maid, had been soaking dirty cloths in buckets of soapy water in the backyard, and luckily she heard the telephone ring. She ran inside to take the call and went promptly to Banarsi Das's house to inform Sharma. Sharma offered his final condolences to Banarsi Das's oldest son, a man who Sharma thought was also soon due for his own funeral, smiled and waved at Nandini from where he was standing, ignoring her stiff gaze, and left for Satyalok Society.

He found Sub-Inspector Arjun Rawat and Assistant Sub-Inspector Jigesh Diwakar waiting in front of the door. Dr. Parmeet Sidhu, the police forensic pathologist, arrived at the same time, accompanied by her assistant lab technician, a young man in his mid-twenties whom Sharma had never met before, carrying a case of pathologists' tools. Sharma glanced at Rawat, who whispered that he had telephoned the pathologist earlier. Although the law didn't require a police pathologist to be present at the crime scene, Rawat knew Sharma preferred Dr. Sidhu's presence in any case of homicide.

Dr. Sidhu exchanged nods with them and introduced her assistant. She was a petite woman with delicate facial features and a soft voice. Sharma always thought she looked too fragile to even see a corpse, let alone perform an autopsy on one. She looked like a college student in her casual outfit of black-and-white cotton *saree* in muted prints with white lab coat on top and oversized trendy sunglasses that covered almost half of her face. Sharma, who was a firm believer of the saying "appearances can be deceiving" knew of her competence, as he had accompanied her a few times during autopsies.

After exchanging pleasantries, Sharma enquired about the incident.

"The maid came at her usual time of half past eight in the morning to clean the flat. She let herself in with a spare key and found the woman dead in one of the bedrooms. She ran to the watchman for help, and he informed the police," said Rawat.

The wooden door of the flat was slightly ajar. Rawat pushed it lightly with his left foot to open it all the way and let everyone in. He led everyone straight to the bedroom on the far left, where the body lay. The curtains were drawn back and the splendid morning sun shone through the vast window, illuminating an exotic nude of *Vishwamitra* and *Menka* on the wall above a huge oak canopy bed. The exquisite jewellery on *Menka's* body seemed to blaze where the sunbeams fell, giving it the appearance of gold. Her face was crossed with red which seemed a defiance to her exotic voluptuous beauty. Somehow, the painting looked unsettling.

On the bed, the woman lay on her back, her eyes, listless and huge, staring into the void, one arm dangling off the side of the bed, her thick hair a halo of glossy black against the whiteness of the pillow. In death, she looked like a plastic statue. Her face was pallid as if drained of every single drop of blood. There was barely any beauty left. In life, she must have been very beautiful, with an enduring, playful sexuality, thought Sharma. The upper lip had a thin dribble of dried mucus on it. A faint but noticeable purplish bruise could be seen on either side of the delicate long neck, where a pair of strong hands had held it, cut off the blood supply to the brain, and squeezed the life out of her.

They looked at her in silence. A sudden hush had fallen over them. Even the faint sound of their measured breathing seemed a defiance to the prevailing authority of death in the room. The spell broke when Sharma stepped sideways to let the doctor come near the body, who bent over her and lifted the woman's head to reveal a small red stain on the pillow.

Ignoring the stain, she turned the lifeless head from side to side to examine the bruises on both sides of the neck.

"It looks like manual strangulation, as you can see bruises on both sides here," the pathologist remarked, pointing to almost-circular bruises around the windpipe. "There are only finger impressions; I can see no fingerprints. Her assailant was wearing gloves."

The assassin came prepared. Could it be a pre-planned and well-thought-out murder, wondered Sharma?

"The way her body is positioned," said the pathologist, pointing to the sprawled legs, "it was done post-death."

Sharma stood, still looking at the body, and took in everything from the woman's pallid face to the full-length, sleeveless pink nightgown with an embroidered neckline and lace trim, which was in shreds. Her partially bare body was displayed vulgarly, as if on exhibition, under what was left of the once-sheer, long, sweeping full-sleeved white robe, her legs spread apart at quite an unnatural angle. She wore two diamond rings on her right hand, and a single, delicate gold anklet on her left ankle. The diamonds on her rings sparkled, creating an uneven aureole of brightness on the ceiling.

An open jar of face cream was lying on its side on the dressing table, and the faint smell of *chandan* from it mingled with the air of death in the room. Death overpowered the ambience in the room. Even the grandeur of the sun could not subdue the powerful presence of death there.

Sharma felt a sense of foreboding in the air. There was something troubling about the whole scene, something unsettling that he could not put his finger on. It bothered him. The scene in the room felt brazenly staged. In the nude painting, the *apsara Menka* sent by gods was seen to be seducing the sage *Vishwamitra* to end his *tapsaya*. Her face, crossed with red, somehow represented something of grim significance, which he now contemplated, seeing as the same red hue was on victim's lips too.

He looked around and took the whole room in: the wall-to-wall wardrobe, two sitting chairs with a small round table in the middle, a dressing table with a mirror and a sitting chair in front, the small tables on either side of the bed. Next to the window, he saw a door that opened to a balcony, and another door to the right opened into a bathroom. A few things were scattered on the floor right next to the dressing table: brushes and combs, a closed bottle of astringent lotion and another one of cleansing milk, two kohl-stained wet tissues, a few makeup-stained tissues, and some jewellery. Everything else in the room looked in order.

Dr. Sidhu took the rectal thermometer that the assistant technician was holding out to her. Sharma turned his head slightly away. He couldn't help but feel like a voyeur when watching this necessary preliminary violation of a dead body's orifices. He had watched autopsies a few times, and they never offended him the way these essential introductory formalities before the actual autopsies did.

Dr. Sidhu got up after taking the temperature of the body, glanced at her wristwatch and said, "Ten to ten now in the morning. I would say she has been dead about eleven and a half hours, perhaps a little longer, so that makes it between half past ten and eleven in the night. The best estimate of the fall in body temperature under normal circumstances is usually about one and a half degrees Fahrenheit an hour. But, as you can see, the window is open." The pathologist continued, pointing to the single vast window in the room. "As it happens, the body's temperature drops much more slowly if it has been exposed to cold. The temperature dropped almost ten degrees last night, as it rained pretty much all night. That means she could have been dead well before ten. But you know how unreliable these time estimates can be. Rigour is almost full and lividity is fixed. I would give you a wider estimate of between ten and half-past twelve. I shall be more accurate once I have cut her liver open to get an exact body temperature, and when I have had a look at her stomach contents to determine the last meal," the doctor concluded.

"What about the bloodstain on the pillow?"

Dr. Sidhu pushed the jet-black hair to the right and pointed to a small gash. "That's the source of blood on the pillow. It happened before she died. But it is a small wound. She probably hit her head on something."

"Could it be a defense wound?"

"From the look of it, that doesn't seem likely. It is more likely that she lost her balance or something similar," concluded Dr. Sidhu.

Sharma nodded and returned to the hallway with Arjun Rawat and Diwakar at his heels, leaving the doctor and her assistant behind. They were distracted by voices outside. A few women and some old people were standing outside the flat talking in excited voices. Diwakar went outside to tackle the onlookers. Sharma heard footsteps and saw the technician team entering the main door. Then, right behind them, a police photographer came in. Arjun Rawat asked him to photograph the body first so Dr. Sidhu could finish her preliminary examination. The technicians started dusting for prints.

Leaving them to their own devices, Sharma looked around. The flat was furnished expensively. It looked cold and impersonal, like a museum. The place seemed devoid of any personal touches. The hallway was spacious; a carved table of antique wood was placed on one side, and its top was adorned with two marble elephants facing each other. Above the table hung a framed painting in vivid colours of turquoise and blue. On the opposite wall stood a tall, pale-brown wooden cabinet. The hallway opened into a spacious-looking drawing room which was over-furnished with expensive-looking rosewood furniture, framed art, and ornaments.

"Sir, everything looks expensive. According to the neighbours, the victim was merely a front-desk receptionist in a hospital," said Arjun Rawat.

"Hmm, that would be worth probing into. Find out whether she owns this flat. Let's not make any judgment in haste, Rawat," said Sharma, and looked toward the dining room at the far end which was equally exquisite.

On the opposite side of the flat was the kitchen, with a big open serving window in the wall next to the door. The hallway opened into another small hall, on both sides of which were more doors.

Diwakar opened the door to the right side first and turned on the light switch. He stepped inside with Sharma on his heels. The room was furnished with a huge oak bed with bedside tables, a dressing table with a mirror and a small sitting stool n front, a sitting chair in the far corner, and next to that stood a tall oak cabinet. A door to the left was closed, and it opened into a small bathroom.

The room was neat and tidy, all the drawers and the cabinet were empty except for a single blanket. Nothing seemed out of place there. This room must never have been used by the owner. The thick, heavy curtains were closed, which gave the room a gloomy look when Arjun Rawat turned off the light.

They came out and continued toward another door which led them into another bedroom. It too was dark, as the curtains were also closed, until Diwakar turned the lights on. It was smaller and furnished more sparsely compared to the previous bedroom, with two single beds side by side. The beds were made, and everything looked to be in place.

Sharma opened the cabinet door while Arjun Rawat went around the beds to look inside the bedside table drawers. The cabinet mostly contained blankets and quilts, pillows, a few plain looking *salwar kameez*, a few *sarees*, and winter cardigans. They looked outdated and old. Arjun Rawat could find nothing except old Hindi magazines and a few electricity and water bills in the top bedside table drawer. The lower drawer yielded a few lipsticks, two nail-polish bottles, packs of multi-coloured *bindi*, a broken kajal pencil, a broken watch, a cotton roll, three old invitation cards for weddings and *jagrata*, and an old album of black-and-white pictures.

"Sir, there is nothing in the drawers except the usual household junk. There is one album containing black-and-white pictures. It looks like these are old family photos," remarked Arjun Rawat as he handed the album to Sharma.

Sharma glanced quickly through the album. It was full of the murdered woman's pictures except for a few empty spots here and there.

"Put it in the evidence bag. We shall go through it later."

Just then Diwakar came to the door and told them that the photographer had finished his work on the body. They all went into the main bedroom where Dr. Sidhu was examining the neck of the victim: her jet-black hair was swept upward. The dead woman was turned on her right side, and a faint purplish bruise could be seen above her right bare shoulder blade. Having seen enough corpses, Sharma knew not to mistake that bruise as an accidental injury.

"As you see, she has bruises on both sides of her windpipe. She was strangled manually." Holding the woman's chin, Dr. Sidhu pushed it up slightly and moved it first to the right and then to the left. There were high discolouration marks on the sides of her neck, and faint, almost invisible, abrasions. "These abrasions, as you can see, are very narrow, sort of semicircular. They were made when the assailant gripped her neck and the killer's nails dug deep into the flesh. The killer was wearing gloves, thin gloves, most probably surgical gloves. So, these abrasions are almost invisible."

Sharma asked, "Is there any sign of struggle? Did she fight with her assailant?"

"The heavy abrasions, as you can see here," Dr. Sidhu continued, pointing to the superficially incised curvilinear abrasions, "came from the victim's fingers as she struggled to pry the assailant's grasp off her neck. They've marked the skin in a single pattern everywhere. She tried to loosen the attacker's grip. Either the assailant was too strong for her or she went unconscious pretty quickly."

Dr. Sidhu lifted the victim's chin up further, exposing the recesses where the carotid arteries lay. "Look at this bruising on both sides of her windpipe." Sharma kneeled next to the victim's face and looked at the contusions. "There's a heavy bruising on the right side of her windpipe. It has come from the killer's thumbs when they squeezed the victim's neck. The thumb generates more pressure than the other fingers, so here, these contusions are deeper as the killer gripped her neck from the front. They must have been facing each other. As you can see, these impressions are less obvious on the other side of her windpipe because the use of the killer's left hand came more naturally than the right one. We can safely presume that the killer was left-handed."

She lifted the woman's head from side to side and said, "There is another sign the killer was standing in front of her at the time of strangulation: look at these smaller finger impressions on both sides that go almost toward the back." She pointed to nearly-circular bruises roughly half an inch in diameter. They were again more obvious on the right side of her neck. If the killer were known to the woman, which usually was the case in most homicides, thought Sharma, there wouldn't be many left-handed people to look for in her known circle.

As always, Sharma was impressed by the way this fragile-looking doctor was so quick to pick up on such a subtle piece of evidence. No wonder she had become his first preference of pathologist on the homicide scene.

Dr. Sidhu pointed toward the left side of the victim's neck, about three inches below the jawline. There was a curious discolouration mark. "That looks like an impression from some object, probably some piece of jewellery that the killer was wearing on their right-hand finger when they tried to smother her."

Sharma bent over the victim's face and studied the curious mark. It looked like a lotus set in the depression of a half moon. That must be the killer's ring, thought Sharma; it was a bit loose on the finger from the look of it. He made a mental note to ask the photographer if he had taken enough close-up pictures of that mark.

Sharma asked, "Do you think a woman could have done it?"

"There's a possibility. But, as you can see, the victim is of medium build and not slight, although her neck is fairly slender. A woman could have done it, a robust woman. It would've needed strength. I've to check if there is any specific internal injury to her neck. Breakage of the hyoid bone, for example—although isn't uncommon, that would have required moderate strength. On the other hand, the fracture of the cartilage of the windpipe or the larynx would've needed a great deal of force on the assailant's part. I can be more specific only after a complete examination of her neck during the autopsy."

Sharma looked at the dead woman, watched her profile from the side. Looking at her lifeless body, he thought about the person who had done this. They must have harboured a deep hatred in their heart for weeks, months, or years. Sharma knew that kind of hatred could be too burdensome to carry around for a long time and thought the killer must have felt the burden of his hate too much to bear. Had they been planning out the murder for a long time? Or had they been blinded by fury, annoyed by something the victim had said last time they met, and had sought revenge?

Now it was up to them to find that person. Perhaps it would take a few days or weeks, if they were lucky, but it could take much longer. They had to go through the formal procedures, searching for clues and witnesses and making meticulous enquiries to get to the killer. He thought about the stacks of unsolved-case files in the backroom storage in the police station. Dust had enveloped them for years. He closed his eyes and exhaled. He did not want to go there. He did not want to think about those unsolved cases now.

"We are ready to take her away now. I shall send you the report as soon I am done with her," said Dr. Sidhu, bringing him out of his stupor.

"If there is anything unusual that seems important, call me, Doctor," Sharma said. He walked the doctor back to the front door and waved her goodbye.

The morgue orderlies came soon after and put the stretcher on the floor beside the bed where the woman lay. They lifted the corpse from the bed and laid it on the stretcher. The harsh rays of the sun pierced through the vast window and shone directly on the corpse baring it to the curious eyes of strangers and robbing it of its last traces of dignity. Sharma gave a sigh of relief when they covered the partially-bare body with a white sheet and took her away.

The photographer was taking his last shots of the bedroom and the painting on the wall before packing up his equipment. The three fingerprinting technicians were carrying out the last of their work quietly, with a measured efficiency that Sharma marvelled at, as this was rarely seen among government employees. The technicians soon left the flat leaving Sharma, Rawat, and Diwakar behind to finish their remaining search of the premises.

They came to the main bedroom and looked for anything of importance. The bedside table drawer had two packs of Zolfresh pills; one unopened and the other with only four pills left in it. The woman might have been an insomniac, thought Sharma. He went to the cabinet and opened both doors. It was filled with a young woman's clothes in flashy colours, fashionable and of good quality; *sarees*, *salwar suits*, blouses, skirts, bell bottoms, and midis. He moved the hangers and smelled orange blossom and jasmine. She must have worn something and put it back on the hanger. Behind the hangers, he found a safe. He searched for the keys which he found in a purse on the bottom shelf in the wardrobe cabinet. The safe had three passbooks of different banks and some gold jewellery in it.

He put his reading glasses on and went through her passbooks. She was a rich woman, or it was more accurate to say that she had become a rich woman recently. A huge amount of money had been transferred into her accounts in the past few months.

"She has accumulated quite a lot of money for herself, Rawat. Find out if she has left any will or not. We need to know who is going to inherit her wealth now that she is no more. People have been killed for lesser money."

Rawat made a mental note to inquire about that and said, "Okay, sir. Everything here looks in place except for a few things scattered on her dressing table. There's no paper or any other evidence that would tell us about her family or her hometown."

From outside, the footfalls of other people could be heard on the staircase going upstairs or coming downstairs. The procedural preliminaries were already over, but they still had a lot of work to do. They had been there since morning, and now it was evening. The building was huge, three stories high with back doors on two sides as well as the main entrance. It was a difficult job. The killer could have left unnoticed through any door.

Sharma knew they had to get all the facts together. Facts were important in any homicide investigation. But during the twenty years of his career, he had learned to listen to his hunches as well. In most cases it was his hunch that had helped him catch the criminals.

"Go to the neighbours. Someone must be close to her. Also, put all these passbooks in the evidence bag. It seems we have got something useful here," said Sharma.

"Sir, Constable Rana is already making inquiries outside."

"Let's pack up here then, as nothing more seems of importance. Let's talk to the girl who found the body."

He could write the inquest report after the interview, thought Sharma.

Chapter 7

"One thing alone not even God can do,

To make undone whatever hath been done."

—Aristotle

Despite the resilience of youth, Kammo had failed to recover from the shock of finding her mistress's body. It was understandable, as the horror of the scene had already been engraved in her mind before she could turn her eyes away from her mistress's face. It was too late now to blot it out completely. Every time she closed her eyes, a ghastly image of Devika's lifeless eyes gazing at the ceiling would come to her mind. The horror she had encountered in her mistress's bedroom was still so vivid. Despite being traumatized, she had refused to be taken home.

When Sharma approached her, she was still sitting in the same plastic chair where the *chowkidar* Narayan Das had made her sit. Sharma offered her a drink which she accepted with gratitude. She kept her hands wrapped around the glass of steaming tea, relishing its cozy warmness.

Sharma asked, "You work here every day?"

"Pretty much, for the last few months. *Ma* has taken more work at another flat. I do Devika madam's flat and number twenty-three on the ground floor every day."

In response to Sharma's inquiries about her arrival in the morning, she described what had happened from the moment she got to the victim's flat to the discovery of the body.

Sharma asked, "The door was unlocked and the light in the gallery was still on. Was that usual?"

"As far as I know, Madam *Ji*, wouldn't have left the door open in any case. She was cautious about these sorts of things. And the curtains in the drawing room were always kept open day or night. Madam *Ji* hated to close the curtains, except the ones in her bedroom, and those only at night. I thought it odd that the curtains in the drawing room weren't drawn apart and the light in the gallery was still on."

"Who had keys to her flat?"

"*Madam Ji* gave *Ma* a spare key because sometimes she has to leave early for the hospital."

Sharma asked quietly, "Did you touch her?"

She replied in a low voice, "No."

"What did you do then?"

"I knew I stood looking at her face for some time. I was rooted to the spot and couldn't move. Then I rushed downstairs to the main hall. *Chowkidar* Narayan Das was sitting at the front desk. I blabbered something about the murder in number sixty-six. He made me sit in one of the chairs, and then ran upstairs. I have this memory of him dialling the telephone and talking about the murder later on. Then everyone came at once and started talking."

"What made you think that your mistress was murdered?" asked Sharma, wondering if the girl was as innocent as she looked.

She glanced at him, startled, as if she had just realized the implication in her words about her mistress's death and said, "Murdered! That's what I said? I don't know why I said that. The way Madam *Ji* was lying there—languid with stony eyes— I must have assumed that she was murdered. She wasn't old or sick or anything like that. She couldn't have died on her own, could she?" She looked at Sharma questioningly.

Ignoring her question, he said, "Would you be feeling good enough to go to the flat with me and see if anything is missing there?"

She said reluctantly, "But, Madam *Ji*... her body?"

"Don't worry," Sharma said. "They have taken her. The flat is empty now."

Kammo nodded in agreement, and they took the stairs to the victim's flat. After going through each room, she confirmed that everything looked in order except the closed curtains in the spare rooms and the drawing room.

"You said Miss Devika used to close only her bedroom curtains at night. At what time did she go to sleep?"

"I wouldn't know," Kammo replied. "When I came here for the first time, Madam *Ji* asked me not to close any curtains in the flat as the gloom filled her with dread. She closed her bedroom curtains at night only she said."

Could the killer have been searching for something, wondered Sharma? With the lights on, anyone could have seen him from the spare-room windows. It seems unlikely that the killer closed the curtains right before the murder. He must have closed all the curtains after killing Devika; before he started his search. Everything seemed neat on the surface except for a little bit of disruption in the victim's bedroom. It was a probability they had to explore, thought Sharma.

"Were there any friends or family who visited her?"

"No, as far as I know, she had no visitors."

"Did she have any family?"

"I know she had a younger sister, but I never saw her. Madam *Ji* never talked about her family."

Sharma asked Rawat to send someone who could drop the girl off at her home. Although she had now recovered from the early shock, she still looked pallid and exhausted. She gave Sharma a warm smile and left. It was already eight in the evening and Sharma decided to call it a day—he would resume the investigation in the morning.

Chapter 8

"Every man must do two things alone;
he must do his own believing and his
own dying."

— Martin Luther

The first thing that anyone noticed about Vishwanath Sharma was his extreme politeness. He had pleasant manners. His face always bore formal expressions of politeness in the company of acquaintances and strangers, a protective shell which kept them at a distance. He brought none of his colleagues home. As often happens with introverts who, despite having nothing against people, find the solitude of their home more comforting as opposed to the company of others, he was thought arrogant by many. Nandini, his wife, knew that being in the company of people for more than a few hours always wore him down, not because he disliked people but because he liked having his own space for his thoughts. Sharma had never considered himself an introvert but, as the years passed by, he started to prefer the seclusion of his home to anything else. He liked its warmth and its comfort. It was a place where he could leave the stress of his job behind, relax, and be himself.

He thought about the victim, her flat where they had found her body. She must have thought her home a place where nothing bad could happen to her, her safe harbour. She must have been herself there, shedding all the masks she wore around people. Had she invited her killer to her home that day? Had she opened the door expectantly, or was it someone who rang the bell and forced themselves in when she opened the door? Circumstances didn't point to an outside intruder theory; no valuables were missing from her place, and there was no sign of forced entry. All the windows were barred with iron grills. Nothing seemed out of place. Her flat was neat and tidy. Some gold jewellery was on the dressing table and in the safe. The jewellery on her body was intact. It was someone known to her, as much as he would have liked to think it was the other way around, thought Sharma, and sighed.

What had she done that had sealed her fate and bound her for the pathologist's scalpel? There were so many questions. He knew he had to unravel each one at a time, thoroughly and meticulously. He had to know her to get to her killer, put her under a knife and cut through the layers of her life, the life she had lived in her last days. He had to learn all the secrets she had guarded, the thoughts she had concealed, and the dreams she had seen. Was she the type who dreaded the spotlight that revealed her layers of secrets or someone who loved exhibitions, he wondered?

"We've checked everyone's alibis in the building, sir." Rawat's voice interrupted Sharma's thoughts as he came in and seated himself in one of the empty chairs opposite Sharma's desk.

It was early morning of Thursday, 14 August and the clouds were pitch-black. The forecast set for heavy rains. Sharma looked out through the window on the street outside and asked:

"Anything out of the ordinary?"

"They all seem to have been home on the night of the murder. They're old occupants in the building, respectable working middle-class families. Devika Singh was the only one who rented her flat. After the last owner's death, his son, who lived in Australia, rented the flat to Devika Singh because he could not sell it. All the units are for ownership only; the owner of the building made special provision for the son upon his request. And the flat came furnished, sir."

"That explains the unusual exhibition of wealth. Were any of her neighbours close to her?"

"There is one woman with whom she was on friendly terms. I have asked her to come to the police station to record her statement."

"Has anyone admitted having seen or heard something unusual?"

"Diwakar talked to a college-age girl who had seen a distraught looking young man often standing outside in the back lane, opposite the building, with a direct view of the victim's flat. He will get the name of the man."

"Let's hope we can get some leads which will put the investigation on a clear track. Have you talked to the manager of the building?"

"According to the manager, the victim started renting the apartment about a year ago and was interested in buying it after the yearly contract was over. She lived alone there. We are still trying to locate her family."

"Have you checked where the watchman was last night?"

"Sir, the building is expensive. They are particular about the watchman's appointment. They hire local men with good credentials only. There are two security guards, and both have worked there for over five years. I have verified their credentials. They are clean. Both are locals and seem trustworthy. They have interesting things to say about the victim. I brought them here to talk to you. They are waiting outside."

"Bring the one who was at the front desk last night first. Let's hope he took his duty seriously and was awake through the night."

The security guard, Narayan Das, was a short, sturdy man of sixty with a tense smile that Sharma suspected was probably due to fear of neglecting his duty the previous night, or maybe he was just nervous. He greeted both men with a brief bow of his head and stood to attention facing Sharma like a soldier on a disciplinary charge. Sharma asked him to take a seat in the empty chair in front of his desk.

In reply to Sharma's questioning, Narayan Das described his movements after leaving his house in Subedarganj until his arrival at the Satyalok Society at six o'clock the previous evening. His account of the discovery of the body matched that of maid Kammo's. After Kammo had come running downstairs and told him about Devika madam's body, he had at once rushed upstairs to the victim's flat. The door was open, and the lights were on everywhere except for the room where the body lay. He had stayed at the threshold of the room and knew at once that the victim was dead. He described the position of the body from where he stood as precisely as he could. He hadn't gone near the body or touched it for fear of getting involved in any legal hassle. He showed them the entry register, according to which, the victim had had two visitors that night both sharing the same surname. The first entry was that of Rajinder Bhardwaj at quarter past eight. The other visitor was Gayatri Bhardwaj. The time next to her signature was entered at nine o'clock.

"At what time did they leave? There is no entry revealing their departure."

"That's not required, Sahib." He flipped through the previous pages and said, "As you can see, there are no entries in the departure column. No one bothers to sign out. Sign-in is required after half past seven in the evening only, Sahib. During the daytime, anyone can go inside without making an entry in the register."

"Were you at the desk all the time?"

"Yes, Sahib, except for a few times when I had to attend nature's call."

"How many times did you leave your desk to use the bathroom?"

Narayan Das scratched his left arm. "I'm a patient of *sugar.* So, I always have to use the bathroom three or four times a night."

In fact, he was probably doing double the trips to the bathroom, thought Sharma and cringed inwardly. He thought about his father who was a diabetic and his frequent trips to the bathroom. And even he himself was making three or four trips to the bathroom every night these days. It must have something to do with age in his case, he mused, as he didn't have diabetes.

"That means anyone could have entered or left when you were not at your desk." Sharma asked him about the arrangement of locking the main door at night.

"The main door stays unlocked, Sahib. That's how Manager Sahib instructed me when I started working in the building six years ago."

"At what time did Miss Devika's first visitor leave?"

"I never saw him leaving, Sahib." He paused for a moment and then said, "I saw no one leaving."

"Could they have left from one of the back doors? I understand there are two more doors for exiting the building."

"That's possible, Sahib. Those doors stay unlocked because some of the occupants prefer to use them, especially the ones whose flats are nearer the south side."

Sharma changed the track of his questions. "Did you know the visitors who came to visit Devika the previous night?"

"Never seen them before."

"Who else visited Miss Devika?"

"She didn't have many visitors, Sahib. I saw no one from her family visiting her. There was a man, around thirty-five, good looking, whom I saw twice in the last fortnight, but both times he left fairly quickly. I would say within an hour. I saw him during my day shift. There was another man whom I saw loitering outside the main gate many times in the last few months. I didn't give it much thought until one day I saw him with Devika madam."

"What happened then?"

"It must have been about ten in the morning when I saw him with Devika madam. He had pressed her against the wall and had his hands around her neck. I ran to help, but Devika madam was laughing, although her face was all red. She asked me not to worry. He looked mad with fury."

"Do you know who that man was?"

"No. He seemed to be around forty, five foot eight or so, stocky, and dark. He was bald. Not bald exactly, but had scant hair."

"You don't know anything else about him—his relationship with Miss Devika or his name?"

"No."

"Very well. You may leave now. You must leave this entry register here. I will talk to the manager about it myself. If you remember anything else, telephone me or come and see me."

Sharma called for Rawat as Narayan Das left his office.

"That's interesting, Rawat," Sharma said as Rawat walked in and settled himself in one of the chairs in front of Sharma's desk. "The dead woman's visitors that night share the same surname: Bhardwaj."

"They might be related, sir."

"They might be. We need to find out if their visit that night overlapped as well. They might have seen each other then."

The other watchman had nothing new to add to what Narayan Das had already told them. He confirmed seeing both the men a few times but had witnessed no violent confrontation between Devika and the men.

It was ten to nine when Sharma finally left for home. Nandini was in the bedroom, a book on her lap, listening to Modi ke Matwale Rahi on the radio. Although she never considered Sharma's detective work of much interest, she loved the exploits of Balwan Singh and Lalit Singh who solved a different mystery in each episode. She looked up at him and smiled. He felt a surge of warmth spreading in his heart. It felt good to be home in his wife's comforting presence. He asked Nandini what was for dinner. He realized that he hadn't eaten all day. He was starving.

She heated up some *aaloo matar* and served him *roti* with *raita*, salad, and green chutney. During the initial years of their marriage, despite his protests, she had insisted on making hot *roti* for him whenever he arrived home. But after spending two years with him, she had learned that he enjoyed good food anyways, cold or hot. He wasn't a picky eater. He liked everything. She was a good cook and usually served delicious meals. However, there were days when she became so engrossed in reading—which was her first interest—that she would find it hard to part from her book even to spare time to cook one proper meal. Those days, she would serve him bread with jam, an omelette, *khichdi* or sweet rice. She could get away with that for a few days until he noticed the lack of a proper meal and the continuous presence of the same bland food, and would complain and grumble until she cooked something good and hearty. That would always calm him down, and he would go about his business happily.

After Sharma had finished eating, he talked about his hectic day at the police station, keeping the news of the killing to himself.

Having been a policeman's wife for over two decades, Nandini had become less sensitive to most of the tragic news, but still, it bothered her. But the cases concerning children depressed her extremely. Even though both their children were grown up now, she still found it hard to hear about any tragedy involving a child. Such news used to depress her for days when their children were younger. With age and maturity, she had learned to control her feelings, though, and she still followed all the case developments through the newspapers.

Sharma never discussed tragic news with her because he was sensitive to her feelings and also because he hated to bring his work home.

She handed him a glass of hot milk and did the last of her kitchen chores. He sat sipping the slightly sweet, frothy milk and scanned the news in the day's paper. Nandini talked about her colleagues at the school and set the milk for the *dahi*. Her voice, steady and flowing in the background, reminded him he was at home. He watched her dip the tip of her finger in the stainless-steel pot. Satisfied, she poured the milk into the jug, added half a spoon of *dahi*, stirred it, covered the jug with a small plate, and wrapped it in a white kitchen towel, carefully and precisely, not letting it spill. She washed the last of the dishes quickly, took her own glass of hot milk, and together they walked to their room. He talked some more about his busy day—sparing her the gruesome details—while she drank. Within minutes he was asleep. She took off his glasses for him, picked up her book from the bedside table, and started reading.

Chapter 9

*"And all who told it added something
new, and all who heard it, made
enlargements too."*

—Alexander Pope

By the afternoon of Friday, 15 August, it had been determined that Swaranlata Devi, Devika's next door neighbour, was the second last person—the last one clearly the killer—to have seen Devika Singh alive. On the night of murder, at half past eight she had knocked at Devika's door and talked to her.

When Rawat showed her inside Sharma's office at the police station, Sharma's first impression was of someone in actual medical distress struggling to breathe. On the second look, he realized that Mrs. Swaranlata was a very fat woman who, because of her ample size and because she had just climbed the stairs to his second-storey office, was only running out of breath. She was wearing a printed chiffon *saree* with a tiny low-cut blouse which propelled her massive bosom up, on top of which her fleshy double chin seemed to rest. Folds of loose flesh from her massive midriff hung out loosely from underneath the blouse and also considerably at the sides.

Nandini had once told him that many of the fattest women preferred to wear tiny revealing blouses because of frugality. A standard blouse-sized piece of fabric measured eighty centimetres. It made a proper-fitting blouse for an average, lean woman but it was the preferred buying choice for everyone regardless of their size because of its availability and the price difference compared to bigger pieces. To Sharma, this frugality contradicted the widespread criticism of those actresses who bared themselves in the pictures and were blamed for corrupting the youth of the country.

She flopped down in the chair and accepted Sharma's offer of *nimbu pani*. It was a humid day and Sharma knew some cold lemon water would do her good. Her face, unlike her body, had kept its youthful contours despite being plump. Sharma waited until she settled in the chair.

There was a low tap at the door and Constable Rane pushed in bearing a tray with a jug of *nimbu pani* and some empty glasses. The whiff of freshly squeezed lemons filled the room. Sharma

Sharma looked at Rawat's notes about Swaranlata Devi's verbal statement and said, "Madam, you no doubt have done us a great favour by coming forward to talk about Miss Devika. According to you, there was someone with Miss Devika on the night of her murder."

She was still a little flushed and breathless when she answered Sharma. "There was someone with her for sure."

"Did you see that person yourself?"

"It's a pity, I could not see the person's face. If only he'd been sitting in the drawing room, I could have seen him from the main door, but the drawing room was empty. I tried to look past the gallery, but the bedroom doors were closed. But one thing is certain, I was the last person to see her alive."

The woman was content to present herself as the key witness in the murder enquiry.

"You mean you were the last person except the murderer, madam?" Rawat could not hold himself back.

"Yes." She continued hesitantly, "Yes, of course, the last person to talk to her except for her murderer. I'm sure it was the same man whom I heard talking to her."

"Could it be a woman, madam? Did you hear the person talk?" Sharma asked.

"Who else could it have been? Not a woman." She continued, "Only a man could do this heinous crime. I'm sure he was the killer. If you ask me, I would say a jilted lover." She leaned forward a little and said in a low voice, "I am not in the habit of bad mouthing people, but she had men friends. A few residents in the building were not comfortable with her friends visiting her at odd hours."

"So, there was more than one person who frequented her flat often?"

"There was a man who came a few times, although he never stayed for more than half an hour as far as I noticed. But there was someone else who only visited her at night, once or twice a week, at least," she said, finally regaining her breath.

"Think carefully, madam," Sharma said, keeping his excitement to himself, "What did he look like? Any idea about his age, complexion, or height? Anything distinctive about his personality that would set him apart from others?"

Swaranlata Devi fiddled in her chair, twisted her *saree pallu* around her fingers, and said, "I heard about it from other women in the building. I never saw him with my own eyes."

He should have known it in advance, thought Sharma. The woman belonged to a circle where everyone seemed to relish gossip without a need to verify the facts first.

"So, there was no one in particular who you saw?" Sharma asked in a soothing tone.

"No, not with my own eyes."

It was, thought Sharma, probable that no one had visited Devika. She was a very good-looking, young woman living on her own. That could be reason enough to start such rumours. Even occasional sightings of any male would have given rise to rumours. But if there was a regular visitor, someone must have seen him. They would know soon. He changed the track of his questions.

"I want you to think carefully," he said. "Try to remember and tell me everything about your last meeting with her."

"You think I could help catch her murderer?" said Swaranlata Devi, clearly relishing the idea. "I would if I could."

Sharma looked at her. The woman was nosy and cunning, not the most reliable witness, given such people have a penchant for exaggeration, but perhaps she could be depended upon to bring forward some factual and rumoured knowledge about the victim. And rumours were sometimes worth probing into, as one never knew what skeletons might be hidden inside someone's closet.

After a momentary pause, she said, "It was about half past eight when I knocked at Devika's door. I remember the time because Binaca Geet Mala on the radio was still on and I had been boiling milk for *dahi*. That's when my husband came back from his clothes shop. I'd realized I had no *dahi* in the fridge. My husband never eats rajmanh chawal without *dahi* and that's what I cooked for dinner that night. I decided to fetch *dahi* from Devika's and went there."

"What happened then, madam?" asked Sharma.

Swaranlata Devi continued, "I knew it was late to go round and ask for *dahi*, but I could hear voices in her flat. But then I heard shouting. I hate to eavesdrop, but the walls are very thin." She paused and looked at Sharma, who understood it was her curiosity and not the lack of *dahi* that made her go to Devika's flat. But keeping his thoughts to himself, he nodded in understanding and prompted Swaranlata Devi to continue with her story.

She went on, "When Devika opened the door, I tried to look past her to see who was there, but she said she had no *dahi* and closed the door. I knew there was someone with her because I heard the loud voices earlier. I knocked again and asked her for *jaag* for the *dahi*. But she didn't have any. She was in a hurry to send me away. I asked her if there was a guest inside, but she just shook her head and closed the door. Afterwards, it was quiet next door except at around ten when I heard the noise in her flat. I could hear the noise because the power was out and it was very silent."

"What happened then?"

"I was in bed trying to sleep when I heard a loud thud next door. I strained my ears to hear more voices, but there was complete silence. I found it hard to fall asleep and I was still half-asleep when I heard someone outside. I thought it was my imagination because the only other flat in our hallway is the Rathods' and they have gone away for a fortnight to attend their granddaughter's wedding in Kanpur."

"What time was that?"

"It was just after half past ten. I looked at the alarm clock by my bedside because I heard footsteps again. It was like someone was walking back and forth. I got up to look and turned on the lobby lights. That's when I heard footsteps come to our main door. The main lobby outside is well lit, but when I opened the door the outside light had gone off. It was creepy."

"What did you do then?"

"I was scared. I locked the door right away. I tried to listen to the sounds outside, but it was quiet. I fell asleep thinking it might have been Devika's guest leaving."

It was as if she had just realized the implication of hearing those sounds. Her body shuddered involuntarily at the thought of the murderer's horrifying act. She continued in a tremulous voice, "Now, if I come to think of it, that loud thud could have been her falling to the floor as she died, and those footsteps might have been those of her killer's."

"Did you, by any chance, hear part of the scuffle next door when you turned off the radio, anything at all?" asked Sharma.

After a good pause, Swaranlata Devi said, "I'm not one of those women who like to keep a score of all the happenings in their neighbours' homes. I despise intruding in others' lives.

But, as the walls are very thin, one can't help hearing a few things here and there." She sighed and looked at Sharma for soothing encouragement.

Sharma's tone was placid when he spoke. "I understand, madam. One can't help it, if one's neighbours are too loud."

Encouraged, she beamed at Sharma and said, "I heard a few words here and there. Devika was warning the person not to try her patience and she said something about facing the consequences soon. She said she wouldn't give up until she had destroyed everything."

"But you heard nothing that her visitor said?"

"No, he must have been talking in a low voice. I have a keen sense of hearing," she said.

"That was very helpful, madam. Now, tell me, what was she like?"

"She was all right, with me at least. She didn't have any other friends in the building. Most of the men in the building were her admirers. The women hated her. She liked attracting men's attention. You know what I mean, right?" She looked at Sharma, who nodded. She went on, "That did not settle well with a few women. Not that she was interested in anyone from the building." Swaranlata leaned forward and looked side to side as though someone else might be listening. "There was someone she had left."

"You mean she had broken up with someone?"

"Yes."

"In the building, madam?"

"No, not from the building. Someone from outside. I saw him once sitting in the gallery outside Devika's door. Before I could ask him anything, Devika came back. She was furious when she saw him and pushed him inside before slamming the door shut. I'm not the type to eavesdrop, but I heard him hurling obscenities at her. Later, I asked her about him. She laughed and denied everything."

"Did you see him again?"

"No, that was the only time."

Swaranlata Devi's description of the man matched the one that watchman Narayan Das had given.

There was nothing more to learn from the witness. Sharma thanked her and instructed Rawat to show her outside. She left the police station with a palpable satisfaction.

74

Chapter 10

"Questions are never indiscreet.
Answers sometimes are."

—Oscar Wilde

Sharma and Rawat drove across the Sanjivani Chowk. There was a narrow road on the right that rose sharply off the main road. It was lined by cedar trees on both sides and led to a tall, impressive two-storey brick-and-glass building that housed the Lifeline Hospital's five-hundred bed facility.

Sharma wanted to talk to Mr. and Mrs. Bhardwaj, but when Diwakar had telephoned the Bhardwaj residence, he had been informed that they had gone out of town and would be back in two to three days. It was evening of Friday, 15 August and Sharma decided to visit Lifeline Hospital where Devika had worked before her death.

They climbed the stone steps to the covered porch which opened into the brightly lit reception hall. The area was functional and pleasing to the eyes. There were a few indoor plants in copper vases, two framed paintings on the wall behind the reception desk which, despite their mediocre quality, were appealing to the eyes with their rich and vibrant use of colours.

The girl sitting behind the L-shaped reception desk was good-looking, but not disconcertingly so, thought Rawat. She flashed a brief superior smile which faded as soon as Rawat explained the purpose of their visit. She went to her companion, a woman in her mid-twenties with a serious face, sitting in another chair behind the reception desk and whispered to her. The woman rose at once, led them to the waiting room, and asked them to wait until she had talked to someone in authority.

The waiting room was full of people, only half of whom, Sharma suspected, were patients. The other half must have been their moral supporters, families, and friends. The room had rows of assorted chairs, all upright and uncomfortable and that looked as though they'd been bought especially to forbid people from occupying them for long periods. They seemed to serve their purpose well, as most people sitting in them appeared to shift restlessly. A few people glanced at them as they entered but went back to their private world of worries, apprehensions, and sorrows.

Rawat asked for the dead woman's employment file, after the receptionist returned with news they must wait some time for the nursing superintendent as she was in the middle of a medical emergency. She found the file, pulled a chair near the reception, and asked Rawat to sit there, as if she expected him to run away with the file. Rawat shrugged, took the file, and started reading it.

Sharma took the opportunity to talk to an orderly passing by with an empty tray. Sharma asked him about the dead woman. According to him, Devika was rude, didn't care about morals, and had been dismissed from her position a few days earlier.

Rawat looked through the dead woman's employment file. It acknowledged her as unmarried, thirty-one years old, a native of Chamba, a stenographer and secretarial assistant, and educated at the Indira Gandhi Industrial Training Institute for Women, Chamba, HP. There was no record of previous employment.

They weren't kept waiting long. A stern-looking woman of around sixty in a checkered cotton *saree* in faded lilac and slate grey approached Sharma, introduced herself as the senior nursing superintendent, Saroj Rani Jaiswal. She led them into a small office. It was an oblong box, ten feet by eight feet, with a single small window that faced the rear entrance of the hospital. Rawat was surprised it could hold so many stacks of cardboard-bound withered-looking files in a neat and systematic order. Clearly, Saroj Rani Jaiswal was a woman of order and efficiency.

She asked them to sit down and settled herself in the single chair behind the desk. Her hair, more white than black, was pulled in a tight bun at the nape of her neck, which gave her narrow face a determined look. Her eyes, although small and dull, had strength in them.

"We're here to talk about Miss Devika Singh. You must know about her death."

"Such shocking news. The whole town is buzzing with it."

"You, I understand, are one of the oldest and most senior members at the hospital. For how long have you worked here?"

"I've been with this hospital for almost thirty years, right from the start when its foundation was laid. Dr. Bhardwaj had just acquired his medical degree. His father built this clinic for him. The building was small, and there was just Dr. Bhardwaj and a few other staff members. But back then, Sanover was also a small town. As the town swelled, our clinic kept getting bigger. The east and the west wings were added to the original building eventually. Six years ago, we had to set up an emergency ward. Big hospitals in Shimla proved to be expensive. We provided the same equipment and facilities, so patients from the neighbouring towns and villages came here instead." Sharma detected a proud glint in her eyes.

"What are your duties?"

"As a nursing superintendent, I am responsible for conducting interviews for the selection of nursing staff, inspecting nursing care, checking the performance of other employees in the wards, and also noting observations for performance and patient satisfaction. Basically, I take care of the necessary administrative work in the hospital."

"Who hired Miss Devika Singh? Was she good at her job?"

"She was hired for a front-desk position. Unfortunately, we received only two applications for the post advertised and the other applicant arrived late for the interview. I selected Devika then. She was efficient, I suppose, as far as her work was concerned. I couldn't find any fault with her there."

"Did she get along well with the other staff members?"

"She did in the beginning, when she first joined us. Everyone admired her for her dazzling beauty, her pleasant and friendly nature, and her willingness to help everyone. But that wasn't her. That was a disguise. She was selfish and opportunistic. She was nice only to those who she thought could do her any good. She had this explicit talent for manipulating a situation in her favour, if it helped her realize any of her ulterior motives."

"So, there were a few with whom she got along well?" asked Sharma.

"No one in particular. She had decided that she was a cut above the rest of us here, and she needed no one. After the first two or three months, she stopped being nice altogether."

"Do you know what brought about this sudden change in her behaviour?"

Sharma's questions, it seemed, made her realize that she had said too much. She stayed silent for a long uncomfortable moment during which Sharma and Rawat sat quietly waiting for her to talk. Realizing she had no other option than to answer Sharma's question, she spoke in what Sharma recognized as a partly reluctant and resigned tone.

"She . . . was close to Dr. Bhardwaj," she said, her voice hesitant. "That made her feel particularly invincible, it appeared."

"Dr. Rajinder Bhardwaj?" Sharma asked.

"Yes."

"Close in what sense?"

"Their closeness . . ." She hesitated. "It was beyond the boundaries of general friendship."

"So, they had an illicit relationship," stated Sharma.

She cringed at Sharma's crude choice of words. Instead of saying anything, she merely nodded in affirmation.

She was one of those witnesses with whom Sharma, on the one hand, loved to deal with because of their truthfulness and unimaginative nature. But, on the other hand, they could prove to be challenging if they decided to shield the one with whom their loyalties lay. Sharma recognized in Saroj Rani Jaiswal a cascade of everlasting devotion flowing for Dr. Rajinder Bhardwaj. It seemed she had no intention of yielding to Sharma's queries easily.

Ignoring her uneasiness, Sharma said, "Devika Singh proved to be difficult, and she was shielded because of her romantic involvement with Dr. Bhardwaj. How did others react to her unrestrained conduct?"

She looked at Sharma and replied in a rigid tone, "There had been a considerable amount of resentment, hard feelings, and unrest among the staff now and then. But there was never any formal complaint that came to light before her dismissal on August 12."

"Was there any pressure on Dr. Rajinder Bhardwaj to remove her from her position?"

"Only he could tell you. I wouldn't know anything about that. He has no reason to educate me about his official or personal business."

Sharma couldn't help but notice a trace of suppressed bitterness which had crept into her voice.

"What prompted her removal?"

"We had a suicide case in the emergency ward. The girl was local, barely seventeen—unmarried. She was brought to the hospital in a state of unconsciousness. She had consumed rat poison because she was with child. Her state was not apparent, but one of the senior nurses checked and knew at once. As you know, attempted suicide is a police matter. If things like this get out, you must know they can create so much hardship for a girl's family in our society. The whole thing was hush-hush, but an orderly told Devika about the episode. Dr. Anju couldn't start the treatment because Devika informed the police. They had to wait for them to arrive; by then, it was too late to do anything for the girl. She was beyond help. Ours is a small town and news like this travel fast. Within days, the town was buzzing with the news of the girl's suicide and disgrace. Her family not only lost their daughter, but they were also left to face the scandal. Poor child! She didn't want her family to suffer. If only she were a little older and wiser!" she said forlornly.

The young, thought Sharma, have this ability to suffer much in the time of grief, unlike the old who have seen enough sorrow and know it shall not stay forever. The young hardly know grief is like a thunderstorm. It comes whispering softly at first, a distant hum, a halo of vehemence in the sky, and then there is a sudden, violent, and copious outpouring; that drenches everything that comes in its way. It darkens the sky and turns every inch of green terrain dusky grey. But they don't realize its ferocity will become less with the lapse of time, and the sun will shine bright and warm, and wash the land golden, and no one would be able to tell there had been a storm. They scarcely understand this essential unfolding of grief isn't meant to last forever, and eventually, it shall come to pass.

"Who took the decision to fire Devika?" asked Sharma.

"The townspeople did not take the girl's death well. The girl's family was enraged: her brother Shivnaik Asthana came to the hospital after his sister's funeral and threatened Devika in front of the reception staff. The hospital's reputation was at stake. To avoid further confrontation, Dr. Bhardwaj scheduled a staff meeting. Keeping the hospital's best interests in mind, the administration took a joint decision to remove Devika from her position."

Rawat jotted down Shivnaik Asthana's name in his diary.

Sharma asked, "How did she take her removal?"

Saroj Rani said in a crisp voice, "She was angry, but there was nothing she could've done other than to leave quietly."

Sharma doubted whether the woman had taken her humiliation kindly. Dr. Bhardwaj was Devika's lover and, him being head of the staff, she must have expected him to support her. Her quietly leaving the hospital was something Sharma deemed unlikely, unless she was a woman of resolute tranquillity. From a few witnesses' testimonies, the picture that had emerged of the dead woman was one of an impatient, loud-mouthed, and cunning person. She must have felt anger at being abandoned by her lover.

Sharma probed her further. "Was there absolutely nothing that she said in her defence? She must have blamed someone, for example Dr. Bhardwaj, who was supposed to be on her side." Recalling Saroj Rani Jaiswal's earlier discomfort, Sharma refrained from mentioning Dr. Bhardwaj's illicit relationship with her. He had a feeling that something vital had happened in the meeting that was relevant to the events that led to Devika's murder later on.

Saroj Rani Jaiswal didn't meet Sharma's eyes. She had decided to look at the wall behind him. She said in a rigid tone, "She uttered insults which were vile, incoherent, and could distress a sensitive person at the least. Anyone with enough sense wouldn't have taken notice of her spite."

Sharma couldn't help but detect a trace of defensiveness in her tone. She was only revealing half of what she knew, he thought. There was something she was reluctant to disclose.

He decided against prodding her further. She could resist his queries and choose to alert Dr. Bhardwaj. Her loyalties lay with him who, at the moment, was a strong suspect. Sharma had no intention of putting him on his guard. Instead, he diverted his queries.

"Who else attended the disciplinary meeting?"

"There was Madam . . . Mrs. Bhardwaj, Dr. Anju, Dr. Namita, Dr. Sanjeev Kaundal, Dr. Naresh, Dr. Rudra Bhardwaj, Assistant Nursing Superintendent Mrs. Sarveen Tomar, Mrs. Shobha Mangal, and Anandmoorti Babu."

"Was it common practice for Mrs. Bhardwaj to attend disciplinary meetings?"

"No, it was the first time for her, just like some of the others. She occasionally attended official meetings. It was also the first time that we had to call for a disciplinary meeting to take a decision about an employee's future. Before Devika, we had no such occurrence in the hospital or any impetuous employees," she said stiffly.

"Did you know anything about her personal life? Did she have any friends outside the hospital?"

"I wouldn't know about that. I've no idea about her life outside the hospital and I doubt if anyone among the staff knew anything about her either. I know she rented a flat in Satyalok Society, a newer and expensive part of the town, and lived alone there. As far as I know, no one from the staff had ever been invited to her flat."

"Was there anyone from the hospital who might have hated her, someone from the staff, or even a patient? Can you think of anything, any reason, why someone might wish her dead?"

"I've no specific theory why anyone might want her dead. I didn't know her that well. All I know is, she had this nasty habit of meddling in other people's lives. Anyone might have done her in. The woman was toxic, sir," she said rather sarcastically. As an afterthought, she added further, "She was one of the most beautiful women I had ever seen. I couldn't believe she was bestowed with such a dazzling outer beauty— a woman who was so ugly inside."

"Thanks for your help, madam. That will do for the present," said Sharma courteously. "We might come again if the need arises."

Chapter 11

"For prying into any human affairs,
none are equal to those whom it does
not concern."

—Victor Hugo

Sharma was confident he would get another person, someone from the staff, who would feel no reservation about divulging any information implicating Dr. Bhardwaj. He was a man of success; he had money, power, and prestige. There must be many who would be wary of his accomplishments and despise him for his success; a few others would've liked to hurt him, damage his reputation, or make him face judgment for his affair. It was unlikely that Dr. Bhardwaj was popular with everyone in the hospital. Not everyone would be in awe of him the way Saroj Rani Jaiswal was. Sharma was confident he would find someone. Later, he would marvel at the accuracy of his own perception of basic human nature. He found not only one but two such people who felt no qualms about revealing the senior doctor's disgrace to him.

The house where Dr. Namita lived was a three-storey brick structure with an angled roof and two large dormer windows. Three high stone steps led to the solid wood front door. Rawat pressed the door bell and it was quickly answered by a fiftyish looking woman with carefully brushed shoulder length hair. She introduced herself as Dr. Namita's mother. After ushering them into a spacious and tastefully decorated drawing room, she asked them to sit down, and went out to call for her daughter. They seated themselves in two plush armchairs each side of the large leather sofa and waited in silence for Dr. Namita.

Dr. Namita was an ordinary-looking girl with a round face and a high forehead from which hair, wavy and the colour of dark cocoa, was swept back and fastened in a high, tight bun. She had small eyes, which drooped at the outer corners and were dark-brown in colour.

She walked in confidently and sat down on the large sofa, her knees together, her chin up, and her back rigid. Sharma could not see any sign of nervousness other than a vein throbbing on the left side of her temple. Was that a sign of inner conflict? Where did she fit in? As far as he knew, she had no close association with the victim. It could just be the excitement of talking to the police. She came out as an honest and good observer. Sharma liked her despite her indifference.

It was from her that Sharma gathered how shocked everyone was by Devika's outburst, and how jubilant Devika had been when she saw the effect her actions had.

Dr. Namita was forthcoming about everything that happened in the hospital. Dr. Bhardwaj, who was a good doctor, Sharma learned, possessed an uncanny talent for seducing young women. During her years working at the hospital, Dr. Namita had seen him getting involved in intermittent affairs. In the last year, she knew at least two staff members who had fallen prey to Dr. Bhardwaj's charms. They were both young, new additions to the staff at the time, and left the hospital after their relationships ended bitterly.

"How did Mrs. Gayatri Bhardwaj take his infidelities?"

"I have no idea. I doubt if she knew about his occasional affairs. She is a strong-minded woman. She wouldn't have stayed quiet all these years. But then, what do I know about their marriage? She might have had her reasons for staying in the marriage, I suppose. Unlike Dr. Bhardwaj, she's from a humble background. Her marriage has provided her with wealth and prestige. She might be carrying the scars from years of disappointments. Or else she might be one of those women who would rather keep her marriage intact, despite everything, as years of betrayals have dulled her senses."

Sharma said, "A day before her death, Devika Singh was removed from her position in a disciplinary meeting. As per my understanding, she was accused of intentionally delaying treatment that caused a patient's inevitable death. Could her relationship with Dr. Bhardwaj be the real reason behind her dismissal?"

"I wouldn't know about that. Despite Devika being unpopular among the staff, no one made any official complaint against her. No one here was so inept as to get involved in any conflict with her, recognizing the hold she had on Dr. Bhardwaj. I don't think there was any pressure on Dr. Bhardwaj from the staff to dismiss her from her position," she replied.

"So, their affair was common knowledge among the staff?" asked Sharma.

She had no reservations in revealing Dr. Bhardwaj's relationship. She said, "No one talked about it, but everyone knew. Dr. Bhardwaj was discreet about it. He avoided being seen with her in the hospital. But Devika had no qualms about disclosing it. She purposely dropped hints about their relationship from time to time. Her attitude toward the rest of the staff had also changed by that time. We had the impression that because of her relationship with Dr. Bhardwaj, she thought of the workplace as her domain; she expected others to treat her as if she was the administrative head and not a mere front-desk employee. Besides, Sanover is a small place. This kind of thing can hardly be kept under wraps for an extended period."

That was not clear-cut evidence, but Sharma didn't disregard it completely. It seemed likely that the change which others observed in Devika's attitude was the upshot of her increased confidence. It coincided with her being sure of her firm hold on Dr. Bhardwaj.

Sharma asked her to describe the events in the meeting.

"Everyone arrived at the meeting before me. I was rather late that day, I was on duty the previous night until ten in the morning. I barely had enough time to take a bath and grab something to eat at home before I was summoned back for the emergency meeting. I saw Devika right outside the boardroom. Everyone looked uncomfortable, including Dr. Bhardwaj. A meeting was not required to take that decision. Dr. Bhardwaj could have sacked her directly. I wouldn't imagine her having a signed contract with the hospital."

"Is it usual practice in the Lifeline Hospital for employees to sign a work contract?"

"Only with doctors. Sanover is not Shimla, sir. Doctors keep looking for better opportunities in bigger cities, so they are required to sign a three to five-year contract when they join."

Sharma asked, "Considering her relationship with Dr. Bhardwaj, Devika's removal must have seemed shocking to others. Did you or any other staff members have any inkling about her dismissal beforehand?"

"Not at all. As far as I know, no one had been thinking along those lines. Most of us were unaware about the objective of the emergency meeting. There was this conflict going on because of this girl's death. We had imagined that Devika might get a warning because of her unsavoury conduct in a situation which called for a more humane approach. But more than that, everyone thought the meeting was planned to discuss implementing clearer guidelines in the wake of the incident to prevent a similar happening. We thought the staff would be directed to follow those instructions. We learned the real objective only after we were handed the agenda."

He questioned Dr. Namita about the accusations levelled against Devika in the meeting. She described how Gayatri Bhardwaj's presence had astonished everyone, as it was unusual for Mrs. Bhardwaj to attend any such meetings. It was only after Gayatri Bhardwaj accused Devika of misconduct, others became confident, and that was when accusations against her flowed in. The senior nursing superintendent, Gayatri Bhardwaj, and she herself were verbal about their disapproval of Devika's conduct, but Dr. Sanjeev Kaundal, could find no fault with Devika's conduct in the death of the patient. His insensitive remarks about the deceased patient had angered the female staff to a great extent which resulted in a furious spat. Dr. Bhardwaj had to intervene to stop the heated exchange.

"Others sat there as silent spectators," she said as she crossed her legs and added, "Although Dr. Bhardwaj wasn't involved in levelling accusations against Devika, he was the one who put forward the final proposal that cost Devika her job. It was a well-thought-out decision. If you ask my opinion, I would say it was Gayatri madam's decision all along."

If Mrs. Gayatri Bhardwaj had gone forward, took the reins in her hands, and directed her husband to throw Devika out of his life, it meant she had learned about her husband's affair. That seemed possible, thought Sharma, considering she had visited Devika on the night of her murder. It made her a strong suspect along with her husband, Dr. Bhardwaj.

Sharma asked her about Devika's reaction to her removal. Unlike the senior nursing superintendent, she had no reservations in revealing Dr. Bhardwaj's disgrace. Interestingly, Saroj Rani Jaiswal had taken her fair share of slander as well when Devika had dragged Dr. Bhardwaj through the mud. No wonder she was tight-lipped about the whole fiasco.

"We were all very shocked when Devika threatened Dr. Bhardwaj in the meeting. But I can see how it all happened. Getting involved with someone shrewd like Devika had been his biggest mistake. I had always known things would not unfold in his favour this time. Unlike his earlier love interests, Devika didn't have the naivety of youth. I never thought she would quit easily."

"How did the Bhardwajs react to Devika's threats?"

"They stayed unfazed. Their reaction was not something that Devika had expected. Devika was angry. She threw a piece of paper at Gayatri madam and threatened to go to a local paper if they failed to pay a large sum," she said.

Dr. Namita hadn't missed a thing.

"What kind of paper?" asked Sharma.

"Only Doctor Sahib or Gayatri madam could tell you about that. It was a folded piece of paper."

"And then Miss Devika asked for a certain amount of cash for her silence?" Sharma had difficulty in keeping the curiosity out of his voice.

"Not exactly in so many words. No direct demand or anything like that. But she made it clear that if they failed to oblige her within twenty-four hours, she would go to a local newspaper." Dr. Namita smoothed her hair and said in a defensive tone, "It was understandable. Devika could not have asked Dr. Bhardwaj to divorce Gayatri madam and marry her instead as early as Friday. The best thing for Devika that could happen in twenty-four hours was acquiring a huge amount of cash. I'm sure that's what she meant when she made her threat."

"So, no direct demand was made that day?"

"No, she did not say it in so many words."

Faced with Sharma's specific question, Dr. Namita acknowledged that no direct demand was made. Sharma knew he could not ignore her indication entirely.

She described how, a week earlier, Devika had been confronted by Shivnaik Asthana who shouted threats at her and left in a rage.

"I know many people here would see him as a suspect, but I cannot see him killing Devika. An impulsive and temperamental person like him could not have done that. He lacked the aptitude to plan and carry out such an ingenious killing. I know the family.

"The person whom Devika humiliated the most was Gayatri madam. Devika was the first woman who had humiliated her marriage in the open. She could have easily killed Devika. One could not blame her, though—slapped in the face like that, in front of the whole staff." Dr. Namita tucked her hair behind her ear and smiled at Sharma innocently.

The girl was shrewd and a keen observer. What Sharma liked most about his witness was how she didn't hesitate to relay her observations to him. He had to depend on others' observations to draw conclusions about a person, something he had learned during the long years of his career.

Sharma continued the questioning with a feeling this might not be the only revelation that his witness intended to make today. She took him through the events of Wednesday evening. She had left for home after the meeting. She was on the night shift again on that day and had taken a quiet walk in the evening. She had noticed Devika with Dr. Rudra. At first, she had mistaken Dr. Rudra for someone else but quickly realized that it was him talking to Devika in hushed tones. She had left unnoticed then. She had not heard their talk.

That was something. Rawat, who was sitting in the corner chair taking notes threw a quick sideways glance at his boss. Sharma knew better than to show his heightened interest.

"What time did you see them?"

"Around half past five."

"Would you say they were on friendly terms?"

"Definitely not. They barely interacted as far as I knew. Anyone else would tell you the same. That's why I was shocked."

"What happened then?"

"I saw them walking toward the Pipli Road, the road that goes toward Devika's apartment building. Later, around eight,

I noticed Dr. Bhardwaj leaving the hospital. He was carrying a briefcase. From my office window, I saw him crossing the street toward Ganesha Road, the road that goes to Devika's building," she said and paused to see Sharma's reaction. Sharma prompted her to continue. She said, "He must have gone to see her, although I cannot vouch for that. I had to leave my office at that point to attend to a patient. That is mere supposition though. I suppose the black briefcase put this idea in my head, as it was unusual for Doctor Sahib to carry a briefcase. He must have gone to pay her off as she had demanded."

Sharma entertained the same notion in his head.

"How did Dr. Bhardwaj seem?"

"Agitated and rather impatient. Usually, he is good at keeping his composure in any situation."

"Are you sure about the time Dr. Bhardwaj left?"

"Yes, I had glanced at my watch when I saw him walking outside. It had shown seven-fifty-five."

She had not seen Dr. Bhardwaj that night again until at four in the morning when he was called in to attend an emergency. He seemed weary, but not agitated or nervous. She had seen Dr. Rudra in the morning a half-hour before her duty ended. He was talking animatedly to nurse Vasudha Haldar. He looked exhausted, although he had this weird animal sheen in his eyes, as if he were high on something. The nurse Vasudha Haldar seemed awestruck with him as usual. Prompted by Sharma to shed more light on the matter, Dr. Namita elaborated that it was common knowledge among the staff that Vasudha Haldar liked Dr. Rudra. The girl was nice, from a good family, and seemed smitten with Dr. Rudra's good looks and intelligent talk. She was sure it was a one-sided attraction, although it was not beyond Dr. Rudra's power to lead her on just for flattery. The last words Dr. Namita said were with a trace of concealed bitterness.

After they came out of Dr. Namita's house, Rawat said, "It's odd that Dr. Rudra was seen talking to the murdered woman intimately. Do you think Dr. Namita is a reliable witness, sir?"

"Composed, meticulous, and a little bit too self-assured, but a keen observer nonetheless, Rawat. I think we need to take a closer look at both the doctors in the Bhardwaj family. Also, check if Dr. Namita had any personal grudge against Dr. Rudra."

Chapter 12

*"We all have strength enough to endure
the misfortunes of others."*

—François de La Rochefoucauld

Mrs. Sarveen Tomar, Assistant Nursing Superintendent, was more than eager to shed light on the whole affair as part of the inner circle who knew things as they were.

She was dressed in a light purple printed *saree* with a sleeveless matching coloured blouse and sat in one of the upright chairs opposite Sharma. Her drawing room was beautifully furnished, apparently in period furniture. Most of it looked eighteenth-century to Rawat's inexpert eyes; he knew almost nothing about vintage furniture.

Talking about Devika, she said in a know-it-all tone, "I've had my suspicions about her sincerity right from the start. I had seen through her long before others recognized her for what she was. She had her eyes on Dr. Bhardwaj from the start."

"So, she was the one who made advances?" asked Sharma.

"Certainly. I had seen her fluttering her eyelashes at Doctor Sahib. Even someone blind couldn't help but notice it. She was hell bent on trying to woo him, as if he needed any wooing. He is a good man, no doubt about that, but a born flirt." She gave Sharma a meaningful smile and continued, "I always knew something would happen between them. Saroj dismissed my suspicions, thinking I was trying to read too much into things. Later, she was speechless when I told her about spotting the pair of them at the cinema." She flashed a winsome smile and leaned back in her chair.

Rawat glanced at Sharma, who kept his face straight. Mrs. Saroj Rani Jaiswal hadn't mentioned the pair being spotted together.

Realizing that Mrs. Sarveen Tomar needed a few words of encouragement to continue further with her story, Sharma said, "That must have been shocking. Did they see you as well?"

"It was more distressing than shocking," she said with a feigned sincerity. "In my mind, I had thought it possible, but to watch them together was unpleasant." She, it seemed, liked hearing the sound of her own voice. After a momentary pause, she continued, "That was sometime in June. I saw them at Prem Gold Cinema. I had gone there with my husband to watch a matinee show of *Rajesh Khanna's Aap Ki Kasam*. I never miss any of his pictures. He is my favourite, along with *Dharmendra*. You must have watched it, I assume?" She looked at Sharma inquiringly. But then, without waiting for his answer—probably reckoning that his police profession rendered him unable to relish any entertainment—she continued, "They were sitting together holding hands two rows ahead of us. I noticed Doctor Sahib walking back to his seat a few minutes before the interval. I expected Gayatri madam there, but it was Devika who was with him. I couldn't believe it at first. But they were there all right. Afterwards, when the picture was over, I wanted to meet them, but my husband asked me to stay back so they could leave first. He didn't want to embarrass Doctor Sahib; he's impossible like that sometimes," she said wistfully, as if she still regretted having missed the opportunity to embarrass the senior doctor. She added, "I wasn't the only one who had spotted them together. Dr. Rudra was also there. I met him outside the cinema gate."

"Did he talk about Dr. Bhardwaj and Devika?"

"Yes, he did. He must have heard us talking about Doctor Sahib. I did not know he was at the cinema. It was him who spotted me first. He asked me not to talk about it to anyone. He didn't want the matter to reach Gayatri madam. He was concerned about hurting her feelings. He is fond of her, I imagine."

But, Sharma thought, she had told the senior nursing superintendent, who mightn't have been her only confidant. Was Dr. Rudra's kind regard for his *chachi's* feelings as candid as he had made Sarveen Tomar believe? Had he heard her talk about the lovers, which had gotten him anxious, or was it his malice that inclined him to find a mean delight in his uncle's predicament, wondered Sharma?

Sharma found this was an opportunity to inquire about Vasudha Haldar's infatuation with Dr. Rudra.

Mrs. Sarveen Tomar had more information than Sharma hoped to learn about the girl and Dr. Rudra. But she had no intention of replying to Sharma's direct questions. She said, "There's a talk about it. You know, her *bua's nanad* is my *dewrani's chacheri behen*. That's how I heard about it."

"You mean people are talking about their relationship?"

She looked around and then said in a low tone, "Their possible marriage."

Instead of trying to fathom the complex relationship between Mrs. Sarveen Tomar and Vasudha Haldar through endless links, Sharma asked her about a possible marital union between Dr. Rudra and the girl. Owing to Mrs. Sarveen Tomar's irksome tendency to sway away from the main conversation, Sharma failed in his effort. Instead of providing a direct answer to his query, Mrs. Sarveen Tomar talked about the girl's misfortune instead.

"I have heard they soon will have *roka* done. The whole engagement matter is hush-hush. But it doesn't take long for these things to get around. Vasudha is a widow, you know. She has *manglik dosha* in her *kundli*," she said in a tone that suggested a slightly mean relish in the girl's misfortunes, although she kept her face grim. "She was married a few years ago, but her husband who was not *manglik*, died in some accident five days after the wedding. People had warned her family against that marriage; the groom was not *manglik*, but they ignored it, dubbing it as mere superstition. We all know *manglik dosha* is unfavorable for any marriage. It always leads to severe conflicts and big health problems and eventually can cause death of the spouse. That's what happened with the poor girl as well."

To Sharma's critical mind, people's fascination with foreseeing the future, and their fear of what was vague and unreasonable, could make no sense. He marvelled at the cunning ability of all those astrologers and pundits who earned their living by manipulating the minds of ignorant people. Ignorance, Sharma reflected, had nothing to do with education. He often had observed conscientious stupidity in the well-educated section of society who, owing to their fear of the unknown, adhered to centuries-old, absurd beliefs. Mrs. Sarveen Tomar was more or less one of them, reflected Sharma. He wondered if a time would ever arrive when people could discard these useless and senseless superstitions and become progressive.

"Dr. Rudra knows everything, I suppose," remarked Sharma.

"He belongs to today's generation. As far as I know, he isn't *manglik* either. The youth nowadays think they know everything. They slam centuries-old beliefs, calling them mere superstitions."

As an investigator, he had learned not to jump to conclusions without collecting data first, weighing the facts and then thinking the matter through thoroughly. He was curious to know how this match had been formed.

"Who arranged their match? How was this relationship formed?" inquired Sharma.

"They must have asked each other, I suppose. Most probably, Vasudha's family approached him. She's too meek to take the reins in her own hands. The girl barely speaks. Once, Devika said something nasty to her, and she cried all day. Anyways, I was talking about their proposal. I've no idea. I always thought it was just a one-sided admiration on Vasudha's part. She, oblivious about her transparency, has followed Dr. Rudra around like a lovesick adolescent for as long as he's been here. I never imagined she would get him to glance in her direction even once."

As an afterthought, or to ease the severity of her harsh words for Vasudha, she added, "The girl is all right, if you ask me. It's just that he doesn't seem the type to marry the likes of her."

She paused briefly to look around, as if to make sure no one else was in the room, and then leaning forward, she said in a hushed tone, "I always thought he would get married to Dr. Namita. Even Dr. Bhardwaj seemed eager for this union. Dr. Namita is Gayatri madam's close friend's daughter. She's like family to her. But if this news about Vasudha is true, then I was wrong about it. He must have his reasons for choosing Vasudha over Dr. Namita. Someday, he will become Dr. Bhardwaj's heir. Dr. Bhardwaj is childless, you know. Knowing that, I would have imagined Dr. Rudra wouldn't have had to think twice about saying yes to Dr. Namita's proposal."

So, that was the connection between Dr. Namita and Rudra, Sharma realized. Those were all rumours though. Mrs. Sarveen Tomar knew nothing concrete, but Sharma knew he couldn't entirely overlook the information she had provided. The woman was shrewd.

He thought about Dr. Bhardwaj's estate. Would it bother Gayatri Bhardwaj if Rudra married Vasudha instead of Dr. Namita?

"Do you think Dr. Namita knows about this?"

"I suspect she is aware. She seems cross with Dr. Rudra nowadays. They used to be on friendly terms."

There was nothing else that she could tell about Dr. Rudra. Sharma changed the track of his questions. "How did Devika get along with the others at the hospital?"

"No one could stand her at the hospital. She was a difficult woman, thoughtless and selfish. Not a soul liked her among the staff. Dr. Bhardwaj was upset with her; the way she went about announcing the pregnant status of that young unmarried girl. You must know about the whole episode." She looked at Sharma questioningly.

Sharma, who had been told about the incident, deemed it better to hear another person's version. In a murder inquiry, it never was a bad idea to get information from different witnesses. On Sharma's insistence, she narrated the whole story. She was of the belief that Devika had done wrong in informing the police. Like many others, she empathized with the young girl. She, Sharma realized, was a woman who took small delights in the misfortune of others, but was not overly unkind.

"So, that was the reason for her dismissal?" Sharma said.

"No, not because of that. But yes, the incident gave Dr. Bhardwaj an excellent excuse to remove her from her position. Gayatri madam had come to know about his affair," she said in a conspiring tone.

"How did you know about that?"

She leaned back in her chair, fixed her *saree pallu,* and said in a scandalous tone, "I heard Devika telling it to Dr. Rudra. They were talking in his office. I was just passing by when I heard Devika telling Dr. Rudra that Gayatri madam had seen her with Dr. Bhardwaj and she was furious."

"Are you sure she was talking about herself and Dr. Rajinder Bhardwaj?"

"Absolutely."

Chapter 13

*"There is occasions and causes why and
wherefore in all things."*

—William Shakespeare

Dr. Rudra's offer to Mrs. Saroj Rani Jaiswal, a lift to home,
was made merely out of curiosity to know her opinion of his
uncle's involvement in the police investigation rather than an
intended act of courtesy. She stood there in confusion for a
few seconds while considering the motive behind his offer. It
was the first time that Dr. Rudra had done this. She lived in
the old part of town, and her house was nowhere on the route
to Dr. Rudra's house in the Kailash Colony. After
contemplating it for a few seconds, she graciously accepted
his offer and sat beside him, wrapped in her nurse's white *saree*
with a blue border, her grey hair in a tight bun, and her
forehead incongruously dotted with a coin-sized red *kumkum
bindi*. She was married, but her husband had dropped her off
at her parent's home—a week after their marriage—on the
insistence of his parents because of an unfulfilled demand for
a Yezdi Roadking motorcycle as part of the dowry. Although
he tried to rectify his mistake later, she had stubbornly refused
to go back to him. They were never divorced and spent their
lives cursing each other and their respective families for their

imposed solitary life. She kept her husband's name and the prefix Mrs. She loved her job in the Lifeline Hospital. Anything else hardly existed for her. Life at home was solitary for her. Her parents had died, and her younger sister lived with her husband and three children in Calcutta.

Dr. Rajinder Bhardwaj, despite his weakness for pretty women, was in Saroj Rani Jaiswal's good books; she had a fond regard for Dr. Bhardwaj's nephew, Dr. Rudra. Dr. Rudra did not like her much because of her brutal way of stating the bitter truth. They hardly interacted with each other. The thought of intentionally avoiding Dr. Rudra had never crossed Mrs. Saroj Rani's mind, but Dr. Rudra managed to avoid her because her duties at the hospital included many erratic jobs other than nursing because of her accommodating nature. They seldom saw each other. Any other day, he would not have cared to talk to her. But today, he wanted to hear Saroj Rani's opinion about the whole case.

He was so eager to know what the head nurse thought of the police investigation he never saw the man on a grey scooter who tried to cut in front of his car. He panicked and almost stepped on the gas pedal instead of the brake but luckily the scooter-driver had been driving fast and was already out of his way. Rudra found himself easing back on the gas pedal. He stole a glance at his companion, who sat there unperturbed by the small happenstance.

To Dr. Rudra, the frustration of getting through the evening rush of cyclists, scooter-riders, pedestrians, *rickshaw wale*, and stray cows seemed a small price to pay for the gratification of his curiosity. Saroj Rani did not speak until they crossed the Krishna Chowk. He'd been contemplating saying something to start the conversation when he heard her stern voice.

"I never thought a bizarre thing like murder would happen in our town. The woman invited it on herself if you ask me. What do you think?"

"A most unusual thing! I hope the police will leave Rajinder *chacha ji* alone. It will be tough on our family. What do you think of the SP who's investigating the death? I forgot his name."

Saroj Rani, who had been wondering about Dr. Rudra's motive, realized the real reason behind him offering her a lift home. She had no reservations in talking about the case with Dr. Rudra. He was Dr. Bhardwaj's nephew.

"SP Vishwanath Sharma. He seems efficient. I have heard he is honest to the core. I am sure Dr. Bhardwaj has no role to play in Devika's murder. People always relish these kinds of rumours. It's very awkward of course, and we all know Doctor Sahib has his faults. He always had them, but I have never seen him losing his head over pretty faces. He's had a few distractions during all these years, but then, this matter is different. He wouldn't hurt a fly if you ask me. I expect the police will clear the matter up soon."

Dr. Rudra thought Saroj Rani was too sympathetic to his uncle's slip-ups but saw no point in saying so. Instead, he asked about her interview with SP Sharma.

"I told him what I knew about Devika. There was not much, but he was interested to hear about the meeting."

"What about the meeting?"

"The threats she made. SP Sharma asked me to repeat everything Devika said. I told him she had always enjoyed hurting people with ugly words," said Saroj Rani in a curt tone.

"None of the staff liked her."

"Yes, that's true. But then, she was hardly likable." Saroj Rani stated the truth.

"It looks like an inside job. What do you think?" asked Dr. Rudra.

"Someone from here? It could be anyone if we come to think of it."

"I wonder what was in the paper that Devika gave to Gayatri *chachi*. I hope no one mentioned it to SP Sharma," said Dr. Rudra, looking at the road ahead.

"Yes, there was the paper. I saw no reason to talk about it because SP Sharma never asked me. Everyone who knows me also knows I am not the least bit interested in other's lives," replied Saroj Rani.

"You did good. I hope it does not give the police any wrong idea about *Chacha Ji* if it comes out later."

"SP Sharma said anything, however small, might be critical in catching the culprit. It is not easy to know what to do for the best. But my policy is straightforward—to keep the matter simple, one should always state the truth and keep one's answers to the point. I wouldn't have lied about it, but I saw no point in talking about it on my own. And even if it comes out later, it wouldn't hurt Doctor Sahib. I'm sure about that."

"True, but the police wouldn't think like that. He is already their first suspect, I assume. He was involved with Devika, they had a fallout, she had something that would be damaging to him, and she threatened to expose him if he would not fulfil her demand." His voice sounded a little too distant to his own ears.

"I am sure Doctor Sahib has nothing to fear. Just the mere idea that Doctor Sahib murdered Devika is ridiculous. He had this weakness of character, but he is not a killer." She almost whispered the words.

"Of course," Dr. Rudra said.

He glanced at her face. It was melancholy. She looked at him with a forlorn expression but did not speak. Despite the chillness in the air inside, Dr. Rudra felt his hands sweating on the steering wheel. He exhaled, and it startled her. She opened her mouth to say something but decided against it. Dr. Rudra stayed quiet as well. The air in the car felt heavy with unspoken questions. Ten minutes later, the car drew up outside Mrs. Saroj Rani Jaiswal's narrow two-storey, stone-and-wood house. As soon as she got out of the car, Rudra bid her a polite goodbye, refusing her offer of *chai*, and gave a deep sigh of relief when she finally disappeared from his sight.

Tied to Deceit

On the way back home, he whistled softly under his breath.
His hands relaxed on the steering wheel. The nursing
superintendent, he knew, was honest and truthful. That was
the reason she had felt no qualms about disclosing the matter
of the threats in the meeting to the police. She had not done
that out of malice or vindictiveness.

He wondered if it was wise of him to talk about the
murder. He was involved in this murder case like everyone
else in the hospital. The nursing superintendent was nobody's
fool. She was a keen observer. Was it suspicious to point out
his *chacha's* first-hand involvement in the murder case? Could
she have seen through his guilty conscience? Was it ill-advised
of him to talk about the case? Suddenly, the air in the car felt
heavy again. His mind was seized by anxiety. A sinking feeling
of fear swept over him and shattered his peace. He must think
about everything calmly and be cautious. There was no point
in getting worried now. The sooner this matter ended, the
better it would be for him.

Chapter 14

"Beside all the small reasons we assign,
there is a great reason for the existence
of every extant fact; a reason which lies
grand and immovable, often
unsuspected behind it in silence."

—Ralph Waldo Emerson

She was wearing a loose, lightly embroidered *kurta* with a plain, tight *churidar* and a matching *dupatta* in faded lavender. She had just arrived at the hospital for her night shift and was about to leave for a change of clothes when Sharma and Rawat approached her. She, Sharma thought, was a woman who wasn't bestowed with any natural beauty and lacked the expertise to make herself beautiful, but she tried to nonetheless. The harsh yellow light of the ceiling bulb revealed the uneven splotches on her powdered face, and her lipstick, in the same shade of lavender as her *dupatta*, intensified her already-blemished dark complexion. She wasn't wearing any jewellery except for small heart-shaped earrings and a ring, on the third finger of her right hand, with a single blue sapphire surrounded by tiny sparkling diamonds set in gold.

Nurse Vasudha Haldar was, Sharma suspected, one of those plain-looking women whose existence had always remained inconspicuous in a group; men wouldn't even notice her. She would draw no attention to herself and would go unnoticed. If the rumour was to be believed, she would soon marry Dr. Rudra. What did she possess, wondered Sharma, which had caught a man like Dr. Rudra's attention? With his looks, combined with his uncle's wealth, he could have gotten any girl. He, in Sarveen Tomar's opinion, was one of those superficial fellows who usually married either for looks or for money. According to her, Vasudha was a nice girl, but Dr. Rudra didn't seem deep enough to marry a plain-looking girl just for her good self.

"We're here to ask a few questions about Miss Devika Singh. It won't take long. There are one or two things which we're hoping you may be able to help us understand better."

"Oh, me?" Vasudha looked tense and rather unsettled. She, apparently, hadn't expected herself to be included in the police inquiries.

She shrugged impassively and then said, "I hardly knew her, but all right. My duty starts in fifteen minutes. I hope your questions won't take long."

It seemed she had regained her composure.

"Could we sit somewhere?" asked Sharma.

She reluctantly led them to one of the empty rooms at the end of the hallway. The room had several empty cardboard boxes lying haphazardly on the floor and a stack of four white plastic chairs against one of the walls. Rawat pulled three chairs out and they settled themselves in.

"Did you like Devika Singh?" asked Sharma.

"We barely interacted. I didn't know her enough to like or dislike her," she said frostily.

"We've heard that you had a small spat with Miss Devika Singh?"

It was an unexpected question, and not welcomed either, thought Sharma, as he noticed a flush of anger pass over her impassive face. She stayed quiet—weighing her options carefully. The pale face had regained its disinterest once again. It didn't reveal her inner thoughts. Sharma waited.

After a while, she replied tentatively, "I don't know who has been telling you things. As I said, I barely interacted with her. We worked in different departments. I usually saw her in passing and that's all. How could I have any conflict with her when we never even shared common pleasantries?"

According to Mrs. Sarveen Tomar, Vasudha Haldar's plain disinterest when it came to Devika had more to it other than the usual dislike that almost everyone else among the staff felt toward the now-dead woman. Sarveen Tomar had spotted them once arguing heatedly about something. Although the woman relished gossip, Sharma saw no reason to discount her version of their relationship. Clearly, there was something Vasudha had decided to hide from him.

Sharma asked persistently, "What was she like? She worked in this hospital for over a year. You must have formed some kind of opinion about her, madam."

"She was a cunning, heartless person. She liked to exercise control over others and thought seducing rich men was the easiest way to get it. You must know about her affair with Dr. Rajinder Bhardwaj?" She stared Sharma questioningly in the eyes but, getting no reply, she went on, "She came from a humble background and hadn't achieved anything academically. Frankly, she didn't have enough intelligence. So, naturally, there was nothing else but her cheap sensuality that she could use to achieve wealth."

Her concealed hostility for the dead woman had come out in the open now.

Sharma changed the course of his questioning. He asked, "Was Miss Devika close to anyone among the staff? Would you say she shared something like a closer acquaintance, if not a good friendship, with anyone. Dr. Rudra Bhardwaj, for example?"

This sudden out-of-context question seemed to touch a raw nerve. When she spoke, her voice lacked her earlier confidence. "Only Dr. Rudra could tell you about it. I have no idea about his personal life."

"But I have heard that you two are soon going to get engaged. He must have told you about his acquaintance with Miss Devika."

Sharma had taken a chance. He wanted to see if she knew of any association between Dr. Rudra and the dead woman.

She stayed silent for a few moments, as if deciding on something. Sharma watched her quietly. She sighed deeply and then spoke. "I don't see how this is relevant to your investigation. I don't have to tell you this, but it wouldn't make any difference to me either way," she said with an air of indifference. "There's no definite plan of marriage as of now. We aren't engaged. But yes, we have talked about the wedding. Rudra wants to ask his uncle, Dr. Rajinder, as well. They were estranged for so long and he has no other family to speak of other than his mother. It's awkward for him to talk about the wedding at the moment. Dr. Bhardwaj is already stressed out because of the latest happenings."

She said this more to herself rather than to Sharma. Talking about marriage plans seemed to awaken an underlying uncertainty in her. On the surface, she appeared unconcerned. Sharma couldn't help but notice an insecure young girl underneath. It was as if she herself needed justification more than Sharma did.

Sharma was blunt when it came to his next question. "And who proposed the marriage?"

Her face reddened. It was difficult to determine if the flush on her face was of anger or embarrassment. When she spoke, her tone was brusque. "Rudra, of course. It had been on his mind for some time."

Sharma couldn't help but notice she hadn't admitted her fondness for the young doctor.

So, this talk about marriage was very recent, as Mrs. Sarveen Tomar had already pointed out. The timing at which Rudra had declared his fondness for Vasudha Haldar was curious, though. Was it mere coincidence or intentional, wondered Sharma?

He came back to his earlier question again. "And did Dr. Rudra share a cordial relationship with Miss Devika Singh?"

"As far as I know, he had no interaction with Devika. Neither was he acquainted with that woman nor was he a close friend. Rudra could never have become friends with her."

She had dropped the prefix doctor from Rudra's name now.

She hesitated briefly and then continued. "If you must know, Rudra couldn't stand that woman. She was so vile; she repelled him."

"Was there any particular reason for Dr. Rudra's profound dislike toward Miss Devika?"

"If you mean anything other than her awful nature, then no, nothing that I know of."

Chapter 15

*"There are no facts, only
interpretations."*

— Friedrich Nietzsche

River Ravi flowed in the east-to-west direction, forming
deep canyons and always posing a flood risk to the town of
Chamba during the months of spring and summer when the
melting snow amplified its water level. The weather had stayed
mild during the summer in Chamba, but early in August the
rain began; for the first few days as occasional showers, and
then as a constant heavy downpour with a strong wind. The
water level in the Ravi rose at a steady pace, threatening to
spill, and encircling everything around it. Schools, colleges,
offices, and factories were closed until further notice; people
were asked to stay alert until the danger was averted.

It was during one of those days, someone took Devika
Singh's life in Sanover. Flooding had hindered the police
inquiry. Sharma knew they needed to investigate Devika's
background. Her hospital file had revealed that she came from
Chamba district and that she had studied for her stenographer
and secretarial assistant's diploma at Indira Gandhi Industrial
Training Institute for Women. But Chamba was a big district.

They did not know about her town or city or village. The Indira Gandhi Industrial Training Institute for Women was closed, as every other college was until further notice. No one from the hospital knew about the dead woman's family. Sharma's only hope now was Dr. Rajinder Bhardwaj who, he was informed, would be back tonight from his out of town excursion and who, considering his relationship with the deceased, probably would know where they could locate her family.

They had talked to Shivnaik Asthana as well. Rawat had assigned Diwakar to trace his movements on the night of the murder. It was astonishing how much people noticed, especially the women. Apparently, he had returned home after his confrontation with Devika at the hospital. Diwakar had been provided with a list of relatives who had stayed overnight with family after the funeral. Two of Shivnaik's friends had visited him later in the evening and stayed with him until midnight. Lalita Rani, his next-door neighbour, had confirmed his friends' visits and so did two other women neighbours down the street. The young man was in the clear as far as the police were concerned.

It was Monday, 18 August. Roughly five days had passed since the woman was killed.

As the afternoon wore on, a gentle breeze blew with a hint of chill. Sharma sat in his office, the window open, the file containing witness testimonies on his desk. His eyes were on the words in front of him, but his mind was unable to grasp anything, when Rawat arrived.

"Has Dr. Sidhu called yet?" asked Sharma.

"She's done, sir. The victim's body is in the morgue now waiting for the family."

Sharma felt his spirits lift and a simultaneous feeling of guilt for feeling elated. He asked Rawat, "Let's hope Dr. Bhardwaj can give us Devika Singh's home address. What does the report say about the time of death?"

"According to Dr. Sidhu, the most probable time of death has to be between quarter past ten and quarter past eleven."

Sharma glanced at the report and asked, "Did she give any closer estimation of the time of death other than what is in this official report?"

"Yes, sir. She's sure about it. Personally, she thinks the victim was dead by ten. Officially, she put it between quarter past ten and quarter past eleven."

It was always difficult to estimate the time of death, but Dr. Sidhu's estimates usually proved to be right. She, with her skill, experience, and probably hunch, seemed to zero in on the exact time of the death.

"Anything else that could be of importance?" asked Sharma.

"According to Dr. Sidhu, the attacker was standing in front of the victim when strangulation occurred. The killer was left-handed and used considerable force. An extensive fracture of the hyoid bone occurred. The victim had taken Zolfresh tablets after her meal. She might have been lethargic at the time of the attack."

"That explains no resistance on the victim's part. With the victim being lethargic, it wouldn't have taken much to kill her. Even a woman could've strangulated her."

"We found an opened pack of Zolfresh in her bedside table drawer, sir. She might have been taking those pills on a regular basis. If it was a premeditated murder and the assassin was a woman, she might know the victim's routine of taking sleeping pills. Otherwise, there was no way she could have imagined overpowering a young and healthy woman like Devika."

"You have a valid point, Rawat. The killer couldn't have been a woman unless she was physically stronger than Devika and knew she could overpower her easily."

It was easy to assume that Devika was killed because of who she was, and what she did. There were people, Sharma knew, who hated her enough to wish her dead. But wishing someone dead was entirely a different matter. The actual killing required a blind hatred. To get to the murderer, he must find out the motive behind the murder. It could have been fear Devika had incited, fear that had prompted her killer to take her life, or she could have hurt someone's fragile ego with her actions, someone who embraced presumed hurts.

If she was killed for who she was, then it could become a cumbersome process. She had hurt many. The way her body was displayed pointed to another possibility. The post-mortem report said she died fairly quickly. Strangulation is often done in a frenzy; it is a crime of passion. But the killer took the time to arrange her body a certain way. It was as if they wanted to cover up something. Sharma sighed heavily hoping it was a straightforward murder.

Chapter 16

*"If you follow reason far enough it
always leads to conclusions that are
contrary to reason."*

—Samuel Butler

By the time Sharma and Rawat started out to Dr.
Bhardwaj's house, the clouds had already cleared. The sun was
shining bright and warm above them. The drive toward the
countryside was pleasing. As far as their eyes could see,
mountains towered above mountains in the distance, with
clouds hanging low. The tiny rows of two-storey whitewashed
houses with their sun-stroked slated roofs in the foreground
looked almost unreal with lush green *deodars* in the backdrop.
Blooms of wild orchids, marigolds, and daisies swayed with
the wind. The whole scene looked like an artist's canvas with
careful strokes in rainbow colours.

Dr. Bhardwaj's house was on the outskirts of Sanover,
almost two miles from the central, main market of the town.

A heavy double iron gate set into an intricate-looking,
seven-foot-high compound wall of ashlar masonry—the
stones trapezoid and in all shades of russet, like burnt leaves—
welcomed them. It looked intimidating. It had probably been
constructed in recent years, Sharma thought, because the

stones barely showed any sign of aging, and the pointing was intact. The blocks were set up in an asymmetrical, yet definite, fashion. The resulting irregularity formed uneven joints between the blocks and generated the effect of artistic intricacy. The wall was a little over two feet thick, its top choked with shards of broken glass—a jaded, old, and rather commonplace barrier that marred the beauty of the stonework, and in no way could it keep intruders entirely at bay. It wouldn't protect, but it would somewhat constrain. This timeworn barrier, exhausted and slightly daunting, Sharma knew, might make any intruder reconsider his dodgy business, but it would hardly stop him from breaking in and getting inside if he'd already decided to carry out his risky endeavour.

The double gate, though unlocked at this time of the day, was provided with a sinister-looking, heavy cast-iron lifting latch which, from the look of it, seemed to require effort to lift. Besides the latch, the gate had a solid cast-iron aldrop which could be secured with a hefty padlock and keys. Rawat, who had already gotten out of the jeep, swung open one side of the gate; its metal hinges in need of oiling, it made a low screeching noise. He let Sharma drive through and closed the gate behind him before getting back into the jeep.

The jeep bumped gently over the pebbled roadway, which had a single row of carefully planted pine trees on its side; their pyramid-shaped crowns swayed quietly in the wind. The trees stood tall and magnanimous, hovering to their full height; their russet-brown bark was scaly and deeply fissured; their needle-like leaves a soft pale green tinged with yellow, long and ever so slender, bunched together to form glistening spirals about the stems. Beyond the avenue of trees, they could glimpse a painstakingly maintained lawn and beyond that just the clear blue sky.

The air moved warm and gentle in their faces. In the distance, they saw the dark silhouette of the Bhardwaj house against the light sunlit sky.

It was an impressively built house and an excellent example of the British era's Tudor style architecture; a mixture of one- and two-storey brick-and-stone buildings with steeply pitched gable roofs, wide carved gable boards, and tall mullioned teak windows arranged asymmetrically. The bay window projecting outside was covered with metal roofing. The painted gables on the top of a single dormer window made the house look like an old English country house.

It stood facing both the west and the south. Unlike the compound wall, where ashlar blocks were used for all the stonework, this part of the house had comparatively expensive granite stonework. The front of the house was considerably raised on a terrace of granite blocks laid out in an elaborate pattern. A flight of six granite stone steps led to the front entrance on the south side. The exterior layout of the house was set to have a good view of the west side that overlooked the carefully maintained levelled lawn, and towards the east and the south as well, the sides that faced the forested area.

The grounds and gardens were charming. Sharma and Rawat mounted the granite steps which led to a grand front entrance with a decorative pediment held by four wide stone pillars.

The door was opened by a stern-faced, small, and frail-looking woman in her late sixties who scrutinized them with suspicious eyes. When she spoke, she reminded Sharma of his late grandmother who, with her four-feet-ten-inch height and commanding voice, had ruled his gentle and meek mother for a good forty-five years of their life together until her death. As they both wore civil clothes instead of their police uniform, Sharma suspected she was a trusted member of the Bhardwaj household: a decades-old servant who had probably served for long enough to be part of the family; she knew who they were and didn't hide her expression of disapproval when she showed them inside and told them to wait for Doctor Sahib.

The drawing room was lavish, imposing, all money—old and ample. The furniture was the finest—in rosewood, teakwood, and ebony, a blend of vintage ambience and modern comforts. The heavy silk curtains were drawn apart. The place, although grand, was devoid of any personal possessions. The room was meant for formal guests, Sharma concluded.

Dr. Bhardwaj was a tall man with a lean athletic build. He had a handsome face despite average features. He walked, straight and proud, toward them. Sharma looked for signs of apprehension but couldn't find any. If he was troubled by their visit, he didn't show it. His handshake was firm.

Dr. Bhardwaj settled himself in a comfortable chair opposite Sharma and Rawat, and without a preamble, he said, "I understand you are here because of Miss Devika Singh's tragic death. I learned about it yesterday when I came back from Khajan. We had to leave here because of a relative's sudden demise. Gayatri, my wife, is still there. She shall be back tomorrow. Dr. Sanjeev, my colleague at the hospital, called me with the tragic news. One of the nursing staff learned about it after the body was discovered, and she told everyone at the hospital." Leaning back, he went on, "Moreover, news in towns like ours travels fast, particularly, shocking news like this. Miss Devika started working with us not so long ago. Everyone at the hospital is shocked after hearing about her death. It is extraordinary! A violent death is both deeply shocking and unbelievable to those who know the victim, even if only slightly."

"But you two weren't just acquainted?" Sharma was blunt. "You knew Miss Devika better than that."

"Yes, of course. Quite well, for a few months at least. She came here to work over a year ago. About two months later, we started our affair which ended a few weeks ago, over six weeks to be precise," he said easily.

A young girl in her late teens arrived with tea and biscuits. Dr. Bhardwaj stopped talking and patiently waited for her to serve the tea. After she left, he took a sip from his cup and said, "I appreciate that you agreed to come here to talk, SP Sahib. Although privacy was not a concern at the hospital, I had made up my mind to take a few days off. As you are here to make inquiries, let's get to the point. I would be glad if I could be of any help."

His brown eyes were cool and observant, noticed Sharma.

"During her entire time in the hospital, both of you stayed close. What eventually happened that led to your break-up six weeks ago?" Sharma had decided to continue to be blunt. He put his cup on the table and kept his eyes on Dr. Bhardwaj.

Dr. Bhardwaj answered without flinching. "She, as you must know, was a very attractive woman. Right from the beginning, she bestowed attention on me. I was flattered. She was young and lovely and had this way of making anyone feel special. As a human male, the vanity I possessed ensured that I was no exception to the rule. I was thrilled. Our affair started. As always happens in such cases, the passion wore off after some time. She was half my age; so young that she bored me. We had nothing in common. She, I suspect, also got weary of my lack of zest for her youthful exuberances which I found dull and tedious. Things just cooled off then."

"Both of you parted ways on cordial terms then?" asked Sharma.

"That's what I believed initially. It seemed we'd both lost interest. At the hospital, we barely saw each other. She was always at the front desk, so it was not intentional." He leaned back, placed his right ankle over the left knee and continued. "I assumed she had met someone younger and more exciting. I had no hard feelings. She seemed happier than she was before meeting me. One of those days, I hinted about ending our affair. She was strangely indifferent to my suggestion as if it didn't matter to her either way. Though my male ego was hurt, I felt relieved. Then, a few days ago, she asked me for some help. It was about her family. We agreed to meet at my villa. My wife arrived there and saw us. Devika pretended we were still lovers. I am sure Devika was behind my wife's arrival that day."

Dr. Bhardwaj, Sharma thought, was too intelligent to hide any obvious facts which others might know and could quickly come to light during the investigation.

Rawat raised his eyebrows a fraction, but Dr. Bhardwaj ignored him.

"What was your wife's reaction to the entire thing?" asked Sharma.

"She was devastated. But she was willing to give me a chance. I took a few days off from the hospital. I thought it was better to avoid any chance meeting with Devika, but more than that I wanted to reassure Gayatri I had realized my mistake."

"From what I have heard, Miss Devika was quick-tempered. She didn't take her rejection kindly." It was a statement Sharma made rather than a question.

It was hard to guess what Dr. Bhardwaj was thinking. If he was perturbed by Sharma's question, he didn't show it. He said easily, "No, she did not. I gather you have already talked to some of the staff at the hospital. You must be aware of all the happenings surrounding Devika's termination. I assume you would like to hear my version as well?" He looked at Sharma expectantly.

"Certainly," replied Sharma.

"Very well then. I will supply you with all the bare facts. Kavita Asthana, a seventeen-year-old, had tried to end her life. Though the girl was in a serious condition when the family brought her in, the hospital staff could've saved her. There was a delay in starting her treatment, and the girl died. It was Devika who had caused this unnecessary delay. Apparently, she insisted on following the proper protocol by notifying the police first. By the time treatment started, it was already too late to do anything for the girl."

"But Miss Devika was merely a front-desk employee. Surely, she couldn't have possessed enough credence to take that decision."

"She hardly carried enough weight to take any decision at all, SP Sahib, let alone on such a matter, but that didn't restrain her from doing so. That she was a mere front-desk employee never hindered her ambition to ascertain control over other staff members. She was assertive and defiant. Assertiveness is a lauded quality, but when one's assertiveness upsets the wellbeing of others, it turns into aggressiveness. I am afraid the same applied to her."

"One of the doctors or any senior member of staff could have intervened and started the treatment. What stopped them from exercising their authority?"

"Dr. Anju, who joined us recently, was there, and she is a pretty conforming person. She tried her best to dissuade Devika, but I suspect her easy compliance was no match for Devika's brazen aggressiveness. Sadly, the nursing superintendent, Mrs. Saroj, was the one who could've dealt well with Devika's unruly tyranny, but she was held up with some other patient. By the time she joined Dr. Anju, the police had already arrived."

Devika's removal, Sharma thought, conveniently coincided with her break-up.

"She was recently dismissed from her position. Had it anything to do with your decision to end your relationship?"

Dr. Bhardwaj hesitated for a moment, but he kept his eyes on Sharma.

"I know it seemed a calculated act on my part, SP Sahib, as it happened when I'd already ended my affair with her. But it was not intentional. As the head of the hospital staff, it's my duty to make a decision in the best interest of the hospital. Devika hadn't felt any qualms about spreading the news of the girl's unwed pregnancy. She didn't have to do that. The patient was no more, but the family had to face the social stigma. People questioned the hospital's role in the girl's tragic death. Her death had brought out many supporters into the open: the very people who would've condemned her alive, wanted to get justice for the family. It was a delicate situation. Her removal was necessary."

"So, she created quite a furor in the meeting?"

"As much as one would expect her to do under such circumstances. She felt that the administration had wronged her. Though what made her imagine that, was beyond everyone's understanding. As the head of the staff, naturally, she held me responsible for her removal. She threatened me. But then, she spared no one. She was sore at the time. Her outburst was not the least bit unexpected."

Dr. Bhardwaj was thorough in stating the facts so far, thought Rawat. But then, Devika had threatened him in front of others in the disciplinary meeting. To come clean about the whole episode was his best bet under the circumstances.

"But she had no intention of parting ways with you, as you believed," said Sharma.

"She had no wish to marry me. She never intended to be a constant in my life. She asked for money—fifteen *lakhs*. Neither my wife, nor I, were likely to kill her because we couldn't afford to part ourselves from a sum which was only a meager amount of our vast wealth."

"I understand she had Dr. Sanjeev Kaundal's support. He had a row with other staff members during the meeting. Do you think Devika had any hold on him?"

"That was just a difference of opinion. Dr. Sanjeev Kaundal is an anti-feminist. He had, altogether, a different attitude toward the whole episode about the girl's death. His misogynistic views angered all the women in the meeting as expected," Dr. Bhardwaj replied, his tone nonchalant.

The same girl who had served tea earlier entered the room again. She picked up the empty cups and placed them carefully on a tray and took it away, closing the door behind her.

Dr. Bhardwaj who had stopped talking on her arrival resumed. "So there was some scrapping. But that meant nothing. Besides, it was quite natural to have a tiff when there were so many of us with different viewpoints. We get along well otherwise. Moreover, Dr. Sanjeev had always disliked Devika for her unconventional ways. She wouldn't have found a supporter in Dr. Sanjeev that day if not for the others. They pushed him to it. The anger spouting from all the feminists drove him to Devika's side. There was nothing personal in his alignment. I wouldn't put too much credence on common gossip in his case."

It was hard to understand if Dr. Bhardwaj, despite everything, still felt possessive and found it hard to entertain his dead mistress's close association with someone else, or if he was stating the facts accurately. Sharma pursued a different line of inquiry.

"I'm told that Miss Devika threatened to go to the newspaper if you failed to carry out her demand. That would've clouded your reputation."

"I admit I have my vices when it comes to women and I'm not proud of it. I never thought love had anything to do with these occasional flings. There were others . . . as well, before Devika." He hesitated momentarily. "I never deceived myself by imagining that no one knew about my infidelities. I don't intend to sound like a male chauvinist, but being a man, it doesn't affect me the way it might affect a woman. As you must know, our society is such that a newspaper story might have carried weight only if people hadn't known about my past affairs. I wouldn't pretend to dismiss the whole matter as inconsequential though. The story in print would have affected my wife and it would have been very awkward for both of us. But it would just be a matter of time before the dust settled. People forget things faster than they believe. You can't think I killed her for something so trifling."

"Was there anyone who hated her for any specific reason?"

"I wouldn't know, SP Sahib. She was an eccentric woman in certain ways, hateful, mean-spirited, and unhappy with everyone. It was typical of her to rub others the wrong way.

You don't believe I was the only one she had snubbed? She was vile. She must have miffed many others."

"You were close to her for a considerable time. You must have known her well."

"In the beginning, I thought she was overly flirtatious and the appeal it held for her, I suspected, lay in her being proven irresistible. You know, one of those women who copiously flirt because they're attention seekers. That was in the beginning, though. I felt she lacked faith in herself, in her abilities, and had this deeply rooted need for reassurance. But as time went by, I started to doubt my own powers of observation. She craved attention, but more than that she was so unlike any average woman. She was unconventional and more like a man—she enjoyed physical intimacy without any emotional connection. Unlike her women counterparts, she despised the emotional dependency they often associated with enduring relationships. Usually, we men are blamed for viewing women as occasional amusements, but that's how she saw men. I'm not ashamed to admit that she treated me as a sporadic distraction, you know, a mere pastime that she occasionally needed to amuse herself with, but an insignificant being in any case whom she couldn't permit to become a constant in her life. She was so unlike any woman I have met, and that was part of her attraction for me. Although most men would've welcomed that attribute of hers, as I had done, it might not have gone down well with a possessive person—an egoist who wouldn't let her treat him like a pastime."

Sharma couldn't help but agree that Dr. Bhardwaj had a valid point. Devika was an enigma. Her impassiveness could easily drive a susceptible person mad. Her relentless behaviour wouldn't have sat well with a jealous, possessive person. After realizing that she had this innate tendency to flirt, someone could have become furious and killed her in rage.

"Do you have any theory as to who could've killed her, a suspect in mind? Was there someone she saw secretly other than you?"

"No, I've no idea. Feeling her disinterest, I imagined there must be someone else. Although I was not the one who took the initiative in the beginning, she was the impassive party in our relationship. After my passion wore off, I started to feel her indifference clearly. She was half my age and a very attractive woman. I had absolutely no delusions she was interested in me for my sake. My wealth, my status in society, must have held a strong attraction for her. She liked indulgence. I felt she was only interested in having a brief relationship with me."

Devika, according to each witness so far, enjoyed men's attention. In Dr. Bhardwaj's words, despite not having any care for romantic relationships and despite her lack of interest in men, she didn't mind playing this game of relentless flirting. There was a chance she had been seeing someone else as well. That might not have gone down well with him. Or it could be her fury at being rejected. She wasn't used to being rejected. An envious person like her might not have taken rejection kindly. The picture that had emerged so far from different sources revealed Devika as a vindictive, egotistic woman who would have gone to any lengths to get what she wanted. Did her fury trigger Dr. Bhardwaj to kill her?

"Did she talk about her family, her birthplace? We know she was from Chamba, but it's difficult to find where in Chamba."

"I'm not sure, but it should be Panchpula. She had a sister, but I don't have any idea about any other family members."

"I understand you went to see Miss Devika on Wednesday night, the night she was murdered."

If he was disconcerted by Sharma's direct question, Dr. Bhardwaj didn't show it. He said in a calm voice, "I went to see her at her flat at around eight to give her the cash—fifteen *lakhs*. I wanted to end the whole matter at the earliest as Gayatri was upset with this new development."

They had found no money in Devika's flat. If Dr. Bhardwaj had given her money, it wouldn't be difficult to prove. There must be a bank transaction from his account. No one kept such a large amount of cash at home. Could it be the killer who took the money? So, whoever killed Devika knew about the money.

"And did you give Miss Devika the money?"

"Yes, I did. I took out the money from the bank. I had all the cash in the briefcase, and I left it there. She opened it once but didn't bother to count the money."

"Could you describe the briefcase?"

"It was a standard size, full-grain leather briefcase in camel colour."

"How did Miss Devika seem at the time?"

"She was astonished to see me when she opened the door, as if she expected to see someone else altogether. I had this impression she was waiting for someone. I explained the purpose of my visit and handed her the briefcase. She opened it but closed it again at once. I told her everything was over between us, and I had no further intention of keeping any relationship going with her. She had the same intention and told me to leave. I left straightaway."

"So, you didn't have a row with Miss Devika during your brief stay?"

"No. As I told you earlier, it seemed she was waiting for someone. She appeared to be in a hurry to send me out which worked for me perfectly well."

"What was the time when you left? Was there anyone who saw you leaving, who could corroborate your statement?"

"I didn't check my watch, but it must have been ten past eight or quarter past eight at the most. If I'd known she was going to be murdered, I would have made sure that someone saw me leaving the building. I would have taken the front entrance and made a point of talking to the watchman for a few minutes. But sadly, no one saw me. I took the staircase and left from the back door, as it was open and situated right next to the stairs."

"At what time did you return home?"

"It would have been around ten o'clock." Before Sharma could question him about his whereabouts after he left Devika's flat, he added, "I drove around after I left her flat. Before I took the decision of paying Devika, I hadn't consulted my wife. I wanted to make things right first and then assure Gayatri I had realized my mistake and was trying to rectify it. So, I arranged to get the money. But, before leaving for Devika's flat, I changed my mind and decided to inform Gayatri of my decision to pay Devika. I called home. But Gayatri had left in the evening to visit her brother. I paid Devika and after leaving her place I drove around, contemplating the whole situation, and wondering if Gayatri would approve of my decision. After I came back, I changed my clothes and went to sleep."

"Anyone who could confirm your time of arrival?"

"Leela kaki. She was awake."

Although he knew the futility of this exercise, because quite some time had passed, Sharma had every intention of questioning the servants in the Bhardwaj house.

"I understand Miss Devika gave a paper to your wife. I would like to know what was written on the paper."

Dr. Bhardwaj leaned back against the plush, soft leather. He seemed to consider his options as if there was more than one answer to Sharma's question. Although there was a momentary hesitation, his face did not change colour. When he spoke, his voice was steely.

"It was a letter, one of the many I wrote to Devika months earlier. It was rather a silly piece of writing. Gayatri already knew about my affair, so there was no point in handing it out to her. And, knowing Devika's aptitude for creating drama, it didn't come as a shock either. She wanted to embarrass us in front of the staff."

Sharma and Rawat sat there in silence. Sharma waited for him to say something more. Without flinching, Dr. Bhardwaj looked straight in Sharma's eyes. He was too shrewd to add anything else to his statement. He held Sharma's gaze as if challenging him to get the truth out of him.

Sharma asked him to write the address in Khajan where they had gone to attend their relative's last rites.

Dr. Bhardwaj was right-handed.

There was nothing more that Sharma could say or ask him.

"We appreciate your help, Doctor Sahib," Sharma said in a calm tone. "We are done for today. And now, if you don't mind, we would like to talk to all the people from your domestic staff."

They could get no useful information from Leela kaki. She answered Sharma's questions with a clear expression of disgust mixed with anger. She gave details of the Wednesday evening meticulously. According to her, Gayatri Bhardwaj had left at around seven for her brother's place. Dr. Bhardwaj had called at a quarter to eight to talk to his wife, but she had already left. He came back at ten past ten, refused dinner, asked her to bring hot milk to his room as usual, and went to sleep. She remembered the time because that was when she took her blood-pressure medicine.

She had then bolted the outside iron gate and the main door inside, put the keys in the drawer of the dining-room chest as usual, turned off all the lights, and had gone to sleep at eleven. That was the usual time of sleep for everyone. She had heard no one going out again.

The other servants couldn't add anything new. The security guard confirmed Leela Kaki's story. Madam had left at seven and came back the next morning. Dr. Sahib had returned at ten past ten and stayed home. After that the house had remained quiet.

Rani, a bubbly and overly giggly girl, however, said an interesting thing that seemed significant to Sharma, although he didn't realize in what context it was important exactly. The security guard, when asked, refused to corroborate Rani's story though.

In reply to Sharma's questioning, she described how on Wednesday night she had been home, helping Leela kaki clean up the kitchen, and had left for her room at half past nine to study for her class 10 private exams as Gayatri madam wanted her to study further. She had seen no one arrive because the window in her room was at the back; the pebbled drive to the porch could not be seen from there. She had heard a car arrive moments before she went to sleep. It must have been around midnight because she remembered looking at the clock and wondering who had come.

"What made you think a car had arrived and not left?"

She was quick to answer: "Well, the engine sound had died down instead of picking up, which happens when a car is started first."

Sharma and Rawat exchanged a quick glance. That could be important. Both Dr. Bhardwaj and Gayatri Bhardwaj had the motive, opportunity, and means to commit the murder.

Chapter 17

"There is nothing more deceptive than
an obvious fact."

—*The Boscombe Valley Mystery*, Arthur Conan Doyle

Sharma liked Rawat's idea of calling on Dr. Bhardwaj junior at his home. He had a few specific things in mind he wanted to ask Dr. Rudra, but more than that, he liked the plan of a sudden, unannounced meeting with Dr. Rudra which would allow him to study the man in his own home. Rawat accompanied Sharma to Dr. Rudra Bhardwaj's house to talk about the dead woman. After Dr. Namita's testimony, they had decided to see the young doctor whom they had excluded from the interviews earlier. They had not talked to him earlier as they knew he was doing the night shift at the hospital on the night of 13 August. There was nothing on the surface about Dr. Rudra that stirred any suspicion, but Sharma had a small, nagging doubt at the back of his mind after the testimonies of Dr. Namita Kaushik and Assistant Nursing Superintendent Mrs. Sarveen Tomar which had prompted him to conduct a detailed interview with the man.

They drove to the Kailash Colony, through the old High Street, and onto the Bhimtal Road. The old Mahadev Temple still stood tall and majestic at the top of the High Street, although stone steps had replaced the old rickety wooden stairways on either side of the temple, which led to the top of the *shikhara*. Rawat had lived in Kailash Colony years ago when his parents were newcomers in Sanover, and they had rented an old two-storey house for four years. He felt a nostalgia for his childhood days when on aching legs he had plodded the streets of this old neighbourhood with his friends. They had wandered around the Bhimtal Road countless times, more often during the summers when the town bustled with travellers from around the country and abroad, and had marvelled at the rows of antique shops while eyeing the foreigners shopping there.

The houses there were rows of two-storied, wood-and-stone structures with steep, sloped roofs and small windows and doors.

Rawat, who had come out of his nostalgic memories, said in wonder: "Does not that look strange, sir, him living here in this locality? He could have rented in Khijjar or Panchpolah. Or he could have lived at the Bhardwaj house."

"Strange! But what do we know about what goes on inside a family?"

It was hard to find Rudra Bhardwaj's house, as all the houses in the street were unnumbered. Rawat knocked on the first house in the lane. A child looked at them from the upper balcony. A large, middle-aged woman opened the door and directed them to the last house at the end of the lane.

Rawat tapped on the heavy wooden door. They waited in silence, but no one answered. From the look of the house, it seemed uninhabited, although a faint yellowish glow showed on the upper balcony.

"It seems quiet, sir. Maybe he isn't home."

"That is possible. Let's ask the neighbours," said Sharma, turning around as he spoke and coming face-to-face with a short elderly woman.

"I saw Doctor Sahib go in an hour ago. Knock on the door again," she said.

To extract information, Sharma asked her if she knew Dr. Rudra Bhardwaj well.

"He keeps to himself. Last month his mother came to stay with him for a few days, but I wasn't here at the time. I had gone to visit my daughter in old Mandi. My daughter-in-law told me about his mother," she replied.

Sharma thanked her and asked Rawat to knock on the door again as the woman went inside her house.

This time they did not have to wait long as Dr. Rudra Bhardwaj himself opened the door. He came with a towel wrapped around his waist, his hair still wet from the bath.

"Come on in, SP Sahib." He stood aside to let them pass and pointed to some bamboo chairs on the small verandah. There was a matching bamboo table in front of the chairs; it was curiously bare except for a small grey-and-black tape recorder and a few cassettes which seemed empty as they bore no label.

"Is that Philips?" Rawat said, pointing to the tape recorder. He was planning to get one for himself and he had heard that Philips was the best brand on the market.

Rawat leaned forward to check the tape recorder, but Dr. Rudra had already gathered the recorder and the cassettes.

"It doesn't work. I was trying to fix it. I shall take it to the electrician tomorrow." He smiled at Rawat. "Give me five minutes. I'll get dressed," he said and went inside an open door to the left of the verandah.

"I would also like to check his tape recorder, Rawat." Sharma kept his eyes on the open door.

Rudra came back wearing a plain blue shirt and khaki flared jeans. He was a handsome man with chiselled features. He was tall and dark, and classically good-looking. The effect was amplified by his lean and athletic build, and he gave an immediate impression of robustness. He had a square face, well-defined jawline, and stood a little over six feet tall. Sharma thought he could see Rudra's uncle, Dr. Rajinder Bhardwaj, in him—but he was younger and seemingly sincerer. Although Dr. Rajinder Bhardwaj had somewhat irregular features, his build, the contours of his face, and most noticeably his eyes—deep brown and piercing—acknowledged their family ties unmistakably. Rudra looked at Sharma and Rawat with a mild, disconcerting gaze. Although he had his uncle's ease of manners and confidence, Sharma detected a strained look pass through his eyes at the mention of the deceased's name.

"I understand you shared something of a cordial relationship with Miss Devika Singh," Sharma began, "and you were the only person among the staff to have a friendly relationship with her."

"You mean other than Rajinder *chacha ji*?" Rudra's amused eyes stared at Sharma.

"We will come to that too," said Sharma and returned to his earlier question. "Considering your friendship with Miss Devika Singh, news of her death must have come as quite a shock to you."

It was a statement rather than a question.

Dr. Rudra Bhardwaj's expression didn't change. "If you must know, SP Sahib, I'm on cordial terms with every member of the staff. I get along with everyone. News of Devika's death is, no doubt, shocking, but on a personal level, it makes no difference. We weren't friends as you have implied."

"Let me put it this way, Dr. Rudra. Miss Devika Singh was a rude person, but she treated you quite well, for example, her thoughtful behaviour towards you in the disciplinary meeting. Any reason for her consideration?"

"I don't know why anyone would think we were on friendly terms. It's a small place. Devika wasn't your typical coy woman. You've got to understand that she was outrageous both in her behaviour and her dealings with others. Her behaviour kept people's tongues wagging, and I'm a person who likes to keep myself away from others' affairs. I never interfere, and I never meddle. That set me apart from others. My guess is, because she never came across someone so detached, she found this quality of mine endearing. And, as far as the meeting is concerned, there was nothing she could have said about me, so she didn't say anything," he replied.

"You talked to Miss Devika on the evening of her murder. Any particular reason that the two of you met?"

Sharma watched him quietly to see his reaction. His expression didn't change. He said, "I saw her. But the meeting wasn't pre-planned. I went for a walk and met her on the way."

"What did you two talk about?"

"We talked about the weather and how August had been pleasant so far," he said, smiling. "She was in a good mood."

"Did you think that was odd—considering the circumstances?"

"I did not think much about it. But yes, after her murder I thought it odd."

"What do you think caused her dismissal?"

"If you want to know the official reason, then she lost her job because of her unsavoury conduct. But you're not interested in knowing the official reason. You know that already," he said. "On a personal level, I think she lost her job because Gayatri *chachi* came to know about her relationship with *Chacha Ji*."

"Do you know that as a fact?"

"I'm only making a guess."

If Assistant Nursing Superintendent Mrs. Sarveen Tomar's testimony was to be believed, the man, thought Sharma, was lying. She had heard Devika telling Dr. Rudra about how Gayatri Bhardwaj learned about the affair.

"When did you learn about Miss Devika's affair with your uncle?"

"I heard rumours in the hospital, and spotted them together in the cinema once."

"What did you do then?"

"Nothing. I am not a person who likes to meddle in others' affairs."

Sharma changed the track of his questions. He asked, "Dr. Bhardwaj is childless and possesses quite a vast wealth. Do you have any idea who, in most probability, would become his heir?"

Sharma watched him.

He flashed them a sweet smile. "I'm the only son in the Bhardwaj family. Naturally, *Chacha Ji* would want a Bhardwaj to inherit all the family wealth, even though I'm not very close to him."

"You are his only nephew. Would it bother you much if he bequeaths his estates to someone else other than you, for example, Mrs. Bhardwaj's nieces or nephews?"

"He would never do that. It's not Dr. Rajinder Bhardwaj's money, not all of it anyways, and I'm sure he is aware of that. My father decided to leave his share when he married my mother. He never cared about money," he said easily and smiled at Sharma. "And I'm my father's son."

Sharma decided to question him about Vasudha Haldar. "There's talk about your marriage with Miss Vasudha Haldar. As per my understanding, your uncle and auntie were keen for you to marry Dr. Namita."

Sharma noticed a look of strain pass through Rudra's shifty eyes once more. But when he spoke, his tone was calm.

"I don't see how that's related to your investigation. But to satisfy your curiosity, I wouldn't mind telling you. Rajinder *chacha ji* is, in no way, a conservative person. He would never force his decisions on me. I don't know who told you this fake news about Dr. Namita. As per marrying Vasudha, that's my personal business. I would rather not talk about it, as I'm sure it has no bearing on your inquiries."

"Have you any idea who could have killed Miss Devika Singh?"

"I wish I knew. But I did not know her well."

Sharma pointed to Rawat, who handed Dr. Rudra his notebook and pen.

"Could you write the name of the last hospital where you worked before joining the Lifeline Hospital?"

Rudra shrugged his shoulders and scrawled the hospital's name.

They watched him. He was left-handed, just like his *chachi*, Gayatri Bhardwaj.

As they turned to leave, Rudra said, "I was doing the night shift on 12 August. You never asked me about that. I hope that will help."

Sharma hadn't liked him. He couldn't say what he disliked about the man, it was just his hunch that had helped him catch many criminals in the last twenty years of his career.

Sharma didn't reply to his comment. "Good night, Doctor Sahib," he said and left with Rawat at his heels.

Chapter 18

*"The virtues and vices are all put in
motion by interest."*

—François de La Rochefoucauld

Rawat telephoned the police station in Khandi and, after a
few back-and-forth calls, he learned about Devika's
hometown. She was from Panchpula. After making sure that
a constable was assigned to inform Devika's family about her
untimely death, he reported back to Sharma. It was noon of
Tuesday, 19 August and, knowing Gayatri Bhardwaj must
have come back from Khajan, they decided to see her at the
Bhardwaj house.

The door was opened by Leela kaki once again. She said in
a curt tone, "Madam has just arrived home. I'll call her."

They followed her into the drawing room and settled
themselves in each of the single chairs opposite sofa.

Gayatri Bhardwaj arrived shortly after. She had her
husband's easy manners and air of authority. She was a tall
woman—a little over five feet nine—big-boned, with a few
extra kilos around her middle. She had a square jawline that
gave her face a masculine look despite her feminine facial
features. She settled herself in the same sofa where her

husband had been sitting yesterday, across from Sharma, crossed her legs, and waited for Sharma to speak.

Sharma said, "We are here about Miss Devika Singh's death, madam. You must be aware of it."

"News like that spreads fast. Your involvement in the matter means the rumours circulating about her death are true; she was killed viciously."

"Yes, we are treating her death as a murder. It was a brutal killing."

"Knowing people often have the tendency to exaggerate things, I didn't believe all of it, not the violence involved. It's terrible. My husband heard it from one of his colleagues, but then different people had different things to say about the way she died. We didn't know what to believe. Anyways, I was expecting your visit, but not so soon. I don't intend to sound unkind, but I didn't know that the death of a person who was a mere front desk employee, however terrible, would initiate such quick proceedings on the police's part," she said.

"We are doing our duty, madam. This is standard procedure." Sharma's tone was nonchalant.

"There would hardly be anything worth doing at the police station for you anyways," she remarked.

It was difficult to decide if her intentional ridicule of their police duties was because she was hurting inside or because she was naturally arrogant.

Without waiting for Sharma to say something in response, she went on, "You're here to make inquiries. Let's go ahead with that."

"I've already talked to your husband. He, I understand, had an affair with Miss Devika Singh which you were aware of."

People often despise tactless, direct, probing questions that get right to the heart of their very private feelings and threaten to reveal what lies beneath the surface. He looked at her face to see any discomfort at the mention of her husband's relationship with Devika. There was none.

"I was expecting this question, but not like this, SP Sahib. I expected you would go about it in a roundabout way, you know, considering our position. Anyways, so much happened in such a short span of time, that I had no time to believe it entirely. I came to know about it only a few days ago. I understood, when I heard Devika had died a violent death, that police would look into every aspect of her personal life, and that her relationship with my husband would come to light. I know many people had suspicions about their relationship, while a few knew about it as fact. People at the hospital respect my husband, but they wouldn't feel obliged to stay quiet about his affair with Devika now, considering the circumstances of her death. People were bound to pass this information to you. I take it that someone at the hospital told you about it?" She looked at Sharma.

Sharma had decided to be direct, but he hadn't expected any direct responses from Gayatri Bhardwaj. Her openness surprised him, but he kept his face passive and said: "Yes, we got this information from the hospital."

"That's what I imagined. No one has said anything, but people already have a very different attitude toward us. Only yesterday evening, when I went to attend my weekly kitty party at the Khurana's house, the low buzz of talk stopped as soon as they spotted me. I could guess the subject of their conversation from their sudden silence. But no one asked me anything. Being rich and powerful does that to you. You don't get a chance to offer any clarification because people dare not ask you a thing. They would prefer to hear someone else's half truth, then make up the other half, and then whisper a twisted version in someone else's ear. The whole matter gets distorted in no time, so much so, that it no longer resembles the actual facts. I shouldn't have gone there in such circumstances, but I was feeling particularly brave. Knowing that I couldn't run away from this horrid situation forever, that someday I must face this unpleasantness, I took a chance. Better sooner than later, that's what I told myself. But it's difficult not to take any notice of these nasty rumours that are going around the town. It will not die down until you catch the culprit."

"How well did you know Miss Devika?" asked Sharma.

"Only as an employee in the hospital. I saw her every once in a while, at the hospital, but I never talked to her. I thought she looked arrogant. All the employees knew me and exchanged pleasantries, but she'd never done that. I assumed it was because she didn't know me. That was before I found out about her relationship with Rajinder."

"I understand you arrived at your villa and found them together. Your husband suspects Miss Devika was behind your arrival that day. Was it a chance meeting or did someone inform you about it?"

A faint flush passed over her masculine features for a fleeting moment. But it disappeared as fast as it came. She said in a soft voice, "It was August 4, when I learned about it. I received a detailed note about the meeting." With no real emotional display, she went on, "Apparently, it had been going on for months. I had received two or three letters along similar lines in the past as well. I disregarded the note at first, but curiosity took over and I went there. However, I would spare you all the personal details. They were there all right. My husband asked her to leave and accompanied me home."

Rawat raised his eyebrows a fraction and glanced sideways at Sharma, whose face gave nothing away. Rawat knew his boss was equally surprised at Mrs. Gayatri Bhardwaj's willingness to be open about whole affair. They hadn't expected it.

"Did Miss Devika leave?"

"She did. She was furious, though. She uttered a few derogatory remarks about Rajinder. He, after all, had blatantly rejected her in my presence."

"Do you still have any of those notes, madam? Any idea who might have sent those letters?" Sharma asked

"No, I tore them apart. I thought it better to discard them for fear of them falling into someone else's hands. There was no clue, nothing at all that would've identified their sender."

"The last note—was it a typed note or a handwritten one? Was there any stamp on it that revealed the location of the post office?"

"There was no stamp on the envelope; the note was hand delivered. It was put in a sealed envelope addressed to me in the letter box outside the main gate. Leela kaki collected it with the regular day's post at around three in the afternoon. The handwriting was almost childish. It was a sloppy note. I felt someone had attempted to disguise themselves. It could be anyone from Sanover or the hospital."

"What about the domestic staff?"

"They are trusted members. We keep getting new people to fill in briefly every once in a while, but they are always the relations of old staff. I suspect no one from the domestic staff. There was nothing to gain from revealing my husband's infidelity other than to agonize me or lower him in my eyes. It must be someone from the hospital, someone who disliked Rajinder."

She could be right, thought Sharma. Anyone who empathized with Gayatri Bhardwaj would've told her in person or spared her the pain altogether by not revealing the affair. But there was one thing, Sharma thought, that she had overlooked. The sender could be someone who despised her and not Dr. Bhardwaj and had intended to cause her pain by exposing her husband.

Sharma asked, "We would like to know your whereabouts between eight and midnight on Tuesday, 12 August. You left home around seven that evening and weren't home until the next morning. According to your husband, you went to see your brother. But you went to see Miss Devika at her flat as well. Is that right?"

She was a woman of intellect. She, Sharma knew, was too shrewd to tell improbable lies. A suspect like her, if they decided to mislead the police, could easily fabricate lies that would be difficult if not impossible to detect. She had signed the entry register at the Satyalok Society. Sharma wanted to see what she had to say about it.

She kept her face impassive. She must have been expecting this question.

"That's what I told Leela kaki before I left. I never went to my brother's place that night," she said and looked Sharma straight in the eye. "I knew I could come under suspicion along with my husband. On Wednesday, I planned to see Devika at her flat. She had asked for fifteen *lakhs* earlier, but I was worried she wouldn't drop the matter even after taking the money. Her flat seemed the best place to visit her in privacy. I wouldn't dare to meet her anywhere else, as I was aware of her aptitude for creating scandalous scenes in public places. I didn't inform her of my visit. There was no point in letting her know in advance. She could have refused to see me. I wanted to talk to her alone to persuade her to drop the whole matter after taking the money. She was upset with Rajinder. It was pointless for him to go talk to her and make her see reason. His mere presence could have made matters worse. Hence, I decided to see her alone."

Sharma asked, "Had you something specific in mind you wanted to try—any offer to make or something specific to say to her? Your presence could've upset her more than your husband's."

The hidden implication of Sharma's question didn't escape her. She replied, "I had nothing I could use to threaten her with, if that's what you mean to imply. In our society, the worst fear of any woman is to lose her reputation, her honour. With an illicit affair, a man escapes unscathed. It's the woman who pays the price. But what could have happened to a woman like her who already had a shady reputation? She, as far as I knew, had no qualms about ruining someone's reputation or what was left of her own, if it came to that. There was nothing I could've said to scare her. My only hope would have been an offer of a larger financial payment. She might have hoped to make money from my husband; riches might've been a major drive for her to get involved with my husband in the first place. Anyways, I left the house at five to seven or soon after hoping to find her at home. I wanted to keep my visit private, so I drove the car myself."

"But you didn't go there until quarter past nine?"

She said in a brisk tone, "No, I kept driving. I kept thinking about how to approach her, what to say to her."

"Was she home?"

"I never went to her flat. I changed my mind. I decided I didn't want to see her so soon after all that had happened. My plan, I realized, wasn't practical. She had lost her job. Although it was a joint decision by the staff members, she would hold Rajinder responsible as he is the head of the staff. And then, Rajinder had refused to acknowledge his relationship with her. She would be infuriated with him and mad at me as well. It wouldn't be the best of times to approach her. I had no wish to confront her again, in case she refused to listen. I told myself it would be better to discuss the whole thing with Rajinder first. We would be able to tackle the matter properly together. We had yet to talk about the whole thing. It wasn't a very comfortable topic. He was too ashamed to face me after all that had happened, and I was too upset to talk to him. I realized we would have to talk things over at some point. I had time to think all this over when driving to Devika's building. So, I decided not to see her. But there was no point in going home and talking to Rajinder. I was still angry at him. All I could do, as I understood it then, was level accusations at him. Hence, I went to our cottage at New Kanauji. It is my refuge to escape to, to unwind. I went there for the night to think things over with a calm and open mind."

"At what time did you leave the building? The watchman on duty never saw you leaving."

There was no hesitation. She said: "If you mean did I loiter around in the gallery contemplating whether to approach her or not, I didn't. I left at once. It must have been ten past nine or quarter past at the most. As soon as I reached inside, I signed my entry because I was still thinking. But immediately after, I decided to give up the attempt. I was standing right in front of the stairs. So, instead of taking the stairs, I left and took the door next to the stairwell which was open. The watchman obviously couldn't see me leaving though he was at his post all the time."

That was, Sharma thought, a thorough explanation and the same as her husband's. Either she had time to think and get all her facts together, or she was stating the truth.

"And did anyone see you leave? Any person who could verify the time you left?"

"No one saw me. I met no one on the way."

"What was the time when you arrived at the cottage? Did you stop anywhere to get petrol or to eat something?"

"Half past ten to be exact. I know the time because I checked my watch when I arrived there. And no, I drove straight there. I stopped nowhere."

"And you must have been alone in the cottage as well, madam?" Rawat said with a hint of unmistakable irony.

She stated in a calm tone. "Yes, for the night. We have caretakers there, a couple—husband and wife—from Kolahari. I met them in the morning when I was about to leave. They come to stay for the night if we need them to."

She had chosen to ignore Rawat's sardonic comment which made Rawat more curious. He was about to say something when he looked at Sharma's sombre face and refrained from saying anything further on the topic.

"At what time did you leave from there?" Sharma asked.

"At a quarter to eight in the morning."

Knowing her answer in advance, Sharma still went ahead with his question.

"Is there anyone who met you on the way there at night, a neighbour or acquaintance who could verify your statement?"

"It was raining hard. I didn't see anyone outside. You've to rely on my words in this matter. No one can corroborate my story," she said in a regretful tone that appeared partly candid, partly scornful to the cynic in Sharma's mind.

"That can't be helped," Sharma replied soothingly and asked for the cottage's address, where she had spent the night of 12 August.

She leaned sideways, placed her hand into the side-table drawer, and took out a folded piece of paper. "I've already written the caretakers' names and the cottage address. I knew you would want to talk to them to verify my story."

Rawat handed her his pen and said in a smooth tone, "Could you write their village name as well, madam, in case they are not at their usual address."

Sharma watched her as she scrawled the name. Gayatri Bhardwaj was left-handed.

Was Gayatri Bhardwaj the one who had killed her? Devika wasn't a slight person. To strangulate her would have needed strength. They couldn't rule out Mrs. Gayatri Bhardwaj. She was a tall, big-boned woman. Besides, he could sense an underlying strength in her. However, to take someone's life, to perform such a vicious act, one must possess a raw physical aggression, the kind that can be unsettling for a thoughtful person. Did she have it in her? It seemed unlikely on the surface. But he would not bet his life on that. She would have felt way more inadequate than ever after Devika entered her husband's life. That was for sure. A woman so strikingly beautiful and more than a decade younger had the power to destroy the tranquility of her life. Either the hatred could have evoked it in her or the fear—fear of losing her husband, losing everything that was her life. People have killed for more trifling reasons.

As if reading Sharma's thoughts, she said, "You are wasting your time and energy here, SP Sahib, while the real culprit is still out there somewhere—free, carrying on with life. I assure you I had no reason to kill her. First and foremost, Devika wasn't the first woman with whom my husband had cheated. There were others before her. They might have awakened passion in him, but they never could form a bond strong enough to break the one I shared with him. Although my husband thought otherwise, I had always known about his flings. Secondly, my marriage is secure. It stayed unshaken in the past despite everything, and it will always be. Devika being dead or alive wouldn't have made any difference at all. My husband would never have left me for her. For all his faults, our marriage isn't an unhappy one."

It wasn't an unhappy marriage? Could a marriage be happy, standing on a shaky ground of adultery and a disregard for the wife's feelings? He didn't say anything; he listened to her quietly.

Unaware of Sharma's thoughts, Gayatri Bhardwaj continued, "I have spent twenty-four years of my life with him, and no one knows him better than I do. He has his faults, I admit, but he is shrewd and practical. Divorce is a taboo in our society. It's essentially off-limits for my husband, for he cares too much about his reputation and family name."

It was as if she herself needed to hear those words more than they did. She laughed all of a sudden. It was a shallow laugh which lacked amusement. She had probably laughed to hide her emotions, thought Sharma, or it could be her usual way of laughing.

She added, as if the words had occurred to her as an afterthought only, "He is not the first wayward husband in the world who has gone out to another woman."

Without bothering to reply to her last statement, Sharma stood up and said, "Thanks for your help, madam. That will do for the time being."

They decided to drive straight to the police station. A cool breeze had started to blow.

"Sir, somehow, I don't see a woman of Gayatri Bhardwaj's social standing opening up to us the way she did."

"That's what I found surprising as well, Rawat. She doesn't seem the naive type either. She is a proud woman, shrewd and well aware of her social standing. Her initial behaviour during the interview revealed her arrogance. Something tells me her openness afterwards was a well-thought-out strategy. There is something she is hiding. We need to look closely at her sudden trip to their New Kanauji cottage."

"Sir, New Kanauji is not that far away. It is merely one and a half hours' car drive from Sanover."

"We need to establish the time she reached there. In Dr. Bhardwaj's case, we have his words that Devika was the one who took the initiative in their relationship, though she never really seemed interested in him much," remarked Sharma. "He suspected her hand behind his wife's sudden arrival at the villa. That could be part of her plan. Let's assume she was only interested in the Doctor's vast wealth. She succeeded eventually. We have a bank statement to prove that Dr. Bhardwaj took out fifteen *lakhs* cash on 12 August. He was seen carrying a briefcase to Devika's flat by Dr. Namita and the watchman at Satyalok Society. But something happened that was unexpected, and he killed her. According to the autopsy, she was killed some time between quarter past ten and quarter past eleven. What was Dr. Bhardwaj doing at her flat from eight o'clock onwards? The neighbour said she heard someone walking around midnight. It doesn't add up, Rawat."

"What if Dr. Bhardwaj's vast wealth shook Devika's pledge to leave him alone after receiving the money?"

"Possibly, but even then, why would he stay at her flat for that long?"

"Suppose Dr. Bhardwaj lost his resolve of staying away from Devika after he arrived at her flat. Gayatri Bhardwaj arrived too, in the meantime, to talk to Devika and became furious after spotting her husband there. Devika might have provoked her, and she killed her in a frenzy. They both arranged her body to make it look like the work of a sick mind."

When they arrived at Gol Chowk near the police station, Sharma instructed Rawat to stop the jeep in front of the *chai wala*. Sharma stayed in the jeep and looked at the people around him while Rawat went in and ordered two cups of *chai*.

"Wouldn't you say it was too rash for someone intelligent like Dr. Bhardwaj? The obviousness with which everything points toward him is making me suspicious; there is more to the whole scenario, Rawat. He is a well-informed man of high intellect. If he planned to kill Devika, he would have planned better," Sharma said sipping hot *chai*.

"Maybe he is too clever, sir. He planned it thinking on similar lines."

"I would not call it a very resourceful strategy, Rawat. It was not a foolproof plan. There was always a chance of someone interrupting him in the act. It was still early for everyone to go to bed."

"He could have done it in blind rage. According to the post-mortem report, the killer was standing in front of her when he strangled her. She might have said something that inflicted his rage. She was known to hurt people with her nasty words."

"He does not seem like a person who would do things on the spur of the moment, Rawat. This murder was not committed in rage. It was cleverly plotted and efficiently carried out. The killer took time to arrange the body as it was. Dr. Bhardwaj, I agree, possesses the ability to carry out such an ingenious plan. But why did he leave traces of his guilt behind? He signed the visitor register, talked to the *chowkidar* on his way to Devika's flat. Considering the time at which he arrived and Devika's neighbour's testimony, someone was there for a couple of hours. His affair was more or less public knowledge. Let's not forget the album that we retrieved from Devika's flat. A few pictures seem to be missing from the album. If he was there to kill Devika, he would have left immediately. It does not add up. There is something amiss; something that is crucial to solving this case. Find which bank deals with Dr. Bhardwaj's accounts. We need to take a close look at his finances."

"Alright, sir. There is another scenario that seems possible. Suppose Devika had a partner in crime, but something unexpected happened and the plan went haywire. Devika might have refused to share the money she might have promised earlier. They fought, and he killed her in a frenzy, then arranged her body obscenely to divert our attention and left with the briefcase containing fifteen *lakhs*. Dr. Bhardwaj said she seemed in a hurry to send him off that night. She looked as if she was waiting for someone. It could be her accomplice."

"We have too many scenarios, Rawat, and that's bothering me the most," remarked Sharma and handed out his empty cup to Rawat who went inside to pay.

Chapter 19

*"The pure and simple truth is rarely
pure and never simple."*

—Oscar Wilde

On the morning of Thursday, 21 August, Mrs. Snehprabha came over from Panchpula with her son-in-law, Vinay Kumar to take her daughter's body away. Arrangements had already been discussed in an exchange of trunk calls between both the police stations, and Rawat had appointed Assistant Sub-Inspector Jignesh Diwakar to meet Devika's family at the mortuary. It had been five days and the victim's corpse still was in the morgue. Considerate of the family's need to take the body immediately away, Sharma had decided to interview them after they had performed Devika's last rites.

Diwakar met Devika's mother, Snehprabha and her brother-in-law, Vinay Kumar, at the mortuary and accompanied Vinay Kumar to look at his sister-in-law's body. Despite being in her fifties, Snehprabha was still a good-looking woman. Unlike most of the women her age, her body had not yet taken a dough-like appearance with the passing of time. Her face still bore signs of faded beauty. She sat in the waiting room outside saying she couldn't bear to look at her daughter's body. Her voice, when she spoke, was rough and devoid of any emotions.

147

Vinay Kumar was a shifty-looking man of medium build in his thirties. He looked around at his surroundings with clear distaste. Diwakar, who had seen relatives behaving strangely in a morgue, decided he didn't like the pair of them.

After Devika's brother-in-law, confirmed the body was indeed Miss Devika Singh, Diwakar came outside and informed Snehprabha it was her daughter.

"Do you feel well enough to answer a few questions about your daughter?" Diwakar asked in a gentle tone.

"What could I tell you?" She spoke in a harsh voice. "I know nothing about her. She stopped talking to me years ago."

Diwakar looked at Vinay Kumar, who shrugged. Diwakar asked him, "Who else is in the family?"

"My wife, Lakshmi, her . . . Devika's sister," Vinay Kumar answered this time. "But even Lakshmi wouldn't know much about her. We did not see Devika. A characterless woman like her . . ." He glanced at his mother-in-law and continued, "I . . . . we wanted nothing to do with her."

Ignoring Vinay Kumar's comment, Diwakar asked, "Do you know if she had any close friends?"

"I wouldn't know," replied Vinay Kumar and, as he glanced at his mother-in-law again, he asked, "*Ma*, do you know if there were any?"

"How would I know? She never told me a thing," she said broodingly.

Ignoring their cruel indifference toward the dead woman, Diwakar asked Vinay Kumar to write his and his mother-in-law's home address. Afterwards, he helped him to arrange with the mortuary to transport the deceased's body to her hometown.

After completing all the formalities, as he turned to leave, Vinay Kumar called Diwakar and spoke in a hesitant tone, "Do you know which lawyer to contact . . . to know if she has left any will?"

Diwakar looked at Vinay's shifty eyes. "I've no idea about that. You've to wait for a few more days. As far as I know, the lawyer will contact you if Miss Devika has left a will."

Mrs. Snehprabha, who had been sitting impassively so far, said in a shrill voice, "It wouldn't go to her husband, would it? She left him years ago."

BOOK 2

"We are so accustomed to disguise ourselves to others, that in the end, we become disguised to ourselves."

—François de La Rochefoucauld

Chapter 20

"The weeping of an heir is laughter in disguise."

—Montaigne

It was the visit of Devika's family which marked the start of a new beginning in the case; what initially seemed a more or less straightforward murder inquiry opened out into a completely different area. Afterwards, when Sharma looked back, he knew that Thursday, 21 August was the day when a series of small obstacles fell in his way which, although they were welcome in a sense, for they enabled him to look with new eyes upon the earlier exploits of a couple of suspects closely, turned the murder investigation into a succession of lengthy delays.

But, at the time, he was not aware of that. It seemed he wouldn't be able to solve the murder in a clear-cut way. He couldn't pursue the Bhardwaj couple directly without solid proof. They had high contacts and influence at the top of the bureaucracy. Dr. Bhardwaj was seemingly forthcoming about providing all the information required, but his wife had expressed her distaste openly at the police's involvement. Without solid proof, Sharma couldn't approach Dr. Bhardwaj again. He knew how the bureaucracy worked. He could simply be ordered to put the blame on someone innocent—of an insignificant background—and mark it as solved or close the file unsolved. He felt anger and frustration at the bureaucratic system, and his own inability because of the fact he couldn't pursue the Bhardwajs directly.

Sharma and Rawat's first stop in the city was the district court building. It was the morning of Monday, August 25. The day was bright and sunny with a cloudless, clear blue sky. The district court building of Dongri was an impressive three-storey historic structure in the center of town. It was built during the first decade of the twentieth century by the *Raja* of Dongri and had served as a place for his judicial administration for the next few decades. After independence, the building had come under the jurisdiction of the Indian government and now stood tall with the majesty and grandeur of the past, and served as a place to carry out judicial operations across the whole district including the town of Dongri.

Sharma and Rawat dropped Diwakar outside the district court building to inquire about the divorce proceedings filed by either party. They left for Devika's paternal house in Panchpula, which was located twenty miles south of Dongri, to talk to her mother.

The residence was a far cry from Devika's flat in Sanover, where she lived before her death and which was as luxurious as one could get in a town like Sanover. Even in the cheerful bright light of the morning sun, it looked desolate and gloomy, as if it knew of the tragedy that had befallen its occupants. It was an old place, probably built in the third decade of the twentieth century, possibly by Devika's past generations or someone else entirely, from whom her parents must have bought it. What once must have been a solid two-storied wood-and-stone structure was reduced to a shabby place. The paint which must have been a radiant lemon yellow once was peeling from the walls and the window frames looked unfastened, probably infested with termites. There was a curved wooden staircase snaking its way to an upper-storey balcony. It must have been, Sharma thought, originally built as an escape route in case of a fire or other natural calamities, but looking at its present condition, he doubted if it could serve its purpose at all. Two steps were missing and so were the wobbly wooden railings in a few places.

Rawat climbed two front stone steps to knock on the door. The woman who opened the door bore no resemblance to Devika and had a thick, stocky body and a harsh-looking square face, from where a pair of stony eyes gazed at him inquiringly. Rawat explained the purpose of his visit and stood at the threshold waiting for her to invite them inside. She scrutinized them for a few seconds too long and then instead of saying anything to him turned around and said in a loud voice, "*Bhabhi* the police have come."

She turned to Rawat then and moved to one side to let him cross the threshold. Without another word, she went to the front verandah from where she fetched two plastic chairs, placed them in the courtyard, and asked them to sit.

Mrs. Snehprabha came from inside. Although her face had withered with age, Sharma could still see traces of loveliness she must have once possessed.

There was nothing lovely about her voice when she spoke. "Have you caught the person who killed her?"

It was a harsh and uneducated voice.

"Not yet, madam. But I need to ask a few things about your daughter."

She said, her voice sour, "You are wasting your time, Sahib. She had been living alone for many years up until now. I do not know what she got up to when she was away."

"She must have visited you sometimes?"

"Not as often as you would expect a child to visit her widowed mother," she said, her voice sarcastic. "I might not be her real mother, but loved her like my Lakshmi. But she never considered me her *Ma*."

"And her real mother?" asked Sharma.

"Her mother, my sister, died when Devika was six years old. Our families thought it best for me to marry her father for Devika's sake."

There was no hint of any pain or regret in her voice of losing a child. Sharma detected a naked bitterness for the dead woman. The old grudges were still there. Nothing was forgotten. She appeared unruffled otherwise. She had had time to adjust to the shock of losing Devika. Nevertheless, Sharma found her sullen resentment distasteful. She was her *mausi* after all if not her real mother. It might have been someone else's daughter killed, the way she was acting.

"I understand she had lived apart from her husband for many years. What happened?"

"How would I know? She didn't tell me. If only her father were alive, he could have put some sense into her. He died a year after her marriage—heart attack it was—no warning, nothing, he just went. Her *babuji* was the only one to whom she would listen. One day she came here and announced she had left her in-law's place. I asked if something had happened, but she refused to say a word and said she would never go back to her *sasural*. No amount of nagging would shake her resolve. Days went by and people talked. Why would they not? She had left her son with her husband. The neighbours asked me to talk to her in-laws. Devika asked me not to meddle in her affairs. Then one morning she announced she was going back to her husband. My mind eased knowing things had fallen into place."

"But later she left her husband again?"

"Yes, she did. I wanted her to stay at her *sasural*. Lakshmi was growing up. I had to find a match for her in a few years. I told Devika that it would become difficult to find a good match for her younger sister if she left her in-laws' house. She could have at least stayed there till Lakshmi got married. And then, Virat *babu* was a generous man; he would have helped with Lakshmi's wedding expenses. But Devika turned a deaf ear to my pleas and left him. I still remember the day when her *sasural wale* sent a marriage proposal for her, Sahib. Her father was so proud; he couldn't hold his happiness in that day. He had never dreamt of getting a proposal from a privileged family like theirs for any of his daughters. Good that her *Babuji* were not alive to see the day when she left her husband."

"Didn't she try to keep her son with her?"

"No, she didn't. The boy was a simpleton anyways," said Snehprabha.

"Simpleton?"

"Mongoloid child, you know?"

She was talking about Down's Syndrome, thought Sharma.

Careful not to show his distaste of her choice of words, Sharma asked, "And he lives with her father now?"

"Of course he does. Devika wouldn't keep him. She told Lakshmi that her in-laws insisted on keeping their grandchild. She would have kept the boy if she had it in her mind. She was always willful, had always done whatever she wanted to do and nothing could ever thwart her from fulfilling her wishes. Even as a child, she knew how to get what she wanted. Her skills at manipulating people advanced with age."

"What did her in-laws and her husband say about that?"

"I don't know, Sahib. They never came here. I learned about the divorce only after the court proceedings started."

"Could she have left her husband for someone else?" Rawat asked.

"You mean another man?" She looked at Rawat and, without waiting for his reply, said, "There could have been. She wouldn't have shied away from doing something like that."

"How was her husband?"

"Virat *babu* was a good man. Theirs was a considerate family. When Devika got married, her *sasural wale* paid for the wedding *pandal* and all the other expenses. We had nothing to give except our daughter. They never made us feel inferior to them."

"Did Devika stay with you after leaving her in-laws?"

"Only for a few days. She then took a private care job somewhere. She had her divorce proceedings in the court. By then, I had given up on her. We were not even on talking terms. Later, she went to work in a hospital."

"Where was that private job?"

"I don't know the details, but she took care of a bedridden patient at his home. They were supposedly very wealthy."

"Would your younger daughter know?"

"She may. Devika might have told her."

"Did you or your younger daughter see Devika later, after her divorce?"

"Barely. When I fixed Lakshmi's marriage, I told Lakshmi to write to Devika to tell her to take a few holiday days for the wedding. Devika asked Lakshmi to visit her instead. She never invited me. I accompanied Lakshmi anyways, couldn't send the young girl alone, could I?" She looked at Sharma, who nodded in understanding. Satisfied, she continued, "Anyways, I wanted to go to the bazaar to shop too, but Devika asked me to stay home. She bought Lakshmi some of the wedding things, but got nothing for me. Neither did she enquire if I needed any help, nor did she offer a single *paisa* for other expenses. People gossiped about her, not to my face though, but it reached my ears, Sahib. Rumours reached my Lakshmi's *sasural* too. She had to listen to her mother-in-law's taunts because of Devika."

"What kind of rumours?"

"Nothing in particular. People talked about Devika's character. Living on her own despite being married, and being estranged from her husband and family was enough to start rumours. People questioned me about her living alone as if I was the one to lead her astray. They told me to make her see sense. They expected me to use my authority as her mother, as if she regarded me as one. If I'd had my way, I wouldn't have allowed her to leave her *sasural* in the first place." She sighed as if in pain.

"Was she close to anyone here? Any close friends to whom she confided everything?"

"No, she had none. She wasn't one to keep friendships. Too full of herself if you ask my opinion."

"When did you last see her?"

She stayed quiet. A deep furrow appeared between her brows. Sharma sat watching her face. He could swear the question had made her uneasy. It seemed as if she already knew the answer but was pretending to think about it for his benefit. Then she replied in what could be described as her shortest answer so far.

"Around eight months ago."

"And where was that?"

"Here, at home. I was about to leave for Lakshmi's house, when she came. It was shocking to see her as I hadn't seen her for four years. I told her she could not stay because I had to leave for Lakshmi's house. But she asked me to leave the keys and said she would lock the house and give the keys to the neighbours before leaving the next morning."

"Do you know why she came, if not to visit you?"

"No. I got worried thinking Devika might be up to something that was no good. I stayed home. She went to the attic, rummaged through all the old stuff, and took everything out. She put nothing back in its place before she left. Lakshmi had to put everything back in its place later. I could not even climb the ladder to get to the attic."

"Do you know what she was searching for?"

"She wouldn't tell me. But I think she was looking for her photo album. She had been looking for something in her old trunk. It must have been her old album because there were pictures of her mother in it. But I'm not sure about that. She rummaged through every single cupboard and trunk, and made a mess everywhere. I kept asking what it was she wanted, but she didn't say; she left raging with fury right away."

"Did she come back?"

"No, she didn't. I stayed home all day thinking she might come back. But there was no news of her. Next day, I went to Lakshmi's house. Devika had been there to get her old photo album. Luckily, Lakshmi had it there. Devika could have told me, but she wouldn't. She treated me like a stepmother. She always did."

"Was there anything special about that album other than her mother's pictures?"

"It had her childhood and class pictures from school and training college. There were only a couple of her mother. She must have wanted those because she became lively after getting it. She handed Lakshmi some money for the children as well."

"That was very helpful, madam," Sharma said with a habitual sincerity and stood up to go. Rawat followed suit.

She accompanied them to the door, and as they stepped out, she enquired in an awkward tone,

"About her house and everything else . . ."

"Yes?"

"Would it come to us or go to her son?"

Sharma gave her a narrow glance. He felt rather sorry that he had tried to feel sympathy for her at all. He tried not to show his distaste. Keeping his face passive, he said, "I wouldn't know. Devika Singh might or might not have bequeathed it to anyone. A lawyer could tell you about it."

As far as they knew, Devika hadn't left a will, but Sharma had no wish to pass this information to Snehprabha.

"But it wouldn't go to her insane son? An insane person cannot inherit." A note of clear disgust had crept into her voice. Sharma couldn't help but notice it.

He also couldn't help but despise her for her heartlessness, her insensitivity, and her disregard for her dead daughter. His earlier conviction that her callousness was most probably consequential, rooted in her unhappiness, went to pieces. The sour, the petty, the unkind in her was natural. Her unhappiness had nothing to do with it.

"I wouldn't know, madam," Sharma said in a flat tone. "You're right though. An insane person cannot be entrusted with money or property. But the deceased's property could still go to her son, not directly, but through a trust. The trusts run by lawyers handle all the finances on behalf of any insane person. And her son, I understand, is merely different and not insane. He could inherit his mother's property no matter what."

"But she left him!"

"Yes, she did leave him. But she also left you and your other daughter, madam."

Before he turned to go, he took a moment to glance at Snehprabha's face and recognized her look of profound distress. He left her standing there, her face devoid of all colour.

Chapter 21

*"Facts and truth really don't have much
to do with each other."*

— Thomas Fuller

When Diwakar went inside, the duty clerk was not at his desk, and he had to wait for almost a quarter of an hour. It was a relief when the clerk arrived just before ten. It took another thirty minutes for the clerk to look for the names and find the file. Diwakar, who was getting impatient, had to wait again as the copyist had gone out for *chai*. The minutes dragged by while he waited for the copyist to return. He was a grumpy little man of fifty with grey hair and who looked at the file with aversion when the duty clerk handed it to him and explained what he needed to do. He merely glanced at the file, and while Diwakar waited, he took his time to clean his desk, which he did thoroughly and meticulously, and which Diwakar suspected was done out of pure spite just to irk him. Finally, the clerk photocopied the file and handed it to Diwakar, who was so vexed by that time he could have happily strangled the grumpy little man with his bare hands.

By the time Diwakar came out of the building, it was almost one in the afternoon. He was feeling tired, irritable, and hungry. To his dismay, he found that Sharma and Rawat had not returned yet. He bought the day's newspaper, sat on a bench under a neem tree, and started reading. He didn't have to wait for long, though. Sharma and Rawat arrived shortly after.

"Sir, you were right. The husband, Virat Singh Chaudhry filed a divorce petition under section 27 of the special marriage act, 1954," Diwakar said and handed the papers to Sharma. "He filed the petition eight years ago in the district court, according to the papers. He sought divorce on the grounds of desertion by the wife and got a decree for judicial separation against Devika Singh Chaudhry. But they reconciled and repealed their case. Virat Singh Chaudhry got another judicial separation order, but there was recommencement of cohabitation between both the parties before the separation period expired and hence, the divorce was not granted. The case is still in court as the husband still wants a divorce."

"That's interesting," Sharma remarked.

It was lunchtime, and they were starving. Sharma asked Rawat to drive back to a small solitary roadside Punjabi *dhaba* that they had spotted on the outskirts of Dongri. Rawat took a right and turned the jeep in there. He parked it next to a Mahindra Jeep, and together they walked toward the *dhaba*. It beckoned them with an array of tricolor flags of India swaying happily in the strong wind. The inside of the place smelled of delicious spices. Sharma picked a round plastic table with four plastic chairs placed on the outside pebbled yard, from where he could see the soaring mountains touch the clouds, their peaks still capped with tiny patches of snow here and there—winter's resolute defiance against the predominant summer sun.

Sharma ordered *palak paneer* and *dal tadka* with *tandoori roti* and *lassi*. Diwakar opted for *aaloo gobhi*, *chole* and *raiata*. Rawat, who had gotten fond of zesty Punjabi food, opted for mutton curry and *dal makhani* with *naans*. They watched the passing traffic and devoured their food in silence after it arrived in steel *thali*. It was an agreeable meal—buttery, spicy, and hot—served with juicy green chilies, hot mango pickle, and onions spiked with salt and lemon juice.

"The strange thing is they are not divorced despite Devika living separately for all these years," Sharma remarked. He had already finished his meal and was washing his hands. "Devika's mother gave the impression that the divorce had already happened. She didn't mention anything about the judicial separation order. Do you think Snehprabha is in the dark about what actually happened?"

"Sir, that seems very unlikely, but then she might not know anything about the official papers. Maybe their living separately was as good as being divorced in her eyes," Rawat said, chewing on a fiery piece of mutton.

"That could be true. She is shrewd, but in a silly way."

"Do you want *chai*?" Sharma asked Rawat and Diwakar, who refused.

Sharma went to order tea for himself and pay their bill. They always kept their accounts balanced by taking turns to pay for the meal whenever they ate out.

He returned with a cup of steaming tea in his hand and continued the conversation. "According to her mother, it was Devika's decision to get a divorce. She had a son, but her mother gave the impression that Devika wasn't the least bit interested in keeping the child with her."

"They didn't get along, sir. Her opinion might very well be biased," Diwakar replied.

"Their son's condition could be the reason for their divorce, sir," said Rawat.

"Yes, that could be the reason. However, in Sanover, Devika gave the impression of being unmarried. No one knew about her marriage or the divorce proceedings. What could be her intention? Surely not remarriage because to marry again she evidently needed to get the divorce first," said Sharma, looking at his watch.

"She might be interested in keeping her marriage, sir. The husband might not be willing to stay with her."

"That seems unlikely if we consider her mother's testimony. And anyways, why didn't she try hard if she wanted to save her marriage? The court papers state they stayed together on and off all these years. He might not be that bad if she kept going back to him now and then. The fastest way of getting a divorce in our country is divorce by mutual consent only. Any other option may linger on for decades. It is not surprising theirs was still in the court after all these years. However, we need to check which one of them wanted to save their doomed relationship. They might not have talked about it to others for their own reasons. Let's find out what Virat Singh Chaudhry has to say about it."

Chapter 22

*"From the deepest desires often come
the deadliest hate."*

— Socrates

The drive to Khandi was short and pleasant. It took them a little over an hour to get to the town and another fifteen minutes to find Jaidev Colony where Virat Singh Chaudhry lived. A *rickshaw wala* pointed them to the Ganpati Road from where they could take a left at a small temple and ask anyone about the address. The Ganpati Road was so narrow a car could barely pass. Rawat, tired of maneuvering the jeep through the narrow zigzag of bicycles, scooters, and a few young boys playing cricket, parked it in front of the temple and from there they walked to their destination.

The house where Devika had lived after her marriage was a two-storey concrete-and-brick structure painted in the colour of the pale sky. They went up to the door and knocked the brass knuckle twice.

Upendra Singh Chaudhry was a sixtyish, stolid, wilting-looking man who stared at them cautiously for a few seconds when they explained who they were and the purpose of their visit, before moving to one side to let them in. He was wearing a white cotton *kurta* and a checkered *dhoti*. He led them through the large courtyard laid with polished terrazzo in dove grey and faded black to the front verandah. As they sat on the bamboo chairs, two boys and a girl came running from the right side of the verandah and halted at the sight of them. The sight of strangers in police uniform had kindled their interest. They gazed at them with curiosity. The girl and the older boy looked to be eleven or twelve, maybe a year or two apart from each other. The other boy holding a hockey stick was much younger, and appeared to be around four or five.

Rawat, who was fond of small children called the younger boy, who hid behind the girl in a purple flowered midi frock.

"How old are you, champion?"

"He is three," the girl replied.

The older boy ran to Upendra Chaudhry and said in a solemn voice, "*Dada Ji* look, I am older than Bunty."

"Yes, you are," Upendra Chaudhry replied fondly.

"They are my grandchildren," he said, pointing to the girl and the little boy. "They are my daughter's children. She lives in Lucknow. Their schools are closed for the holidays." Then he pulled the other boy to his lap and said, "He is Sahil, Virat's son."

"Do they visit you every summer? That's quite a distance to travel!"

"Yes, they love to spend their summer holidays here. With my wife gone, it has become a family tradition. I tell my daughter we manage fine, but she still worries. Every summer, Veena comes and stays with us for a month," he said.

"It's natural for children to worry. At first, we are their parents, and then they become our parents," Sharma said.

"Where is Veena?" he asked the children.

"Mummy has gone to Rama *mausi's* place," the girl, who had already lost interest in their presence, replied in a bored voice.

"Durga *beta*, you make three cups of tea," said Upendra. Probably aware of her reluctance to do any household chores, he added in a gentle tone, "Come on! You are my good girl."

She opened her mouth to protest but thought better of saying anything and made a sullen face instead. She turned to leave when Sharma refused the offer of tea. He did not intend to trouble the child. The girl nudged the younger ones who were leaning on their grandfather's shoulders, and motioned for them to go inside with her. Although reluctant at first, they took notice and followed their sister's lead inside.

"We have a boy who helps with household chores but now that Veena is here, he has gone to his village for the holidays. Durga helps her mother with the smaller chores, but she's still a child. And the children, as you must know from your experience, prefer play to anything else," said Upendra Chaudhry.

Sharma, whose own children were adults now, realized for the umpteenth time he knew nothing about children. Although both his children were close to him, they sought their mother whenever they needed anything. Nandini had raised them almost single-handedly, from changing their *langot* to helping with their studies. Slowly, she had come to terms with the fact that he was not one of those husbands who help with children and other household chores. His only contribution to their upbringing had been the frequent conversations he'd had with them during their growing years. Nandini, who was a solitary person by nature and preferred books to a conversation, appreciated the time he spent talking to them. There were times when she had wished for him to do a little more, but never resented him for not doing it.

"It's perfectly alright, sir. It's a hot day anyways."

Rawat's voice brought Sharma back out of his reverie.

Upendra Chaudhry asked, "So what's it that has brought you here to talk about her?"

Sharma had no reservations about disclosing the news to him. "Devika Singh is dead. Someone killed her at her flat in Sanover."

Upendra said nothing for a few seconds, just looked at them, his expression sceptical. Then it came—the realization—the news, it dawned on him. He laughed. It was a mellow laugh which surprised Sharma.

"So that's how she went. She must have moved on to bigger things since the last time we saw her, to die like that," he said. There was no grief in his voice. "Anyways, SP Sahib, if you don't mind my intrusiveness, I am curious to know when that happened?"

"A few days ago, on the night of 12 August. We would like to talk to your son as well. Where is he?"

"Of course, that must be your priority. He is at one of our shops now. I'll send for him," he said, his tone earnest.

He called his granddaughter, "Durga, come here, *Beta*."

He had to call her twice before she answered. "Coming, *Nana Ji*."

The girl came running with the younger children at her toes.

"Go to the big shop and tell your Virat *Mama* to come home. Tell him it is urgent. He has to come at once."

The girl left to go, with both the boys at her heels. Aware of their desire to stop on the way and to look at things or eat something, Upendra Chaudhry added, "Don't stop on the way to eat *kulfi* or *thanda gola*. Go to the shop straightaway."

He turned to them and said, "I always thought there was no one else whom she must have troubled so much. Obviously, there was someone."

It took a moment for Sharma to comprehend that Upendra Chaudhry was talking about Devika's murderer.

Upendra Chaudhry said, "If you want to ask me anything, I am happy to assist."

"What kind of person was Devika?"

Sharma asked it again, the question he knew was as absurd as it was vital for every murder investigation. Most of the victims were killed because of who they were, and to determine that, he had to ask this question. What they thought about the victim was of no concern. What they said about the victim's actions and reactions was significant. It was a meticulous procedure, and a vital one. Sharma would listen carefully, gather facts, put them together, analyze them, and only then would he see a definite shape emerging from the mist from what once was only a faded silhouette in the dark. The final image, although it was never entirely objective because it was based on his own presumptions, would serve its purpose well. It would help him to establish the reason behind the murder and to find the identity of the murderer in the end.

"Don't think wrongly of me if you feel I'm speaking ill of the dead. But I have nothing good to say about her. She came from a destitute family, a different background altogether. We pointed that out to our son, but he wouldn't listen. How could he? He saw nothing beyond her fair beauty. Then we thought the girl was coming to our house. What difference could her background have made? Knowing money is something that comes and goes, I agreed to talk to her father for Virat's sake."

"How did things turn sour?"

"She was only nineteen when she came to our house after the marriage. She refused to do any household chores, wouldn't help her mother-in-law either. And then she had no shame or any respect for us elders. Tell her not to do something and you could bet that she would do it for sure. We overlooked all her mistakes thinking she was still a child. But she never came around."

"I understand she was stubborn and refused to listen to her mother as well."

"Don't let me start on her mother. All children make mistakes but good parents make them aware of their blunders and guide them in the right direction. Her father was a good man, but he didn't live for long after the wedding. If he had, things might have turned out different. Her mother was a different story though. She had no concern for Devika's wellbeing. After her husband's demise, she came here and talked about her intention of borrowing money from us to set up her shop. Not very bright, I told myself. Devika possessed no humility. She was inconsiderate—where did that come from? From her mother, of course. Where else? I know she wasn't her birth mother, but they shared blood. We overlooked all her mistakes, but what grieved me the most was Devika's callous disregard for Sahil."

He glanced toward the door and said, "Here is Virat. He can tell you better about her."

Virat Singh Chaudhry was no taller than his father, who had shrunken an inch or two with advanced age. He was a stocky-looking, short man with scant dark-brown hair that gave him the appearance of being somewhat aged. But that was the only thing old about him. Although Sharma guessed him to be nearing forty, he looked much younger from the look of his youthful face. He had a friendly face that seemed placid. Sharma didn't detect any anxiety on his face. He wore neat navy-blue casual jeans and a plain dark-green cotton shirt. He held out his hand to them and gave a warm smile. Virat Chaudhry fitted the description of the man given by security guard Narayan Das. He must be the man who visited Devika a few times and had an altercation with her on a couple of occasions, Sharma thought.

The children must have told Virat Chaudhry everything, as he said to them in a cordial tone, "Just give me five minutes. I shall get *chai*." He appeared relaxed and gave no outward sign of worrying about the police's sudden presence in the house.

Sharma declined *chai*, saying they'd already had tea at a tea stall in the market.

"Are you sure?" he asked, and at Sharma's assurance made himself comfortable in one of the empty cane chairs.

"We are here to talk about your wife. I'm not sure if you are aware of her death, but she was killed at her flat few days ago." Sharma watched him in silence to see his reaction.

His reaction to his wife's murder did not differ much from his father's. He looked at them in disbelief for a few seconds and then smiled a sad smile. It was the smile of a man who had been through sorrows and sufferings, who had endured much, and had held up.

"Murdered you say? So, that is how she died. Such an unpleasant ending to something so pleasant to look at!" he said in a mocking tone. "Her beauty was absolute, but just on the surface. She was the ugliest woman I have ever known."

Sharma watched his face in silence as he continued.

"You must be aware of her loveliness, SP Sahib, that impeccable beauty? You must have seen her?" He looked at Sharma and then, realizing she had died a violent death, added, "Her photograph maybe?"

Since last seeing Devika in death, Sharma had heard about her from so many people, and he'd formed an image in his mind of someone who was unscrupulous, menacing, and conniving. He had thought about her often in the last few days; he imagined Devika as a woman who was provocative, someone serpentine. The word 'lovely' had not entered his mind. 'Lovely' he associated with a sweet, amiable, and beautiful woman to whom none of these subjective expressions could possibly apply.

"Yes, she was a beautiful woman," he replied.

"She was one of those voluptuous women who provoke strong inclinations in men. She had this sensual, intoxicating beauty that would drown her admirers, leaving them devoid of their sensory perceptions until they could see the shallowness within, the ugliness underneath that beautiful face. It happened to me as well. I had fallen in love with the mask she donned; I was unable to see the viciousness behind it. When the mask came off, there was nothing but ugliness," he said and flashed Sharma a defiant smile.

Sharma glanced at Rawat, whose eyes were on Virat Chaudhry—he seemed to be studying his face to find out if he was acting up. If only there was another way, Sharma thought, to read the mind by a mere look at the face. Virat Chaudhry looked intelligent enough to know he would be one of the chief suspects. He was the victim's estranged husband.

He would not be so carefree if he were involved, if there were any chance of him failing to prove his innocence. Sharma couldn't detect any sign of grief or sorrow. He wondered about Virat's casual reaction to Devika's violent death. Was it because he hadn't done anything and had no concern? Or was he too clever to display fear? Was he trying to delude them?

As if reading Sharma's thoughts, Virat Chaudhry said, "You must think of me as a callous person; I was related to her once. It's heartbreaking, SP Sahib, when a young person dies. A violent death is always sad. But I'm not sad that she is dead. I was never one for pretences. I would not pretend now. Moreover, it's pretty hard to feel sorry for someone who has given you nothing but aches and miseries."

"I understand she was estranged from you for many years," said Sharma.

"Yes, a little over eight years ago. Although I had fallen out of love with her by that time, I asked her to reconsider her decision, hoping she might stay for Sahil. She was supposedly feeling burdened in our marriage and wanted to leave. And she left. It was her decision. She always did what she wanted to do anyways. You might think of me as an insensitive person, condemning her now that she is dead, but she knew nothing about emotions, and she cared nothing for feelings. Affection, attachment, love, and family—all the things we ordinary people hold close—she never let these interfere with her life."

"What about your son? Did not she want to keep her child with her?"

"No, she didn't. Sahil was precisely the reason she left," he said, his tone grim. "Things were fine at first. Later, when she became pregnant, things got worse. She hated everything about it; the bouts of morning sickness, weight gain, all those inevitable inconveniences that every pregnant woman has to suffer. Pregnancy drove her mad. After Sahil's birth, she was dismayed when she realized Sahil wasn't a beautiful baby. She refused to nurse him, saying it would ruin her figure. I had no desire to strain her, thinking she found it hard to cope with the pressure of being a mother at a young age. She was barely twenty-one. I did not want to force her to do anything against her wishes. I did not make demands. My parents thought I indulged her too much. Sahil wasn't an easy child. She took care of him but with a clear disregard. There were times when she would let him stay hungry or wet for hours until one of us intervened. If questioned about her behaviour, she would come up with plenty of excuses or just feign innocence. She was an expert at concocting tales. The days dragged on, and her attitude stayed unchanged."

"What happened then?"

"I realized that she was not the person I thought her to be. The only time she would indulge Sahil a lot was when someone came to visit her. She would feign motherly love, talk as if nothing had happened and she was a typical loving mother. I lost my patience, and our fights started. She threatened to leave us and went to her *mayaka* leaving Sahil behind. I was tired by that time. I didn't object to her going there, nor went there myself to fetch her back. She came back on her own after two months, but her behaviour toward Sahil stayed the same."

"When did she decide to file for divorce? What prompted her eventual departure?"

"Within months, we suspected something was the matter with Sahil. Doctors told us to wait for a few years. That's when she expressed her displeasure openly. According to her, it maddened her to sit at home all day and take care of a child with whom she couldn't feel connected to. It was difficult for her to contemplate a future for herself just being a wife and a mother. She wished to study for a nursing aid's diploma. Even though I was sceptical, I sent her to college much against my parents' wishes, who didn't like her leaving our son so soon after his birth. We had already hired a young girl to take care of Sahil, and my parents were always there for him. I saw no point in not letting her study further. I imagined she had too much free time on her hands, and it would do her good to get a job after completing her diploma. But she didn't complete it. She wanted to do a secretarial course instead. I paid for it as well. As soon as she finished her course, she refused to come back. By that time, I had become tired of her ways. It did not come as a shock either. I suppose I had expected that. She sent me the divorce papers. I signed them quietly. I didn't feel the need to ask questions. I knew she would twist the whole situation to her benefit. Anyways, when it was time to finalize our divorce, she decided she wanted to come back. She assured me she had realized her mistake. Foolish as I was, I trusted her once more for the sake of Sahil. You could consider me one of those people who in reality find it hard to comprehend the depravity of the human race, and get their hearts broken countless times. I had always been a romantic at heart, and in stories and real life, a romantic has to suffer. I was no exception. We took our case back."

"Didn't she want to remarry, settle down? She was very young when she left your house."

"She was a vindictive woman, SP Sahib. She could sink to any depth to get revenge. Her happiness lay in the sufferings of others. Family, relationships meant nothing to her. There was only one person she cared about, and that was her precious self."

The strength of his anger against the dead woman surprised Sharma. He had, Sharma thought, no qualms about revealing his underlying hatred toward his dead wife to them. Was it because he had done nothing? Guilty seldom have the nerve to exhibit such boldness. Or he could be shrewd.

As if he had read Sharma's thoughts, Virat said in a quiet tone, "I was angry with her for her ruthlessness, her insensitivity, and her conceited nature. But more than that I was mad at myself for failing to see through her to her real self. I felt that way for a long time."

"What happened then?"

"Afterwards, she left again. I got the judicial separation decree from the court. When there were two months left for our separation period to end, she came to stay here, forcefully, of course. After the separation period expired, she left. My lawyer obtained another separation order, but she repeated the same dirty ruse. Every time she would come and stay forcefully: long enough, a month or more, so the judicial order became automatically null. It became a ploy for her to torture us. She had a great ability to enjoy other people's sufferings."

"How did you feel about her coming and staying with you during those times?"

"The feelings of inadequacy, of frustration, of anger were something I had become familiar with after I married her, but it was no less difficult for that. At first, it was maddening to see her manipulating the whole situation in her favour. Then, as time passed, her ploy became merely irritating considering there was nothing worse she could have done, had it not been for Sahil. We resented her presence, but Sahil suffered the most. He does not react to unsavoury situations the same way as other children his age do. We had no choice but to send him to my sister's in Lucknow each time Devika came to stay. Each time it happened, he would lose his sense of security. An unfamiliar environment is hard to adjust to even for us adults. Sahil is a child, and a special child. It was difficult for him. We could not trust that woman with him. I'm glad for Sahil that it's finally over now."

"Was she close to anyone? Anyone, a friend to whom she confided everything?"

"No one, as far as I know."

"She must have had at least one?"

"No one from here, at least."

"Do you have any idea who could have killed her?"

"It could be anyone, SP Sahib. I'm sure many people wished her dead. She was a wicked woman. She must have hurt many others."

"When was the last time you saw her?"

"It must have been a month or more ago. I don't remember the exact date." His face was impassive.

"Not after that? Maybe recently?" probed Sharma.

"No."

He was lying, Sharma knew, but he decided not to pursue the matter further at present. He asked, "What did you talk to her about?"

"I wanted her to reconsider her decision as the court date was approaching," he said, his tone evasive. "She refused. The conversation lasted for a little over two minutes. I left then."

"That was very helpful," said Sharma out of habitual politeness. "Hope you don't mind disclosing what were you doing on 12 August from eight until midnight?"

Virat stayed quiet for a long uncomfortable moment. Sharma, who was watching him in silence, noticed his evasiveness. He could have sworn the man already knew where he was at the time but had been thinking of an excuse.

"I went to the cinema that night to watch *Dharmendra's* new movie. It was a matinee show at Basant Cinema. I asked the boys—my employees—to close the shop on their own. I left early to buy the ticket in advance and came home rather late after the show ended, some time after twenty to one. I went there alone, and I did not talk to anyone. As far as I remember, I saw no one familiar. No one can confirm it for me."

Upendra Chaudhry shifted in his chair. Rawat couldn't help but notice the old man's discomfort.

"Good enough," said Sharma.

"And I ripped up the movie ticket after I left the cinema hall. Old habit, SP Sahib."

"There's not much you can do about that. We shall take our leave now."

He was candid about everything except his visits to the deceased's building. He hadn't mentioned all of his visits and had kept quiet the details of his angry brawl with Devika.

Despite that, Sharma liked Virat Singh Chaudhry. He seemed open. But a budding liking for a suspect, he understood, was an indulgence in his profession that could do no good but cloud one's judgment. Sharma knew better than that. The truth was that Virat Singh Chaudhry had become one of their prime suspects after they came to know about his bitter divorce proceedings. He had a strong motive and the opportunity to do it. They couldn't give him clean chit unless he could provide himself with a solid alibi.

Virat Singh Chaudhry walked them to the door, held the door open as they stepped out, and then stood looking at them until they turned the corner of the street.

Chapter 23

"Truth is in things, and not in words."

—Herman Melville

"Do you think he was telling the truth, sir," said Rawat.

They were sitting in Sharma's office. Sharma stood up and walked to the window. Evening sun had coated the sky orange-red. Sunshine moved in patchy broad strips through the stained westward window of his office.

Without waiting for Sharma to reply, Rawat went on, "About going to the cinema and having no one to corroborate his story? He had a strong motive and also opportunity to do it. Sanover is merely an hour away from Dongri. He had enough time to go there, kill her, and come back with no one spotting him. We only have his words about his whereabouts on the night of the murder. And he lied about visiting his wife the last time as well. *Chowkidar* Narayan Das saw him."

"That he did, Rawat. But for what reason, it's hard to say."

Sharma leaned on the second storey window of his office and surveyed the chaotic scene outside. Pedestrians, bicyclists, scooter-riders, and *rikshaw wale* weaved in and out of the evening traffic. The municipality had dug up the middle of the road and left it like that. It lay open like the big gaping mouth of a monster. The traffic seemed to move in perfect succession around the hole. He walked back to his desk, settled himself in his chair and said, "I would say most of what Virat Chaudhry told us about his marriage was true. He didn't need to lie about it anyways. It was public knowledge. They were fighting a bitter court case. He provided the information that we had already got from the court documents. There was nothing secretive about it anyways. He must know that. But what surprised me most was his straightforwardness in voicing his frank opinion about Devika. He did not need to reveal his abounding hatred toward her. Why would an intelligent man like him give away an emotion so risky? Wouldn't it be wiser to stay quiet to remain on the safe side, Rawat? If he lied about going to the cinema, he didn't have to do it. There was no way for us to know he wasn't home until after midnight on the day of murder."

"Obviously, sir. He just had to say he was home. His father was astonished after hearing him stating that he went to the cinema that night. Do you think the old man knows something? I had the impression he expected his son to say something else altogether."

"We'll check his story. Ask Diwakar to enquire about the picture playing in the cinema that night. Get his photograph from the wedding album that we got from Devika's mother. There's always a possibility that the ticket clerk might remember his face. Someone else from the staff might recognize him and put him on the spot, right there, in the cinema, where he said he was at the time."

"I would put my money on that. It seemed like a hate crime, sir. Look at the way his wife's body was violated afterward. It seemed it had been done in a frenzy. I believe he didn't have enough time to enjoy the actual killing. He, in any probability, couldn't have taken his own sweet time to kill her. Other people lived in that building. There was always a chance that someone would've heard him or interrupted him in the act; it was risky."

"I find it hard to see him as a sadist or a psychopath, Rawat. Sadists enjoy cruelty because their distorted minds welcome it. They don't lack emotions. They do possess them. They can feel. They know that their victim is in pain, and it arouses them. And psychopaths commit brutal murders because they are remorseless. They don't have any emotions to speak of, and have no concern for the feelings of others. They are cold and calculating. Somehow, I'm finding it hard to see him in either of the two categories."

"But, sir, every killer doesn't have to be a sadist or psychopath. They can go unnoticed in everyday life. They are often adept at keeping their dark side hidden. Virat Singh Chaudhry looks relatively normal on the surface. It is hard to see what a person can do in reality."

"A person doesn't essentially have to be a psychopath or sadist to commit the murder, Rawat. A vicious act like murder could be incomprehensible later to the one who committed it."

"You think the post-death violation of Devika's body could be the perpetrator's ploy to mislead us?"

"We shouldn't discount any possibility. It could be a woman as well. According to Dr. Sidhu, a woman could have killed Devika too."

"You mean Gayatri Bhardwaj could have done it? Well, she's a big woman. But surely a man has done it."

"Gayatri Bhardwaj had a very strong motive, Rawat. She had the opportunity and strength to strangle Devika. And she's left-handed. We cannot rule her out. But to take someone's life, one must possess a raw physical aggression. I tell you the mere thought could be unsettling for any thoughtful person. On the surface, it seems unlikely. But Devika, according to witnesses' testimonies, had a cruel way of making others feel inferior. She had the ability to evoke immense hatred in others' minds. Let's not forget Dr. Rajinder Bhardwaj had the classic motive.

"But he is right-handed. According to Dr. Parmeet Sidhu the murderer was left-handed. And we know Dr. Bhardwaj doesn't wear a ring; there was a specific ring mark on Devika's neck."

"Despite that we cannot rule him out. Not completely. The bank statements proved he told us the truth though. He took fifteen *lakhs*, but he didn't make any fixed monthly deposits in Devika's bank account. She had money deposited in her account on the fifth of every month for the last eight months. Who was depositing money and why?" Sharma knew there were too many questions and no answers yet.

"Sir, what about Devika's family members? They will inherit her money now." Rawat's voice stirred Sharma from his thoughts.

"Let's see what Devika's sister and brother-in-law have to say. We will check their alibis as well."

After a momentary pause, Rawat added, "You seem to like Virat Chaudhry, sir."

Rawat hadn't spent five years of his service with Sharma in vain. He was smart enough to know what went on in his boss's mind.

He couldn't be that transparent, thought Sharma, and cursed himself under his breath. At times, he couldn't decide if he admired Rawat for his sheer intelligence or disliked his ability to read his mind with almost utmost precision.

Was he trying to overlook what was evident with Virat Singh Chaudhry? Had he taken an unprofessional liking toward Virat Chaudhry because of his sheer admiration for outspoken and candid people? The thought was disconcerting.

Despite his confusing thoughts, Sharma found it hard to believe Virat Chaudhry had something to do with Devika's murder.

"He loathed her, yes, but wouldn't you say it would have been rash of him to leave behind such obvious traces of his immense hatred after he killed her? He seems too intelligent to do something daft like that. And, if he'd killed her, he wouldn't have dared to reveal his tremendous hatred to us. He already had a messy divorce case in the court. He knew he would come under suspicion just because of that. Why would he make it worse for himself then? There was no need to divulge his innermost feelings of hostility for her unless . . ." Sharma left his words unspoken.

"Unless he is too shrewd and did it because he knew we would think along the same lines, sir," added Rawat. "We wouldn't suspect him because of his display of open hostility for his wife. Or he is confident it would be impossible to put him at the murder scene."

"Or unless he is innocent, Rawat," said Sharma.

To suspect everything and trust nothing in a murder investigation had always been Sharma's motto in the two decades of his police career. But in all these years he had learned to trust his instinct as well. Most of the time, it had proved right—not always though. There were times when he had been led astray by following his instinct, but that was during the initial years of his police career. With Devika's husband, things were pointing suspiciously toward him, but his instinct told him otherwise. In any case, he couldn't ignore that Virat Singh Chaudhry had both the motive and the opportunity to commit the murder.

"He seemed candid though. But that doesn't mean a thing. Appearances can be deceiving as you yourself say, sir. For all his openness and honesty, he could be our man," said Rawat.

And Rawat, Sharma knew, could be right.

Virat Chaudhry could be someone who had a clear and strict mindset about romantic relationships; he took pride in caring, did thoughtful things for her, but at the same time expected reciprocity in everything. Could he be one of those people, wondered Sharma? Such people usually prefer predictability in their relationships. They have a distorted perspective of love, where they not only like to set specific rules in their relationships but also like to enforce them. And when things don't transpire their way, they usually feel threatened and become violent. Virat Chaudhry had retreated. He had let his wife go. But was he able to forgive her? In his own words, he hadn't stopped her. But was he telling the truth? His father would, no doubt, verify his son's story. The only other person who could say what had actually transpired at the time of their break-up was Devika herself. They had had violent confrontations later on, during Devika's stay at Sanover. Had he lost his patience with Devika and killed her in rage? Was he really capable of that kind of brutality, wondered Sharma?

Chapter 24

"Never trust the teller, trust the tale."

—D. H. Lawrence

In the afternoon of Tuesday, 26 August, Sharma and Rawat drove to New Kanauji to talk to Sukh Ram Thakur and Asha Kumari, the husband and wife who kept the New Kanauji cottage for the Bhardwajs. It was a short, twenty miles drive from Sanover.

They decided to visit the Bhardwajs' cottage first, where Gayatri Bhardwaj had supposedly spent the night on the day of the murder. It was a detached villa overlooking the river Satluj and surrounded by apple orchards, the trees bearing their fruits heavily at this time of year, their trunks thick with rutted taupe-coloured bark, and their branches gnarled and craggy and bent with the weight of ripe apples.

"A nice, secluded place for Dr. Bhardwaj to have his clandestine excursions, sir," remarked Rawat. "And this is where Gayatri Bhardwaj spent the night at the time of murder, to get away from all the strain, the exact place where, days earlier, she had found her husband in bed with the murdered woman!"

"Curious indeed!" said Sharma, "I wonder what she thought about when she got here. In her own words, this cottage is her refuge to escape to and unwind. Very curious!"

"I wonder if she really came here. Her brother confirmed she didn't visit him that night. Maybe she just drove around or went home. The servants at the Bhardwaj house might've been coached to say otherwise."

"Her brother might be lying. Suppose she went to her brother after midnight or early morning and in great distress? He would naturally lie to us. The problem is he has given his statement and there is nothing we can do to change it," said Sharma and got out of the jeep. Rawat had parked their jeep in front of a small quarter where Sukh Ram Thakur and his wife, Asha Kumari, lived.

The quarter was merely five minutes away from the cottage on the Dhar Road. Sukh Ram seemed both puzzled and apprehensive about their visit, but Asha Kumari, who was a short, robust-looking woman in her fifties, was keen to answer their queries about Mrs. Gayatri Bhardwaj's visit on the day in question.

She gave them details of the morning of 13 August when she went to the cottage to clean. Usually, she would go there at around nine to clean on Mondays; Monday was the day when Asha Kumari did weekly cleaning at the cottage. But she had gone earlier that day, at seven in the morning. Gayatri Bhardwaj had been her usual self when she met her, although she looked preoccupied, as if something was on her mind. She had her morning tea before leaving for Sanover. It was usual for her or Dr. Bhardwaj to arrive suddenly and spend a night or two at the cottage.

"What time did Gayatri Bhardwaj come at night?" inquired Sharma.

"As I said earlier, Sahib, I went to the cottage in the morning when Madam was about to leave. We are poor people. Doctor Sahib and Madam treat us well, but we couldn't expect them to share their personal business with us, could we?" Her tone was sarcastic. She looked at Sharma and went on, "We've no idea at what time she arrived or what she did after arriving there. When I reached the cottage, Madam was getting ready to leave. She asked me to make a cup of tea for her and then she left."

"That means you don't know at what time she arrived at night?"

"I don't know the exact time, Sahib." Her answer was too quick. "But it must have been half past nine or later. It was raining hard. I saw a light on in the cottage from our balcony window. I told my husband that Sahib and Madam must have arrived. We stayed awake in case they needed us, but no one came. That's why I went to the cottage early in the morning. I told Madam it must have been inconvenient for her to spend the night alone at the cottage and she should have called us. But she had eaten before she left home and hence, she saw no point in troubling us at bedtime."

"Was it usual practice for Mrs. Gayatri Bhardwaj to stay alone for the night at the cottage? It's pretty isolated here. As far as I could see, the nearest neighbour is a good kilometer away."

"It wasn't the first time that one of them had stayed alone for the night. Moreover, this area is safe, Sahib. Even children know there's nothing of value here or in nearby cottages," Asha Kumari said tartly, suggesting Sharma's question had been both stupid and irrational.

"These all belong to wealthy people, but they come here only occasionally. They wouldn't think about stashing any jewels here, would they? If someone has plans to rob, he would rather go to the city to their homes where they live."

"Is it a usual practice for Dr. Bhardwaj to come here often? Sometimes accompanied by some woman?" asked Rawat.

Asha Kumari's face was impassive. "We are here to take care of Doctor Sahib and Madam's villa and that's what we do. Not a thing more. Not a thing less."

They couldn't gain any useful information from the interview. Asha Kumari's answers seemed a little too pat. She, Sharma thought, had rehearsed them in advance. She had been informed about their visit and most probably had been coached as well, he suspected.

"Sir, they were lying. Gayatri Bhardwaj must have coached them ahead of our visit. These old servants are loyal people," Rawat echoed Sharma's thoughts as their jeep approached a steep hill. "Gayatri Bhardwaj might very well have called upon Devika that night."

The same thought had crossed Sharma's mind many times as well. She could have visited Devika in her flat that day. Devika was malicious. She was known to cut people with razor-sharp words. Was it possible that Devika had enraged Gayatri Bhardwaj to the point where she couldn't control her fury? She was a big woman, strong and robust. She could have easily strangled Devika. A dead body, though, is heavier than a live one; Gayatri Bhardwaj had the strength to arrange Devika's body post death. She was a practical, clever woman but did she possess enough callousness to strangle her rival in fury and then arrange her body in a certain way post death, wondered Sharma?

"We have no way of knowing that for sure, it seems," replied Sharma.

There was another scenario, thought Sharma. Gayatri Bhardwaj visited Devika's flat and found that the woman was already dead. In that case, the door to the flat must have been slightly ajar. After looking at Devika's body, she suspected her husband of the killing. That could also be the reason behind her openness during the police interview. She knew the police would come to know about Dr. Bhardwaj's affair in time. By revealing she was aware of her husband's affair, she had turned things slightly in his favour.

Leela kaki was not a woman given to gossiping. She had been working for the Bhardwaj household for over two decades.

She was still thinking about the police's visit. SP Sharma had asked her about Doctor Sahib's time of arrival on the night of the murder. Did that mean they suspected him, she wondered? She was still in deep thought, a slight furrow between her brows, when Rani came and sat beside her.

"Do you think I did right by talking to the police? I didn't want to, but that policeman started asking questions," said Rani.

"That's all right. SP Sharma even asked me about that night. They were just doing their duty."

"How should one know what to do for the best? I hadn't even thought about it until I talked to the police. Now I don't know what to think. I hadn't dreamt of telling it to the police, but it slipped off my tongue. Now I suppose it's important for Madam to know? But I dare not tell her, in case it's of no concern. I don't want to burden her unnecessarily."

Leela kaki wasn't a fanciful person and had no patience with any jumbled talk. She also knew of Rani's tendency to wander too often into a meaningless babble during an important conversation.

"Stop talking in riddles now. You'd better tell me what has happened."

"They asked me if I heard anything on that night. I blabbered about hearing a car arrive around midnight. Now I'm scared. Do you think I should tell Madam about it? Would she be upset?"

Leela kaki looked gravely at Rani's plump face. "Don't bother with it. I will tell Madam myself."

Chapter 25

"When you have to make a choice and
don't make it, that in itself is a choice."

—William James

Sharma glanced at the little piece of paper with Lakshmi's address on it. The weather on the morning of Wednesday, 27 August seemed good with a clear blue sky and mild wind. The village of Niligarh was located twenty miles south of the Chamba. They decided to pay her a visit.

Niligarh was a tiny village. Finding Devika's sister's house was easy. It was at the end of a narrow street of two-storey wood-and-stone houses with slanted roofs. The house had a pair of small wooden doors, barely five feet high. Sharma and Rawat went through the door with their heads bent and entered a small courtyard. Lakshmi's mother-in-law was a sturdy and short woman in her late fifties. She asked them to sit down and called her daughter-in-law.

The door opened, and Lakshmi came in with a sleeping baby in her arms. Her husband was behind her. Her mother-in-law got up at once and took the child from her arms. The boy was chubby with a round, cute face and Sharma envisioned him being eight or nine months old. But then, he didn't understand a thing about small children. He was never good at guessing children's ages anyways. He used to have occasional difficulty in recalling his own children's exact ages when they were growing up. On those occasions, he always had to check with Nandini. Later, when the children were a little older, they took command and would put their father right. The child wailed at the first sight of the strangers. His grandmother patted him on the back, left the courtyard, and went inside to put him to sleep.

Lakshmi looked weary but composed, sad though, thought Sharma. She was a good-looking woman. She could be called pleasing as opposed to being beautiful. She was of medium height, slender, and on the dusky side. Her features, although unremarkable, were regular and gave her face a serene look. She shared no similarity with her dead sister except for her eyes which were big and kohl-black.

It would be a difficult conversation, Sharma knew. They hadn't pressed her husband or her mother, when they came to take the body, but now it was important to know everything possible about the victim.

While his wife looked grief-stricken, Vinay Kumar was sitting well forward on the chair, his hands clasped, face tense, and his eyes, fixed alternately on his wife's and Sharma's faces, were jittery. He, no doubt, did not differ from many others, thought Sharma. This untimely tragic death of his sister-in-law could be his only chance of realizing financial freedom. He must fear losing that large amount of money to someone else. In all probability, he wanted to get his hands on his late sister-in-law's property and had nothing to do with the murder inquiry. Once the money came in, all this hassle of getting involved in a police investigation would be forgotten.

Sharma would've liked it better if Vinay Kumar wasn't present during the interview, but he didn't press the issue.

"I still can't imagine that I won't be seeing her again," Lakshmi said in a grief-stricken tone, "it's been so many days. I find it difficult to accept that Devika will never come back. When the police came to give us the news of her death, I hoped that when we reached Sanover, the police would inform us it was all a mistake, that the woman who died was someone who just shared her name, and my sister was alive and well. Even during those last few minutes when they were ready to light her pyre, I imagined she'd wake up any moment, come and console me. She looked as if she had been merely resting."

She gave Sharma a rueful smile.

"It's always difficult to believe when someone close to our heart leaves us forever." Sharma, who always found words of condolence difficult to utter, remarked in an awkward tone.

She looked at Sharma. "Is there any news of who did it to her?"

"Not yet, madam. We are still enquiring. With a murder investigation, we need to know as much as possible about the victim. You were her family. We're hoping you might tell us something significant about your sister. Do you know if anything important happened during the last few months? Something out of the ordinary she mentioned?"

"She never confided in me. There were things she liked to keep to herself. She wasn't the forthcoming type, not Devika. She had always been like that."

"From our investigation, we got the impression she did not see you much. Was there any particular reason behind this estrangement?"

The result was unexpected. Lakshmi started crying. Sharma hadn't anticipated this sudden meltdown. Tears slid down her cheeks. She did not wipe them off. Her body shook noiselessly. Silently, they sat there and waited for her to recover herself. Her husband, who had gotten up and gone inside, returned with a glass of water. He held the glass out to her and she took it with a docile acceptance, but didn't drink from it. Instead, she wiped her eyes with her *saree pallu*.

When she spoke, her voice was hoarse. "I don't know if you are aware that Devika was my step sister." She looked at Sharma.

"Yes, your mother mentioned it. Was that the reason for her estrangement?"

Lakshmi said, "It wasn't like that. My father married my mother, his late wife's younger sister, when Devika was six. Both families—his and *Ma's*—forced him into the decision. He agreed to the marriage for Devika's sake, but took a long time to warm up to *Ma*, too long, in fact, because by that time *Ma* had lost her patience—of which she had little in the first place. Devika, who never was an easy child to deal with, taking a cue from *Babuji*, gave her a hard time and refused to accept her once-beloved *mausi* as her *Ma*. Instead of trying harder, *Ma* gladly agreed to the title of a mean stepmother and took an indignant dislike to Devika, and because of that it became easy for Devika to reject *Ma*. The more *Ma* begrudged Devika, the more *Babuji* indulged his daughter. By the time I was born, *Ma* and Devika had already grown far apart."

"Did they get close later?"

"No. They never could get along. After *Babuji's* death, Devika distanced herself more than ever. Devika was always a beautiful child, but she grew up strikingly beautiful. On the one hand, Devika had *Ma* criticizing her looks all the time: her nose was too big, her lips were too thick, her hair was too coarse, she was fat. It never ended. On the other hand, people only talked about how beautiful she looked. She wasn't the best person, but no one ever told her so; no one looked beyond that beautiful face." Lakshmi smiled at Sharma. It was a smile of longing, of pain, of loss. She continued, "Devika was never the obedient child. *Ma's* hair-splitting criticism, forced her to become a willful, stubborn person. She stopped caring and started doing things on a whim. Although we sisters loved each other, *Ma* did her best to create an air of jealousy and resentment between us. *Babuji* favoured Devika. *Ma* favoured me. It was bad enough to live in the shadow of a perpetual cold war between my parents. For me, the worst part, however, was to witness enduring hostility between my sister and my *ma*. It seems strange, but my sister and *Ma* were very much alike in temperament, and they never even realized it. Each thought of herself as a victim of the other's hostility. They both blamed each other for destroying each other's lives. I wish they could have recognized how much they had in common and had been kind to each other. Now, it will never happen. She'll never return," said Lakshmi in a sad voice.

Sharma asked, "Did she have any close friends who might have stayed in touch with her until now?"

Lakshmi said, "I can't think of anyone who might have been her confidant, or close enough to stay in touch for all these years. She always had plenty of girls surrounding her, but no one was her friend. She was never one to bond. Even when we were young, she always had these reservations about confiding in others."

"Was there anyone who'd threatened her?"

"I can't imagine her being scared of anyone or anything. She was one of those women who couldn't be intimidated, a quality I so admired but sadly lacked myself," she said, without looking at her husband, but the meaning wasn't lost on him; Sharma could tell from his tight-lipped and taut expression. The couple appeared to be at swords' points. Something must have happened during all these days. She must have recognized her grief as an opportunity for him. Diwakar had disliked Vinay Kumar from his last visit; according to him, the man was greedy and opportunistic. Vinay Kumar hadn't tried to hide his curiosity about his late sister-in-law's last will while her body was still lying in the morgue.

Vinay Kumar, who had been quiet until now, turned to Lakshmi and said in a disapproving tone, "She always acted all high and mighty. If you're forgetting, let me remind you. She herself had declared that she didn't want to keep up any relationship with us."

Lakshmi opened her mouth to reply to his scornful comment, but thought better of it. Sharma watched Vinay Kumar. Was he one of those men who believed they were entitled to rage, that it was solely reserved for them? If she stood up to him, would he make her pay for it? That seemed unlikely considering what was at stake. Vinay Kumar understood he might reap financial benefits from his dead sister-in-law. He might have been able to belittle Lakshmi at times, but now she knew that she could bring financial freedom to him through her sister.

He turned to Sharma and said in a measured voice, "There's not much that we can tell you. We wish to help you with your investigation if we can, but I don't see how. I don't think you have an exact idea of her relationship with us, Sahib. My sister-in-law was obstinate and strong-willed. She was unhappy after her son's birth. Free-spirted as she was, she felt burdened with the responsibilities of motherhood. She went to study further after her son's birth and left him and her husband afterwards. But that was a few years ago. After she left her husband, she had no contact with us."

Vinay Kumar, Sharma thought, couldn't be bothered to show any sorrow. He couldn't be expected to feel any personal loss for his estranged sister-in-law; he barely knew her.

Sharma turned to Lakshmi and asked, "Would she have told you if she'd felt threatened?"

Lakshmi looked guilt-ridden. Was it remorse she was feeling now? Was she tormented for not doing enough for her sister, not seeing enough of her? But now, as she must have recognized, it was too late; too much time had passed; too much damage had been done to restore what was lost. It seemed she had lost the fight in her.

Looking at her husband sideways, she spoke, her voice gloomy, "It's difficult to say. I imagine she might have if we had seen each other more often."

Her husband barged in and said in a heated tone, "It's good she never came to see us. I care about my reputation." He turned to Sharma then and said, "The first time the police came, they were in uniforms. Everyone in our locality came to know about it. Scandalous news spreads fast. People are saying all sorts of things now. When she was alive, we had to hear all kinds of things, and now that she's dead, she still won't let us live in peace. We are respectable people, Sahib. I have a younger sister of marriageable age."

Perhaps it was this contemptuous disregard for her dead sister or the harshness in his voice that brought Lakshmi back out of her despondent misery. His scornful words seemed to have diminished whatever anguish she was cosseting and, for now, she seemed conscious of her tears. She held her *saree pallu* with grace and wiped them away.

Then she turned to her husband and said in an angry tone, "Devika didn't come to visit not because she didn't care but because no one in your family wanted her to come and visit me. You looked down at her because she was living separately from Virat *Jija Ji*. Did I ever visit her? No, I didn't." Her voice trembled and tears flowed down her face once again. She sobbed, her body shook. "I couldn't see her because of you. You never wanted me to keep any relationship going with her. Despite that, she never stopped caring for me."

Sharma turned to Vinay Kumar and said, "What were you doing on August 12 from eight o'clock to midnight?"

"I was at home, Sahib. You can ask our neighbours if you wish." Vinay Kumar smirked. "We had held *jagrata* that night at home."

The neighbour two houses down, a woman in her sixties who sat on the front steps of her two-storey house, confirmed Vinay Kumar's testimony about *jagrata*.

"Sir, at least we can eliminate Devika's family from our suspect list now," said Rawat.

Chapter 26

"The senses do not deceive us, but the judgment does."

—Johann Wolfgang Von Goethe

Virat Singh Chaudhry had the purity and naivety of youth when Devika came into his life. He had seen her at his friend Prakash's wedding and decided she was the one. His love was fiery, intense, and passionate, as usually happens with the first genuine love of youth, and it had consumed him altogether. The insane scale of her intoxicating beauty had blown him away. He used to be, he recalled bitterly, a frivolous young man who thought beauty was goodness. He had been turning twenty-nine at the time. More than a decade ago, it was a matter of concern for everyone including his family, relatives, and neighbours. *Ma* and *Babuji*, who were not keen for the alliance because of Devika's less-privileged background, had finally given in to his wish.

He felt bad for her for she had had an unhappy childhood. She was inconsiderate and selfish. He blamed it on her absolute beauty; her being so young. He always had excuses ready on her behalf. He had faith she would change with the passing years. And then, *Ma* and *Babuji*, thoughtful and decent as they were, opted to become mute spectators in their house. For months, he had foolishly believed he and Devika suited each other well. He never could fathom that it was him, in reality, who suited Devika well. He was a good husband for her; he made no demands, asked for nothing in return, and loved her with a selfless devotion, which was the only way he could love. He had believed in this ideal, old-fashioned notion that the one whom you love has to always come first and before your very own self. In the process of loving her, he had forgotten that he existed—that he was special too. Devika had known the intensity with which he loved her. It was important to her, not to love in itself, but to know she was being loved, to know she was being cherished. More than anything else, she had this overwhelming need to be admired. It had taken him a good few years of suffering and plenty of heartache to understand that she was as happy with him as she could be with any other man.

Things were fine at first. Later, when she became pregnant, things got worse. She hated being pregnant and then after Sahil's birth she had hated her husband with equal intensity. But then, it was his fault that he had expected her to love their son. A woman like her—who was so full of herself, who couldn't see anything beyond her precious self— would not love any other person even if it was her own flesh and blood.

After she had left him for good, *Babuji* and *Ma* had asked him to marry again. They worried for Sahil. But he had lost faith in love, in the institute of marriage. He was scared of stepping into another bad relationship. But it had consistently become difficult for him to handle things on his own after *Ma* got bedridden and then died of her illness. Veena lived in Lucknow. She had her family, her children, her household to manage. He had to take care of their shops. *Babuji* could not manage Sahil on his own. That's when Neelam came in their life. She was Veena's childhood friend and was a divorcee. They were so alike, Virat and Neelam; they had suffered misfortunes; they had seen pain. Sufferings had taught Neelam to be more sympathetic and compassionate toward other people's pain. She loved Sahil like her own. Devika had become suspicious about Neelam. She had to spoil everything for him. She had refused to give him a divorce then.

He had kept that information from SP Sharma. He couldn't let the police know about it. But then, that wasn't the only thing he had kept from them. There was another bigger and more damaging secret that he had kept to himself. He had visited Devika more than once in Sanover. No one at home knew about it, not even Neelam. But what would happen if the police came to know about his other visits, he wondered? They would suspect him at once. With his divorce still pending in court, he knew he could be one of the main suspects on their list. The *Chowkidar* had seen him lashing out at Devika once. Sooner or later, he reflected, police would find out about his altercation with Devika. Suddenly, the air felt terribly oppressive, and his earlier confidence vanished in an uprush of terrible anxiety. He had to tell this to Neelam somehow, he realized.

He wondered how he could break this news to Neelam. She wouldn't take it kindly, him visiting Devika stealthily. She had met Devika once, years ago, when they were newly engaged. Unaware of Devika's inherent nature, Neelam had believed she could talk sense into her. But Devika, true to her nature, had hurled insults at her. Their brief encounter had established Neelam's belief that nothing could thwart Devika from trying to destroy their life. Afterwards, he had contemplated visiting Devika himself, but Neelam had put her foot down. It was of no use, she had told him, but he had ignored her advice and visited Devika many times before their last court date. Although he had married Neelam in a small ceremony in the presence of both their families, they couldn't call it a lawful wedding. He had bought a house next door in Neelam's name, keeping in mind Devika's unpredictable occasional visits. Their life kept shuffling between both the houses. Townspeople knew, but no one questioned them. Knowing Devika's vindictive nature, he dared not relax and live with Neelam in peaceful bliss. Despite being married and despite being in love, their marriage was still illicit in the eyes of the law. They couldn't live like a normal couple. Neelam, although she never complained and was happy, would feel the burden from time to time. He himself had loathed this arrangement, and it was in desperation he had approached Devika so many times in the last few months as the court date was getting nearer. But things had quickly gone out of control during his last visit. She had provoked him with her poisonous words and refused to free him from their doomed marriage. He had lost control then.

"It's all your fault. You were hell bent on marrying her." His father's voice interrupted his thoughts. For the last nine years, Upendra Chaudhry had blamed his son for their combined misery.

Veena found it hard to take her father's ranting. She said, "*Babuji*, for how long will you keep blaming *Bhaiya*?"

Upendra Chaudhry had no intention of stopping. He snapped, "She came from a destitute family. Do you even have any idea how it bothered us, especially your *Ma*? We pointed that out to him, didn't we? But he refused to listen. How could he? He saw nothing beyond her fair beauty. Look what she has done to his life."

"*Babuji*, don't start on that again. It wears me out to hear about Devika's background again and again. Her background had nothing to do with what she was."

"If only I had put my foot down. It's all my fault. Your *ma* kept telling me not to bow down, but I thought the girl was coming to live with us. Of course, the family background makes a difference. They weren't equal to us in any way. She hadn't seen wealth. When she came to this house, she indulged herself and spent money as she wished. But this *sahibjade*! He wouldn't say a thing."

"There's no point in recalling that now, *Babuji*. Let bygones be bygones. We've to think about this new problem now," pleaded Veena. She turned to her brother, who was sitting on the verandah step, and said: "Why did you lie to them about your whereabouts, *Bhaiya*? What will happen if they come to know the truth? They will inquire at the cinema. Soon they will know you never went there."

Virat said in a furious tone, "What else did you expect me to say?"

"You could have just stated that you were home all night. We could have vouched for you. What was the need to cook up this story about *Dharmendra's* picture when you don't even know if that picture was indeed playing in the cinema that night?"

"As if that would have helped me! You are my family. If they suspect me and decide to arrest me, they will not consider your evidence, Veena."

"Don't utter these ominous words now. It would have been better to disclose your relationship with Neelam then. She could have vouched for you."

"They will not believe her either. And it wouldn't serve any purpose other than providing a bigger motive for me to kill Devika in their eyes. With the divorce still pending in court, I could be one of the main suspects on their list. If they come to know about Neelam, they will not even look at anyone else."

Chapter 27

*"A good face they say, is a letter of
recommendation. O Nature, Nature,
why art thou so dishonest, as ever to
send men with these false
recommendations into the World!"*

—Henry Fielding

Sharma felt anger and irritation at the unnecessary delay.
He was getting tired of the whole thing.

"Sir, the days are dragging by and, despite new
developments in the case, we are unable to get a hold of any
concrete lead. The list of suspects is just getting longer. I
would still put my money on Devika's husband," said Rawat.

"I agree, no one saw him at the Basant Cinema in
Dongri on 12 August, Rawat," remarked Sharma.

Virat Singh Chaudhry, despite his candidness, was on their
list of suspects now.

After a brief pause, Sharma continued, "We can arrest him,
but the way he felt no qualms about revealing his immense
hatred toward his dead wife, I think the man has something
which would prove his innocence if the matter reached his
arrest."

Although Rawat thought otherwise, Sharma had faith
in his theory. Despite being evasive about his whereabouts,

Virat Chaudhry appeared confident they couldn't get him for the murder.

"Sir, what about Dr. Rudra?"

"He has a tight alibi for the night of the murder. But I would like to know the man's past, Rawat."

Dr. Rudra was not the main suspect, but there was a nagging doubt at the back of Sharma's mind that bothered him. The man seemed connected to the case somehow, but in what way, Sharma could not fathom. He couldn't ascertain any motive that would justify his suspicion. Besides, Dr. Rudra was doing the night shift on the night of 12 August. They couldn't put him at Devika's flat at the time of the murder. Sharma should have dropped the matter, but it was his hunch that prompted him to look into Dr. Rudra's past carefully.

Even Rawat, who usually was vocal about voicing his displeasure, raised no objection when Sharma informed him of his decision to look into Dr. Rudra's past.

"If you say so, sir," replied Rawat.

The wind was blowing strongly and the sky seemed heavy with murky clouds. Sharma and Rawat had started early.

After a series of failed attempts at telephoning Sharma, not knowing the phone was out of order as usual there, Inspector Dogra of Sadar Police Station had sent a telegram last evening with Dr. Raghav Prasad's address at Shimla.

Rawat was in the driver's seat and had insisted on taking a short cut that went through the village of Khandi and linked Sanover through GT road directly to Shimla. Rawat had taken that route once before and was overly enthusiastic to take Sharma through it despite Sharma's warning of flooded village streets in the monsoon weather. He had to suffer the consequences for his zest early on when he had to push their jeep all the way through ankle-deep muddy water—the aftermath of three days of a monsoon storm—with his freshly tailored trousers folded above his knees and his shoes safely tucked inside the jeep. He had cursed himself inwardly for his self-inflicted plight. Sharma, who had taken the driver's seat, was in good humour and seemed content to maneuver the steering wheel. They had almost reached levelled, dry ground when the engine started. Mercifully, they were still in the village, so Rawat had time to wash at a nearby villager's house.

"I guess this journey through the shortcut has taken a toll on you, Rawat," said Sharma, in good humour, glancing sideways at Rawat who seemed weary.

"I should have known better, sir," answered Rawat in a sullen voice, which made Sharma laugh.

The rest of the journey went by hurdle-free. The sky had cleared sufficiently to expose a shy sun with a promise of a bright day ahead. Sharma, who disliked driving, offered to drive all the way to the old professor's house. Sharma's offer cured Rawat's grouchiness at once, and he took the opportunity to doze in the car for an hour.

They passed a few attractive old houses with tin roofs along the way. Most of the early European houses in Shimla had roofs of beaten earth. Locally cut slate, quartzite slabs, shingles, and the tiles were used to give them an aesthetic appeal. Later, the old roofing style was replaced with a roof which was made of galvanized iron. The steady drumming of rain on the roofs of houses presented a constant low humming sound when it rained. To their right, they glimpsed the well-preserved impressive exterior of the *burj* with its slate-cladded walls, orderly gables, and tall chimney stacks.

Dr. Raghav Prasad, who had moved back to Shimla, his hometown, after retirement, lived in an impressive two-storey, old stone house on the outskirts of Shimla. His drawing room was old-fashioned in a familiar way, furnished with expensive rosewood and teak furniture from the fifties, a trademark of the upper middle class these days, thought Sharma, who was accustomed to seeing such furnishings. The only different feature in this traditional setting was a huge wall-to-wall bookcase with glass doors that was packed with massive leather-bound volumes, medical books, and old classics arranged in a haphazard way which Sharma believed was not for effect but for the quality. It was a reader's house.

Dr. Raghav Prasad had taught at B. R. Ambedkar Medical College for thirty years, as a visiting professor and later as the head of the Psychiatry Department. He remembered Rudra as a brilliant but wasted student. According to him, Rudra had a sharp academic mind, a charming personality, and in the beginning he'd had an excellent rapport with students and staff members. That did not last long though. There was a scandal over drugs in the college campus and another one over a break-in to steal examination papers. He escaped punishment in both the cases, although was rusticated later over cheating during the final year's exam.

"Selling drugs on the college campus should have made his suspension possible, but he was cleared. For the break-in, he was given a warning which obviously was a mistake as he was caught cheating in exams later. He had a shrewd mind and knew how to get himself out of all kinds of situations, although his cunningness got him into those situations in the first place. Absolute waste of brainpower, that's what I would say he was. What has he gotten into now? A financial fraud case or scandal involving a woman?"

"We're inquiring about a murder at his workplace. He is not a key suspect, but we're looking into everyone's history."

"Ah, poor bugger. What a waste of intellect! No wonder his murky past has gotten him into trouble now," remarked Dr. Prasad.

"So, he never finished his degree?" asked Sharma.

"I have no idea about that. I was there for only a year more before I went to teach at another college."

"I don't imagine he would've completed it somewhere else, any other college or university?"

"He was rusticated from college. He couldn't have gotten into another medical college that came under H. P. University without getting a conduct certificate from us. There are only three government medical colleges in our state. To get into another university, he would've needed a migration certificate. But, getting it issued is rather a cumbersome process. He would've needed to apply for it from our college while he had still been studying there. You might want to check with the university office. I could not see him completing his degree in any other university unless he started all over again. There was no way he could've completed it from his final year, the year from where he left."

His employment records showed he did his MBBS at B. R. Ambedkar Medical College. Sharma made a mental note to tell Diwakar to check with H. P. University.

Sharma asked Dr. Raghav Prasad's opinion about Rudra committing a serious crime like murder.

"I can't imagine him doing something like that," said the professor in a reflective tone. "But he never had much of a conscience. I wouldn't put it past him completely. With time and age, people with criminal tendencies often advance their skills for the worse. There must be a reason for you to look at him more closely, I believe?"

"We are exploring all the options at present. It's difficult to say anything at this point."

"He was an odd person. Sheepish. Disruptive. Inconsiderate. To achieve what he wanted, he practised means we ordinary citizens would be wary of doing. He was considered a startlingly handsome guy— jaw-dropper-kind-of-handsome—and there were rumours of his involvement with a professor's wife who got him a part-time sales job at a pharmaceutical company where she worked as sales manager. Despite his busy schedule at the college, he did exceedingly well at his job, and soon he outshone his colleagues who worked full-time at the company. He made quite a lot of money through commissions and was eventually dismissed from his job after they found out many inconsistencies in his account. He was selling drugs at prices much below the actual cost. The company had to suffer a considerable loss. He was shrewd enough to cover up his tracks for months until it was time for the final audits."

"What happened later?" asked Sharma.

"The woman had to lose both her job and husband because of him. Rudra left her as well. She was left alone to face the shameful scandal. Afterwards, there were rumours about his involvement with the only daughter of the head of the Anatomy Department. The girl was two years his senior. She mercifully finished her degree during his third year and was sent to another state to complete her residency."

There was nothing else to be learned from Dr. Prasad. Sharma thanked him for his time and they left for Panghera, the next place where Dr. Rudra had worked for eight months.

Chapter 28

*"Did you ever observe to whom the
accidents happen? Chance favors only
the prepared mind."*

— Louis Pasteur

Nalgar, where the Sanjeevani Life Care Centre Hospital
was situated, lay about ninety miles from Panghera. It boasted
three lakes, an old temple, a wildlife sanctuary, and a museum
featuring miniature paintings. The hospital was located in the
new part of the city next to the Polytechnic College, one of
the oldest technical institutes in the district which
accommodated hundreds of students from nearby towns.

On Sunday, 31 August when Sharma and Rawat reached
the hospital, it was noon on a typical hot day in late August,
humid and static. The hospital was a drab concrete-and-glass
building in dull grey and lime white. It was a good-sized
structure.

Dr. Rudra had worked there before he went to work in
Panghera, where he had spent eight months and where they
couldn't get any useful information except that he had left his
job suddenly without any notice. Bansidhar Gupte, the head
clerk, a heavy, sullen-looking man in his fifties who answered
their queries rather crossly, had kept Dr. Rudra's biodata as it
was the policy of the hospital not to destroy records of

previous employees for a minimum of ten years, which he told them with apparent irritation.

Although they had learned a few things from Dhagla, where Dr. Rudra had worked for a very brief period after completing his medical degree, the information so far was arduously identical at the core. In a nutshell, he had worked satisfactorily and wasn't involved in anything slightly shady that would justify a police investigation—a statement that Sharma and Rawat received with a grain of salt at first and with a stoic weariness later.

Some years were also missing from Dr. Rudra's employment record and, despite their best efforts, they couldn't get any information about Dr. Rudra's whereabouts during that time.

Rawat, who usually had an absolute belief in his boss's insight, found his faith shaking, and he wondered if their investigations into Dr. Rudra's background were becoming those of a pair of wanderers in the wilderness. They were not getting anywhere. But Sharma was in good spirits. Sharma believed there was more to him than meets the eye. He, with a growing conviction, felt that Dr. Rudra had something murky in his past that could be their missing link in the case.

Dr. Rudra had worked at the Sanjeevani Life Care Hospital for a little over a year. Short, chubby and youthful Banhi Asher informed them of what little she knew about Dr. Rudra through the grapevine before steering them through a series of narrow, stark corridors that smelled of phenol and chemicals and leading them into a small office. A medium-sized desk in white sunmika was placed in the middle with a wide, low-backed, solid wood chair with a cushioned seat on it and two similar but seemingly narrower seats to its front. Two steel cabinets against the south wall and a large drawer unit of steel on the opposite wall seemed to hold many rows of well-organized files. The only window on the south wall overlooked a small square of uncut grass, a few cedar trees, and a considerably full parking plot beyond the trees.

Devesh Gaonkar was an ancient-looking, spectacled man with a round compact figure, a chubby face, humped nose, and a small mouth that widened into a gentle smile at the sight of them and which denoted genuine sincerity and openness. Rawat found himself liking the man at once.

"I am glad I could be of any help in Dr. Rudra's matter. But first let me order tea for you," he said without a trace of the feigned sincerity that people always practised with the police.

Sharma refused the offer of tea. It was a hot, humid day, and they had no desire to look at anything that screamed steaming hot. Devesh Gaonkar called the *peon* then and asked to get three glasses of *nimbu pani* instead.

"You must have been working here for many years?" Sharma asked, sensing that Devesh Gaonkar was anxious to get on with the matter of Dr. Rudra.

"Yes, sir. It has been a little over eighteen years now. I started working the same year this hospital opened. It was not this big at that time. We began with a thirty-bed capacity, and it kept expanding as our city grew."

The *peon* returned with a tray carrying *nimbu pani* glasses. It was a relief after a hot, humid day. They savoured the peculiar taste of black salt in the squeezed juice of sour lemons and thanked the old man.

"For how long did Dr. Rudra Bhardwaj work here?"

Devesh Gaonkar took out a file from a drawer and handed it to Sharma. "As you can see, I've kept all his employment records. It's the policy in our hospital, which only a few people follow, but I do." Pointing his finger to the entry, he continued. "He joined us on September 28, 1960 and left a year and three months after on December 25, 1961."

"Was he good at his job?"

Devesh Gaonkar hesitated. It was as if he had already considered how he must answer but still had to prepare himself to give that answer.

"He worked quite satisfactorily as far as I know, although there were a few incidents where the administration became concerned. But there was never anything concrete that pointed to his involvement. There was a small scandal where he was directly involved. We couldn't fill the position of the pharmacy manager after the sudden demise of our earlier manager. Rudra Bhardwaj volunteered his service and handled the job for a few months, a most unusual decision on the administration's part. At that time, he received the drug quotations from different suppliers alongside his doctor's duties. The nursing supervisor accused him of accepting inferior quality products at a higher price from a supplier when there were better offers. The assistant administrator who enquired into the matter took no action against Dr. Rudra except issuing a warning. He was the same man who had approved Rudra Bhardwaj's volunteer service as the pharmacy manager."

"Were there any other occurrences of the same sort?"

"Another incident was of a theft at our central dispensary. A few boxes of morphine worth seventy-five thousand rupees went missing. The lock was intact on every cabinet and Dr. Rudra had the keys. But the keys were kept in the desk drawer along with other keys in the inventory-record room in case he was off duty. And also, most of the staff knew of their general location. Although the supplier had the exact entry record of medicine boxes sent to the hospital, and the delivery driver had a spotless record to his credit, Dr. Rudra insisted the actual number was different. One of the nursing staff, who was on duty that night, corroborated his story. Conveniently, there was a small fire at the inventory office on the same night the theft was discovered. A few catalogues including the delivery register were destroyed in it. It was supposedly caused by a burning cigarette butt left by one peon. They could not prove anything though."

"So, he was suspected of causing the fire?"

"He was. The fire incident followed the inquiry so closely that it seemed too much of a coincidence. But of course, nothing could be proved. There was no proof he was behind that fire.

"There is another thing, sir." He paused as if contemplating his choice of words. "I suppose you already noticed my hesitation. There was an interesting thing about the girl, one of the nursing staff who corroborated his story. There were rumours that they were closely associated; they were allegedly spotted together a few times after work hours. After his marriage, the rumours died though. She left her job soon after him."

Sharma and Rawat exchanged a quick glance. So, that was it: Dr. Rudra had kept his marriage a secret so far.

"When did this marriage happen?"

"I think it was four or five months before he left his job. His wife was supposedly the only daughter of a wealthy businessman. He kept working after his marriage. The girl had married against the wishes of her parents and was estranged from her family. He left his job a few months later, to join his father-in-law's business after his wife's reconciliation with her family."

"What was his wife like?"

"She was a sweet child." Devesh smiled as he remembered her. "Very young, looked sixteen. She must have been older than that though. She was thoughtful and gentle. She had this genuine sincerity about her that is not seen often in today's girls. She was humble and simple despite her affluent roots."

"Do you think he married her for money?"

"Urvashi, his wife, she seemed full of him, as far as I could tell. It was hard to say what Dr. Rudra felt about her. He doted on her with almost a feigned sincerity that is so typical of two-faced people. But then, that's my opinion. But, sir, her wealth was difficult to ignore. People regarded it as a key incentive for his marriage. He was not what I would call a sincere person. Although he was a charmer, many of the staff members knew just how little work he did for his money. To his credit, he was educated, intelligent, and polite, but he was dishonest. He used to borrow money from his colleagues despite earning well. He could be very persuasive if it suited his purpose. He continued practising this habit after his marriage. He had borrowed a hefty amount from a few people after his wedding, saying his wife was finding it hard to adjust to his moderate standard of living. She never seemed like someone who would mind hardships though. That was the general impression about her, sir. I could be wrong. It takes ages to know a person's true self, and she was here for a few months only."

"Were they happy in their marriage?"

"They looked happy. That, I suppose, was typical of the first year of the marriage. They were an odd couple though. He was shrewd, well versed in worldly matters. She seemed so unlike him, kind and straightforward. No one could fathom what it was except his looks that had prompted her to marry him. Of course, she was a plain-looking girl, but that would not have stopped her father from finding a match for her considering how much wealth he possessed."

"Dr. Rudra's wife, she must be from the surrounding area?"

"I would not know. It's been many years now." Devesh paused, as if trying to recall something, and then said, "If you permit, I can call Gajanand babu. He is one of the oldest staff members, joined a few years after I did. He works in the dispensary. His wife was friendly with Urvashi. They lived on the same street. He might know."

Sharma nodded his approval and Devesh Gaonkar went outside to fetch his colleague.

"He kept his marriage a secret, sir. No one knows about it in Sanover. What do you think happened to his wife? Do you think she is still alive?" asked Rawat.

"I hope so, I really hope so. Let's talk to another employee first. Once we get the name of where she lives, it won't be hard to locate her. In towns, everyone knows of everyone else's business, and theirs was an affluent family."

"If she hailed from a big city, then it would become difficult to locate her, sir."

"Difficult, not impossible, though," said Sharma.

"The case is becoming more interesting day by day, sir."

"Although it could be another complexity in the case, my instinct says a breakthrough might be near. I have this peculiar feeling we're getting close to something that is linked to Devika's killing, something that's more sinister than the actual murder."

Gajanand Babu was a tall, heavily built man; Devesh Gaonkar's junior almost by a decade. The few sparse hairs left on his nearly bald head were dyed jet black, and Sharma suspected that was the outcome of Godrej liquid hair dye which had been launched a few years ago and was equally popular among men and women who tried to look younger, although it did no such thing to Gajanand Babu's paunchy appearance. He greeted Sharma politely and brought an extra chair from outside in Sharma's direction.

He placed his chair next to his colleague's and said solemnly, "Sir, I don't know her city's name." He paused for good ten seconds and then added, "But she was from somewhere close by where my wife's *bua's* younger daughter's *nanad* was married."

He sat staring at Sharma.

"We could go to your house to talk to your wife," said Sharma.

"She has gone to her *mayaka* for a fortnight, sir. But . . ."

Sensing there was more to come, as the man seemed to have a panache for creating suspense, Sharma prompted him, "But we can talk to her?"

"I could make a telephone call to her *mayaka*, sir," he said, beaming at Sharma.

"Excellent, that would save us lots of time," Sharma said encouragingly.

They all went to the reception desk and a trunk call was made. The whole process of telephoning did not turn out as simple as it had seemed to Sharma an hour ago. The call was placed to a neighbour's house, who apparently was the only person to own a telephone in the locality and lived ten-minutes away from Mrs. Gajanand's maternal home. A child was sent to fetch Mrs. Gajanand, who still had not arrived when they made a second trunk call after thirty minutes. A third call was made after a further fifteen minutes and Gajanand Babu, who asked about Rudra Bhardwaj's wife at once to hurry things up, was greeted with angry bellowing, although faint, but perfectly audible to Sharma's ears. Apparently, Gajanand babu's unusual telephone call had made Mrs. Gajanand and her family anxious about his well-being. All the women in the house had rushed to accompany Mrs. Gajanand leaving Jaimala halfway, their favourite program on Vividh Bharati Radio.

Sharma imagined a troop of *saree* clad, fat women, trying to walk and talk simultaneously as fast as they could, arriving at the neighbour's house gasping for breath. Instead of answering his wife's questions, probably knowing he did not have enough time on his hands to calm her down, Gajanand babu passed the receiver to Sharma, who patiently explained who he was and got the information about Dr. Rudra Bhardwaj's wife despite the commotion of chaotic female voices still inquiring about *damad babu's* wellbeing. Sharma, who had a strong urge to hang up the phone, thought better of it, imagining Gajanand babu's plight if he failed to answer his wife's pending queries about the police involvement in Dr. Rudra's case, and thoughtful as he was, he handed Gajanand babu the receiver.

While Gajanand babu was still on the phone, Sharma thanked both of them for their help, pushed back his chair and got up. Rawat followed his suit. Together they walked out of the hospital.

Urvashi, Dr. Rudra's wife, was from Sambhalpura.

Chapter 29

*"Something unpleasant is coming when
men are anxious to tell the truth."*

—Benjamin Disraeli

It was afternoon of Wednesday, 3 September when the
envelope arrived. The clouds outside were sinister black,
screaming heavy downpour. Sharma and Rawat were sitting
together in Sharma's office, drinking steaming *chai* in tiny
glasses.

Sharma was so hopeful they might get vital information
from Sambhalpura that could be their breakthrough in the
inquiry, but the whole thing appeared to reach a dead end.
They couldn't locate any Urvashi from an affluent family who
had married against her parents' wishes in the last decade.
There was, in fact, no girl in Sambhalpura who had a love
marriage in the last decade, the mayor, who was a short, fat
man in his late forties, informed Diwakar in a smug tone.

It was an ordinary white envelope and contained a clipped
sheet of typed paper. The note was neatly typed in Hindi,
although a single space was used after the period which made
the reading of it cumbersome work for Sharma, who still was
waiting for his new pair of spectacles to arrive after breaking

his last pair. He cursed himself for not listening to Nandini, who always asked him to have two pairs at hand.

The address bore Vishwanath Sharma's name with the affix SHO instead of SP, which failed to irk him, as it was not for the first time he that he had been demoted from his rank of Superintendent of Police. He had been known as SHO Sahib for the last fifteen years in the surrounding area despite him climbing the ladder from the rank of SHO to SP. It could very well be the sender's ploy to make himself look ignorant.

The note stated that the attached sheet of paper was the report that Miss Devika Singh had given to Mrs. Gayatri Bhardwaj in the meeting. The report was issued by Dr. Kalpana Aggrwal Clinic, Shiva Road, Shimla and confirmed the pregnancy status of Mrs. Devika Singh of 66, Satyalok Society, Ganesha Avenue, Sanover.

"Rawat, look at this!" said Sharma as he handed over the clipped sheet of paper to him. "That's someone's answer to our riddle!"

Rawat glanced through the papers.

"Nicely typed note," stated Sharma. "A little bit too brief, perhaps. But it serves its purpose well."

"I wonder why he even bothered to send this typed note. You are right, sir. This medical report would have accomplished the sender's goal. He wanted us to know the Bhardwajs were aware of Devika's pregnancy. And he made sure it reached us; it came unstamped."

Heavy rain had started pouring down. Sharma sat quietly and looked out through the barred window onto the wide, pebbled street where the big raindrops looked like a king's crown after they hit the ground and bounced off the surface of the road.

"Sir, this means that this anonymous person believes one of the Bhardwajs to be involved in the murder and is trying to steer us in the right direction by sending this medical proof."

For Rawat, the truth or falsehood of the information was mostly irrelevant, as he usually believed what he saw, heard, or was told. So, he could believe the most outrageous lies sometimes.

Sharma, from his experience, knew things were not always what they seemed, especially when they were purposely presented to be perceived a certain way.

"That could be true, Rawat. But let's not jump to conclusions so fast. There could be something hidden behind all this. Either the sender of this letter wants it to stay hidden, or he wishes it to come to light. It could be anything."

"That means whoever sent this letter could be Dr. Bhardwaj's adversary. Someone who wants to steer us in his direction. It could be a set-up to frame him, sir. In that case, it could be possible that this paper was not the one that was given to Gayatri Bhardwaj in the meeting."

Despite Sharma's advice, Rawat was quick to jump to another conclusion again.

"It could be. But I strongly feel that this paper is the correct one although precisely it may not be the same one; I think this is a copy of that paper. The original one has to be the Bhardwajs. Whoever the sender is, there is a possibility the person might be close to Devika Singh in order to have possessed that knowledge, false knowledge though. Otherwise why would he assume Devika was pregnant? Devika must have told that person herself. Believing the information to be true he decided to send this report. Knowing Devika Singh, I doubt if she would have shared information of a crucial nature with anyone. We are aware Devika Singh was never pregnant. Her post-mortem report didn't say so. It's time to make another visit to Dr. Rajinder Bhardwaj."

Dr. Rajinder Bhardwaj occupied one of the largest rooms at the rear of the west wing. It was comfortably furnished but lacked all evidence of personal taste except for a couple of framed pictures in black and white of Dr. Bhardwaj with a few distinguished-looking men on the wall behind the desk. As they entered, he motioned them to the two low wingbacked chairs placed in front of his desk. He leaned forward and extended his arm to shake hands with Sharma but did not bother to get up and ignored Rawat completely. He looked relaxed and completely at ease. Sharma could not detect any sign of apprehension in his face.

"I assume this is an official visit once again. How can I help?"

"I want to confirm something, Doctor Sahib. Although you answered differently the last time I asked you this question, I still want to ask you the same question again. I am hoping you will choose to answer otherwise today."

Dr. Bhardwaj said, "Please ask."

"Did you know about Miss Devika Singh's pregnancy? Was her pregnancy report the paper that she gave to Mrs. Bhardwaj in the disciplinary meeting?"

Sharma didn't know how he had expected Dr. Rajinder Bhardwaj to react to his question. Dr. Bhardwaj had shared things with Sharma with an apparent frankness during their last meeting, but only those things that could easily come to surface from other sources. Sharma understood the delicate nature of his question. But Dr. Bhardwaj's reaction was surprising.

He said, his tone calm, "Yes, that's what it was: Devika's pregnancy report. Last time, I didn't consider it necessary to talk about the matter which no one had previous knowledge of. It was a fake report, after all; she was never pregnant. But, of course, you know."

"How did you know about it being fake?" Sharma asked, keeping his surprise to himself.

"Knowing how Devika's brain worked, I telephoned Dr. Kalpana, who is an old colleague, right after the meeting. That was the place Devika got her report. They didn't have any record under Devika Singh's name in their clinic. Devika probably bribed someone there to get a false report."

Dr. Bhardwaj then leaned forward, clasped his hands under his chin and said, "I hope you understand. And now I must attend to my duties. If you have nothing else to ask I would like you to leave immediately."

Getting to his feet, Sharma extended his hand to shake Dr. Bhardwaj's and left the senior doctor's office with Rawat at his heels. And Dr. Bhardwaj, with a stoic weariness, watched Sharma and Rawat as they walked away.

Sharma knew Dr. Bhardwaj could be lying about telephoning Dr. Kalpana on 10 August. In all possibility, he could have made inquiries later. Knowing Devika Singh wasn't pregnant at the time of her death, they couldn't pin another major motive on him. His admitting to the fact wouldn't pose any danger to himself or his wife at this point.

Rawat echoed Sharma's thoughts. He said: "Sir, he could have confirmed it later from Dr. Kalpana."

"That's what I think. But his lying now has no bearing on the case. The important aspect of this whole fiasco at this point is, who is this person who wants us to look closely at Dr. Bhardwaj? He or she must be close to Devika and has no idea that Devika lied about her pregnancy."

"It could be because of his hatred for Dr. Bhardwaj."

"Or just a ploy to divert attention from the real murderer, for example, himself."

BOOK 3

"The Devil hath power

To assume a pleasing shape."

—*Hamlet*, William Shakespeare

Chapter 30

"The intellect is always fooled by the heart."

—François de La Rochefoucauld

On the morning of Friday, 5 September, Sharma had just finished his breakfast of two plain *parathas*, *dahi*, butter, and mango pickle when the morning newspaper was delivered. Things had come to a standstill in the ongoing inquiry.

After two weeks of a hectic schedule at the police station, Sharma had leisure time at hand today. He had no suspect interview planned for the day. He took the newspaper and habitually opened the editorial section and there it was, the article about last year's renaming of Vadodara from Baroda. The article was about the trend, which had started after the independence, of renaming of towns, cities, and even states from anglicized versions back to their original names. According to the article, people were awakening to the spirit of nationalism and wanted their cities' and towns' names to portray local culture and their language. Sometimes, cities weren't renamed in the native language, but they were merely respelled in official Indian English.

That's when it came to Sharma. He left at once, calling out to Nandini, who was washing clothes, to say he had urgent work. He went straight to the newspaper stand on his way to the police station and bought the new state map and all the individual district maps for Himachal. He was right, as he found one Sumbhalpore in district Lohit, the English spelling of Sambhalpura in local dialect. He called for Rawat who was already at the police station and a few telephone calls confirmed Sharma's theory.

Luckily, it was the middle of the week and their journey was only six miles to Sumbhalpore. The narrow stretch of road seemed more like a walking trail widened to accommodate vehicles, and it was devoid of traffic except for a few solitary cars crawling at a snail's pace. Even though the road was sufficiently wide enough to accommodate the width of their jeep, Sharma drove with the utmost caution. A trucker would have to be extra cautious so as not to get too close to the rough edges. At regular intervals, there were steep inclines, but the jeep's engine was strong and took them in its stride easily. Sharma, who never had a problem with vertigo, glanced at his companion, who was sitting staring straight ahead, his knuckles white against the black of his trousers, a nerve throbbing in his left temple, revealing the stress he was feeling at present. Sharma knew of Rawat's fear of the steep mountain roads. He drove in silence. Soon the steep decline started, and they came to the open widened road. He could feel Rawat relaxing.

It was just after three and the afternoon was slipping into the evening after a sunny day when Sharma drove them into Sumbhalpore. It was an ordinary town. They passed the city's historic temple where several labourers were working on its surrounding walls, probably to protect the precincts of this old place. The old, originally constructed walls of rounded fieldstones flattened with mortar seemed badly in need of an overhaul. The pointing, owing to countless seasons of rains and storms, was missing at places where joints had first cracked, and then crumbled completely, to let the aging mortar seep out along with the inner mud filling, leaving nothing but unmistakable rifts behind. The latter seemed to be nature's defiance against man as the stone itself had been laid out well enough to stand through generations of rain and storm.

It must have been a stone temple once, Sharma thought, looking at the massive stone pillars, the only remnants of its historic elegance, that stood soaring all around the drab new building. Separated from the temple grounds was a sheltered concrete chajja where a few old men were playing cards. They gave Sharma and Rawat a curious glance as their jeep passed. On their right side, a small herd of cows was grazing. They crossed a narrow stream where buffaloes were lying in the water enjoying their leisurely bath. Although the air was crisp, the drizzle of the day before had left its lingering presence in the air which smelled of parched clay soaked in rainwater.

After they had driven a few miles, leaving behind the town of Sumbhalpore, which stretched across the main road, a stone archway announced the Estate of Malabar Hills. Like every other town and city, Sumbhalpore had its class system and everyone knew the wealthy lived in the Malabar Hills, the Lodhi Colony or the Ambay Estate.

They were not long in finding the house they were looking for. It was an impressive villa and it lay a little back from the road in a cone-shaped plot. Sharma drove through the rows of *deodar* trees. The majestic Himalayan cedar, the *deodar*, Sharma knew was considered a sacred tree during ancient times. Its impressive form was an object of veneration and the name *deodar* came from *Devadaru; Deva*, the first half of the Sanskrit term, means divine and the second part, *Daru*, was related to the word tree.

The house lay before them—tall, elongated, and impressive with an air of thriving elegance as they crossed the pebbled driveway. Sharma parked the jeep in the covered porch. They mounted the series of steps, went to the door, rang the doorbell, and waited. A small forty-something woman opened the door and showed them inside to the drawing room. The huge, tall, westward window looked out over the courtyard and beyond the zigzag road to the wild green fields blooming in the monsoon. It was soothing to be away from the frenetic hubbub of town life and to hear the distinct hum of the gently blowing wind outside.

The interior of the drawing room was expensive and tastefully personal. Someone had taken time to arrange the objects of sentimental value which connected the past to the present and gave a sense of lasting eternalness to their surroundings. The furniture was solid wood in dark mahogany. Sitting on the tanned leather sofa, Sharma looked around and took in the furnishings which, although expensive, seemed unpretentious by the presence of many personal belongings. Opposite the sofa was a square oak table with two armchairs in tanned leather on either side. On the wall opposite the tall window was a fitted bookcase, which ran floor to ceiling and seemed weighed down by the bulk of personal pictures, family possessions and sentimental souvenirs.

They sat in silence and waited for Urvashi's *bua*. There was something imposing about Kamla Devi when she came walking toward them. She was a tall, well-built woman with an air of vitality about her that surprised Sharma, who knew her to be in her late seventies. He had imagined Kamla Devi to be a small, frail-looking, conforming, and elderly woman. The reality was different—commanding and noteworthy. She was wearing a pale taupe *salwar kameez*. Her silvery hair was brushed back, twisted into a bun at the back of her head, and was covered with a Bemberg silk *dupatta*. She greeted them in a firm yet soft voice.

Without wasting time on preliminary formalities, she came to the point. "Urvashi shall be back soon as she must have informed you. I understood from her that you wish to talk about her marriage and her ex-husband. I would like to make a request, SP Sahib. This matter, that your visit is about Rudra, shouldn't get out. It wouldn't do us any good if this whole affair about him living a different life somewhere else gets out."

"Don't worry, madam, we've no reason to talk about it. Even if a need arises, which I seriously doubt that it will, we shall try to keep your family name out of it."

"You've lessened my burden by saying that. But why you are interested in Urvashi's marriage after all these years? What has happened?"

"We are investigating the murder of a woman who worked at the same hospital where Dr. Rudra works."

"Is he a suspect?"

"Anyone who had any connection with the victim is on our radar at present. We are exploring every possible avenue, madam. But Dr. Rudra's questionable past had made things interesting. We are watching him more closely now."

The woman who had opened the door returned carrying a tray with cups of tea and biscuits. Kamla Devi waited for her to serve tea to everyone. The woman placed the plate on the table and offered them steaming cups of *chai*. Then Kamla Devi whispered something in her ear, and she left.

Sharma asked, "How did the marriage happen? I understand your brother was against this marriage."

"My brother raised Urvashi single-handedly. She lost her mother when she was very young and in trying to protect her against any more disappointments, he gave her a sheltered life. That, precisely, was the reason for her being naive despite her intelligence and sensibility. My brother shielded her from the harsh realities of life but, as you must know, the parents ought not to pluck the thorns out before they hand down the roses to their children; it is not always possible to shield your child against all the disappointments that life bestows. A day comes when a child has to face life on her own and, as a parent, one has to make sure that the child is ready. But Urvashi was not ready. She was good at heart, and so was everyone else; for her, the word 'bad' existed in faraway lands which couldn't reach her."

She sipped her tea and then continued, "When she met Rudra, it was as if she had just awakened to the world and discovered its wonder. She knew a lot about dreams and a little about wickedness."

The maid came back with an envelope and handed it to her mistress. She took a photograph out.

"My niece, Urvashi. That is Rudra with her."

It was a black-and-white photograph of them together.

"She, as you must have noticed from her picture, was not bestowed with any physical beauty. She was just another plain-looking girl. Everyone advised her against this marriage, but she listened to no one. Whereas my brother noticed Rudra's arrogance, his pretence, and his insincerity behind his intelligent talk, Urvashi could only see his candour. Although she didn't understand what it was about her that had so whimsically caught Rudra's fancy, we feared he was after her money. They were together for a little over three years. Those three years of her marriage were a time of intense joy for her. He seemed devoted to her, but we never could shake off a bit of uncertainty about his true intentions. They seemed happy, although I could sense her restlessness sometimes. She must have felt dubious about him because, for all her gullibility, she is an intelligent girl."

Sharma glanced at her, at the watery eyes and the strong face creased with wrinkles that denoted experience and strength of character, and thought how each crease on her skin was etched from wisdom learned from wrong steps taken in life. If elders could bequeath their experience and knowledge of life to children without the children making any mistakes, they would save them from a lifetime of heartaches.

"What happened then?"

"Rudra started looking over the accounts at our factory, and though everything ran smoothly on the surface, the head accountant pointed out the irregularities in the audits. Rudra, when asked, was furious and blamed Urvashi for not trusting him. There were other incidents. Our worst fears turned true one day. He had married her just for her money and, when he found out he would get nothing out of that marriage, being the fraud he was, he just took off."

Sharma looked at the picture again. A happy newlywed couple. The wife an awkward, slight, and plain-looking girl with a big, happy grin. She looked like an ignorant schoolgirl next to her broad-shouldered, virile husband, who was all charm with a contagious smile and a startlingly handsome face. While she had her face slightly turned toward him, he was looking at the camera with a confident expression. Sharma couldn't detect any trace of menace behind those eyes. But exceedingly deceptive people, he knew, were experts at hiding behind a mask of charm. Underneath that smooth exterior, there was a conniving mind at work. Was that what her father and *bua* saw? They couldn't talk her out of that doomed marriage though.

"How old was she?" Sharma asked. Urvashi looked so young, barely in her teens in the picture.

"Twenty-one, too young to get married in her father's eyes. She was a sensible and mature girl, though. Only if she'd had the caution of the old and the experienced, could she have seen through his scheming exterior."

"What prompted his sudden leave?"

"Rudra must have been in need of money. He had tried to mortgage a piece of commercial land which was in Urvashi's name. He went to a private moneylender in Birjpur. Luckily, an employee at the business knew my brother. They sent their people to my brother to inquire. When asked, Rudra made a feeble excuse. My brother immediately consulted his lawyer and bequeathed all his estate to Urvashi and children in such a way that Rudra couldn't touch the money or sell any property. He wasted no time after that, just took off after two weeks but, before that, emptied their joint bank account and the locker. The worst thing he did to her was give no warning.

Everything was normal as far as she was concerned. She had no clue that he meant to do that; their marriage, their togetherness, and the children—their sons—meant nothing to him. It was extraordinary, the way he betrayed her."

A clear picture was forming now, of a man who was cold, calculated, and cruel—a man incapable of remorse—a man who felt no guilt in making a promise he never meant to keep.

"Did you contact the police?"

"We did. The police found his burnt car in a trench, but there was no body. Urvashi was mad with grief. We suspected he had faked his accident. But Urvashi wouldn't believe it. To her, he was so kind, so caring, and so unpretentious. She didn't understand why everyone else was suspicious of his sincerity. We came to know about the theft of the safe in their room in the meantime. A considerable amount of money and jewellery was missing. That's when we knew with certainty that he was alive and had left Urvashi for good, although Urvashi thought otherwise."

"Why you did not contact his mother?"

"We thought he had no family," Kamla Devi said with disbelief in her voice. "He told us that his parents were no more."

Chapter 31

"Do you not see how necessary a world
of pains and troubles is to school an
intelligence and make it a soul?"

—*Letters of John Keats*, John Keats

It was twelve minutes past three before Urvashi reached home. For the most part of her morning, she had been in the hospital talking to the doctors, and then later, in one of their lumber mills in Durgeshwar, industrial town thirty miles from Sumbhalpore, as five labourers had been seriously injured.

She could not remember very much of the whole day except for the tear-stained, anxious faces of the families of those injured at the mill. Urvashi had worked tirelessly with the staff at the mill later that day, glancing through all the insurance policies, and signing the necessary documents. She had felt a sigh of relief in the late afternoon when all the accident victims were declared out of critical danger at the hospital. It was a frantic day for her, but she supposed things had gone reasonably well considering the chaos of the early morning.

Sharma and Rawat were waiting for her in the drawing room when she reached home. She excused herself for ten minutes to freshen up, asked the maid to make tea, and went upstairs. From her picture, Sharma knew she was a small woman. But her slightness somehow astonished him. Although she was in her early thirties, she looked like a college-going girl. She was nothing like her *bua*, Kamla Devi, who despite her age was a good eight inches above five feet. Urvashi barely reached her shoulders. She put on a change of clothes and appeared dressed in an off-white, loose cotton *kurta* and *churidar* with net *dupatta* in pale yellow, which stole the colour from her face and made it look very pale. She was not wearing any jewellery except a dot-sized diamond pin in her nose. Her hair was dull black, parted sideways, twisted in a low ponytail, her face gaunt and her features less than ordinary. The only thing big about her were her eyes, dark brown, hooded, and kind.

When she spoke, her voice was clear and confident. There was no trace of an awkward college kid. "I am sorry I kept you waiting. I have been tied up all day. Unfortunately, there was an accident last night at our mill in Durgeshwar, so I had to go there this morning. Although Amarnath uncle, our manager, is efficient to deal with any emergency, I felt it would uplift the concerned workers to see me there in person," she said as she sipped her tea.

"I hope everything is fine there?"

"Thankfully, no one is seriously injured." She looked up and smiled at Sharma. It was a gentle smile.

"I appreciate that you agreed to see us on short notice," said Sharma with genuine sincerity. "As soon as we got your address, it was important for us to talk to you at once."

"No problem at all. *Bua* must have told you about the circumstances under which I got married and later parted from my ex-husband. I haven't seen him for years, not since he walked out on me. I assume he hasn't changed at all," she said in a nonchalant tone. "People, I know for a fact, never change, not their soul at least. He must have done something awful that brought you here to talk about him."

"There has been a violent death, and the victim worked in his hospital. We are looking into everyone's life who works there. During our investigation, a few interesting things about Mr. Rudra Bhardwaj's past came into light which compelled us to look closely at him."

"I would like to show you something," said Urvashi heading toward a back door. "This way please."

As she walked ahead of him, Sharma thought that she was older than she had appeared initially. The room into which they were shown looked out over the manicured lawn and was filled with bright light. There was a large window and another door to the right. The large sofa which dominated the room was made of leather and looked expensive. The only other piece of furniture was a large oak desk and a leather chair behind it. Unlike the other room, this room was devoid of any personal possession as if its owner has no interest in coming here. The walls were bare except for Dr. Rudra Bhardwaj's picture with a garland of dried flowers around it. Sharma was stupefied.

He said awkwardly, "But you know he is not dead."

"I know. And that garland around his picture. . .frankly, I keep forgetting he's still alive, going about his usual business somewhere else. Of course, he is not dead. I know it. That's kept as a fond reminder of lessons I have learned. I keep it for the sake of *Bua*," she said simply without any hint of resentment. "It would distress her if people get to know the reality. She is old-school and fond of keeping up appearances in front of children and extended family; the priority for her, of course, is in the reverse order. *Bua* dares not let relations know how her only niece was duped in her marriage."

She laughed then, it was a genuine, happy laugh. Sharma thought he liked her.

"And unlike Daddy, she's always been an aficionado for tough love. The picture, according to her, would always act as a good reminder of my past idiocy. It would also help me decide any matter wisely in the future," she said, smiling.

Sharma couldn't help but smile back. He asked, "Your *bua* has already told us about the circumstances under which you got married. Did you not have any inkling about his real intentions? Any warning signs?"

"Let us sit in the drawing room." She walked back to the drawing room. They followed her lead.

"You know how your intuition warns you about someone, but you bury it because it shows the darkness underneath which you wish to ignore; the bright and shiny on the outside is so inviting, you don't want to look anywhere else?"

"I know what you mean."

"That's what happened. There were warning signals alright, but I ignored them. I was one of those gullible and naive people who are essentially unaccustomed to the ways of the world. He was a remarkably striking man, the most handsome of all. Flocks of girls chased him. But he pursued me only. He adored me like no one had done before," she said, reflecting, "I was much pampered at home, but I'd barely known the world beyond home. I was raw. He fretted about me and demanded only my company. I was enthralled. So, I married him against Daddy's wishes."

"When did you realize that Dr. Rudra was alive?"

"I had no proof, if that's what you meant to ask, but yes, I knew of him being alive right from the beginning despite being in denial for a few months. But *Bua* and Daddy knew right away. They weren't the sort to get duped."

"Didn't you try to look for him then? You must have felt angry?"

"I was upset to realize that he was alive and well somewhere. I had not expected that. Was he not supposed to be suffering for what he did to my heart? I couldn't bear the thought of him living his life somewhere as if nothing had happened. I wanted to find him, confront him, ask the reason for breaking my heart. But then, I realized it was pointless. He wouldn't have any answers I wanted to hear. There was nothing out of character in his treachery. He intended to do it when he married me. I realized that he'd never changed. When he walked out of my life after three years, he was the same person who had entered my life three years earlier. I'd formed an image out of my perception. I thought he was what I wanted him to be."

Sharma looked at her intelligent eyes. They reflected understanding and kindness. He listened to her quietly. He had no particular wish to interrupt her discourse which, he knew, deserved silence.

She continued, "Gradually the hatred, the anger, the resentment dimmed, and I felt a dull contemptuous indifference toward him. But my indifference is absolute unlike the indifference we feel for strangers, because occasionally, we might feel a wave of dispassionate pity at their misfortunes. But the callous indifference, you know, that we feel for autocrats, for predators, and for everything evil, the harsh apathy which makes us gloat at their misfortunes, it's rather that absolute indifference I feel for him now," she said.

"You must know you can register a case against him for fraud," Sharma said.

"I should have done it years ago. But now, as I told you, I only feel a contemptuous disinterest in him. It would delight me to see him suffering, but I would rather not get involved in any matter that concerns him. I don't care one way or another what happens to him," she said with a smile that was as genuine as she was herself.

"I can understand."

Sharma had already heard a lot about Rudra Bhardwaj, but the things he had learned today were alien to him before or even to those who thought they knew him.

"Sir, do you think he is involved in Devika's murder too? We know the man is a fraud," asked Rawat, who seemed tense with excitement after hearing Urvashi's version of Dr. Rudra's past.

"He seems connected to this case, Rawat. In what way, that's not clear yet."

"We can charge him, sir, now that we know about his early life."

"Nothing of that sort is possible without Urvashi's cooperation. Faced with this new evidence, he might just become more cautious or bolt. I don't want to take any risks and jeopardize the whole investigation. It's better not to talk to him at this point. And moreover, it is difficult to put him at the murder scene. Remember, he was doing the night shift in the hospital at the time."

"The hospital is merely ten minutes on foot from Satyalok Society, sir. He could have left unnoticed."

"No one saw him leaving the hospital, Rawat; we don't have any witnesses who saw him leaving that night. We can't just arrest him because of his murky past."

Chapter 32

"A very little key will open a very heavy door."

—*Hunted Down*, Charles Dickens

"It came to me to this morning, Rawat. I ought to have thought of it. What we need now is a list of all the girls who were Devika's classmates in training college. Tell Diwakar to get on it at once," said Sharma.

"The list wouldn't be hard to get, sir. The college must have kept records. But it wouldn't be easy to trace all her classmates. They must have moved to God-knows-wherever after getting married."

"I'm aware of that, but we might just get a break here. According to Devika's mother, the last time she visited her, she was frantically looking for an old album. She took considerable trouble to search for it, visited her estranged mother after four years, and went all the way to her sister's house to get it when she had once sworn never to set foot there. Why did she go to such considerable lengths to get just an old album? The album had pictures of her with friends from her college and a few pictures of her mother. But we know she wasn't a sentimental person. Apparently, there was something in the album that was important. We found another album with family photos in her flat, but there are pictures missing in the one she had got from her sister's. One of her old classmates may know something that might help us to break this case."

"That means she was killed because there was something in that album that her killer didn't want to come to light. Whoever killed her took it after the murder."

"She had a sensational life in Sanover and we know all about it. There are a few people including her husband who had both the motive and opportunity to kill her. Dr. Rajinder Bhardwaj is too intelligent to do something so evidently foolish right after that big public showdown with her. Gayatri Bhardwaj had the motive, opportunity, and the physical strength required to strangle Devika. So far, she is unable to provide us with any satisfactory alibi, but then, wouldn't you say she is too intelligent—like her husband—to do something so foolish? Kavita Asthana, the girl who committed suicide, her brother Shivnaik Asthana made threats against Devika. But his alibis are solid. We have thoroughly checked them. He couldn't have done it. Virat Singh Chaudhry lied to us about his whereabouts. But why did he wait so long? If he had wanted to kill Devika, he could have done so years ago. And their divorce proceedings are still in court. He must've known he would become an obvious suspect; he seems too intelligent to take any risk in such a situation. Still we cannot rule him out. Then, we have the senior nursing superintendent, Saroj Rani Jaiswal. Devika insulted her in the meeting, but I cannot see her killing Devika for that."

"People have been murdered for smaller reasons!"

"Wouldn't you say she lacks the physical strength to strangle a healthy and young person like Devika? She is too old to overpower Devika. To suspect that she has done it is a stretch too far."

Neena H. Brar

To trace Sarita Joshi had proved less trouble for Diwakar than Rawat had predicted earlier. The senior office clerk at Indira Gandhi Industrial Training Institute for Women, Mrs. Gandhari Joshi, was a plump woman in her late forties and she had worked at the college for almost fifteen years. She went through the old records promptly, took out the admission register for the year of 1963, and instructed the typist who was a slight-looking twentyish woman to get the full list with names and addresses typed.

"We keep former students' complete records as it is a customary practice, although it's rather a nonessential cumbersome process if you ask my opinion."

Before Diwakar could say anything, she went on, "Why do you need the list, though? Does it concern any serious matter?"

He told her about Devika's brutal murder. She was dumbstruck at first, and rather upset later, to know a former student of their collage had met her end violently.

"Are you sure we are talking about the same person? The woman couldn't have studied here."

She clearly was of the belief that a student of the prestigious Indira Gandhi Industrial Training Institute for Women could in no way fall prey to such a terrible fate. Devika's succumbing to her death like that was an unfortunate and rare occurrence in the history of the college.

To Diwakar's positive affirmation, she replied in a grim tone, "Really, what a weird thing! I thought no one from here could meet such an end."

"Do you remember who were her close friends?"

"I can't remember. Honestly, I couldn't have recalled Devika either, if not for her flawless beauty. She was very lovely as far as I remember."

The typist was back with the list. The list had thirty-five names, none of them local among them. All the girls were from different parts of the state. It would be a lengthy process, thought Diwakar, to trace each of them to their respective homes, as almost everyone must have moved to a different place after their marriage.

"Can you recognize anyone close to her on this list?" Diwakar asked hopefully.

"I wish I could tell you more, but as you can see, this list is a decade old and hundreds of students come to study here every year. I remember a few of them, but they are the ones who achieve something—top-achievers at university level, or who managed to get good posts in reputable hospitals, or were exceptionally beautiful like Devika Singh. As far as I remember, hers wasn't a very distinguishable batch. Not even one of them achieved something worth mentioning," she said in a regretful tone.

Diwakar had another idea. He asked her about the hostel warden and Devika's boarding arrangements in the college hostel. He hoped that the same warden still worked at the college and could provide the name of the girl who had been Devika's roommate. But that proved to be a dead end, for Devika had lived as a paying guest at a private residence in the city.

"I remember because it wasn't common for any student to live on her own. We had enough rooms for all the out-of-town students in our hostel. If you ask me, it was most unusual. Any respectable parent wouldn't have allowed it. And she was a married woman," she said in an accusing tone, as if Devika opting to live as a paying guest was an immoral act and essentially her husband's fault who had failed to keep tabs on her, the way her parents would've done.

Diwakar started his enquiries about Devika's classmates with the two names Amba Raj and Latika Sastri. Both the women were from Kolwara, the town twenty miles from Khandi, the closest one. He believed that the women, in all probability, must have known Devika well considering they were from the same district.

To Diwakar's disappointment, Amba Raj's family had moved to Delhi five years ago, and the house had been sold.

He tried Latika Sastri's address then and learned from her mother, who was a proud-looking woman in her mid-fifties, that Latika Sastri, who was Latika Grover now, lived in Paonta Sahib with her husband and son, and she was expecting her second child.

Diwakar left for Paonta Sahib early the next day, but it took all morning and the best part of his afternoon to meet Latika Grover in person because she had gone for her routine checkup to the doctor. She was a pleasant-looking, slight woman, and it was hard to tell if she was expecting. She knew Devika well but wasn't close to her in a real sense. She directed him to Sarita Joshi who had been Devika's roommate and a fellow resident of Khandi, Devika's *sasural*. Devika shared a rented room in the city with Sarita Joshi because she didn't want to stay in the hostel. Diwakar thanked her for the address and left.

The address provided by Latika Grover was Sarita Joshi's paternal home, Diwakar already knew. He found it without any difficulty in Khandi. Her parents knew Devika well and knew of her death. They had been very forthcoming in giving him their daughter's home and her work address in Saloh, where she lived with her husband and children.

Instead of talking to Sarita Joshi on her own, an excited Diwakar informed Sharma, who asked him to carry on with his further queries about the victim's other classmates in case something of importance could be learned from one of them. Diwakar's further queries amounted to nothing but a long, futile process as none of the women knew much about Devika. She was not close to anyone.

The telephone rang only once. He knew Gayatri would call.

"Hello," Pratap Kaushal said in a thick voice.

"Did they come around?

"Yes, it was some ASI from the police station. I told him you never came here."

"Did he ask *Bhabhi* as well?"

"He wanted to, but I told him it was not necessary. Your *bhabhi* would have said the same thing, Gayatri. Now don't worry. No one needs to know about it."

"But what if they come to know about my visit from the Mehtas?"

"No one needs to know we had guests sleeping at our house when you came over after midnight. They never saw you. And the Mehtas have gone back to Chandigarh; as far as the Mehtas know, you never visited us on the night of 12 August. Just stay calm." Her brother's voice was soothing.

"Good." Gayatri Bhardwaj was relieved.

Chapter 33

*"No facts are to me sacred; none are
profane; I simply experiment, an
endless seeker, with no past at my
back."*

— Ralph Waldo Emerson

Sharma hoped Sarita Joshi might know some important information, considering she had been the victim's roommate in the city for two years. During those two years and afterwards, Devika had stayed away from her in-laws and her paternal family. They knew nothing of her life after she went to study for her diploma until she went to Sanover and met her end there. Sarita Joshi, Sharma hoped, could provide them with a much-needed breakthrough in the case.

Sarita Joshi was of medium height, fair, and appeared to be in her mid-thirties. She wore a figure-hugging, bright-red short *kurta* with *churidar* that would have suited her better if she were younger by a decade. She had a thin top half that seemed to widen dramatically right below her waist. But her problem wasn't just her large hips and generous thighs. She had a small heart-shaped face that looked disproportionate compared to her lower half. She could have looked mediocre if not for her *Sadhna-cut* hairstyle which, Sharma suspected, she had been sporting since her youth and which certainly had looked gorgeous on *Sadhna,* but the front fringe seemed to throttle her forehead, to such a degree that her pointy chin appeared awfully squeezed and made her already-narrow face look narrower.

"I still can't believe Devika is dead. It seems unreal. She was full of life," she said with a hint of incredulity in her voice as she led them through a narrow hall to the drawing room located on its left.

Sharma's eyes roved round the room. It was the drawing room of an average middle-class family. It looked comfortable and cozy. The furniture was outdated but of good quality, hand-embroidered cushions were placed on the sofa, and framed hand-painted art decorated the wall. It looked somewhat on the small side with all the knickknacks and a few personal possessions accumulated over the years. The focus of the room was a small television set covered in a white lace cloth. It sat on a square table.

Sharma at once started with his queries. "Were you very friendly with Devika Singh?"

"I wouldn't say we were very close," she said, her tone reluctant. "But, we were good friends. She was a secretive person. What little she shared about herself she did with me. We shared a room for two years. She was doing her nursing aid's diploma during the first year. Then she joined a stenographer and secretarial assistance course in a nearby college while I was studying to be a registered nurse in a nursing college."

"Were you acquainted with her before you went to study?"

"I knew her by name. And, in Khandi, everybody knew Devika. It was hard not to know her." Sarita smiled feebly. "Although the college had its hostel where I lived during my first year, I had a hard time there. The warden was an old hag who believed in issuing severe reprimands for small mistakes. It turned out I had become her favourite to pick on because of my carefree nature. Devika, who joined a year after, opted to rent out a room somewhere in the city because she wasn't one to follow any rules. My parents knew her in-laws. I rented the room with her because my parents wouldn't allow me to live on my own. It worked out well."

"What kind of person was she?"

"I don't want to imply that she wasn't a nice person. She was good, but not always, and certainly not to everyone." Sarita seemed uncertain. "She was . . . well, she differed from the usual crowd."

"Don't worry, madam. The talk we are having now shall stay between us. It will not go on record," Sharma said in a soothing tone, sensing Sarita Joshi's uncertainty. "Outside her family, you knew her intimately. Family, because of their presumptions, can be biased. I'm hoping I can get a neutral impression of her personality. It's important. It might help us catch her killer. Just try to give a sort of outline of her personality."

"I understand. It's just that . . . well, she died a violent death. It seems cruel to say unkind things about her now." She took a deep sigh.

Sharma nodded in understanding and urged her to go on.

She said, "I'm sure everyone in Khandi considered her vile, but she was not that bad . . . if you weren't a very sensitive person. Yet, it was not easy living with her. Well, it's not easy to live with a self-obsessed person. Everything with them is about their precious self. Their arrogance and self-importance force them to live two lives simultaneously. You find yourself entangled between their real self, which you live with day and night, and the other imaginary self which they stage for their audiences. You do not know which part of them is genuine and which part is an act for the benefit of onlookers."

"Did she lie a lot?"

"It was hard to tell with her. Like a chameleon, Devika effortlessly feigned the role she sensed the other person expected to see, subject to what she wanted in return—mere admiration, for which she had a vast appetite for, or to get something she desired at that particular moment. She could feign any emotion which she thought would suit the situation. One of the lecturers who was in charge of the practical exams for her year had a stillbirth. Devika visited her every day, did all kinds of chores, cooked, and took tiffin to her for days. She was sad for her. A few weeks later, I was telling Devika about one of my relations who fought with severe depression after her second consecutive miscarriage. The woman had a congenital uterine abnormality and the doctors advised her not to try for another child. Devika was shocked. She could not comprehend why such a situation would make anyone depressed. The problem with her was that she couldn't see anything beyond herself. Not that she was devoid of empathy, but it was difficult for her to experience any genuine compassion for others in light of her self-importance."

"How was her marriage to her husband?"

"He was good to her, but after their son's birth, their relationship started dissolving into resentment and bitterness: contempt on his part and bored indifference on hers. As far as I understood, their relationship was one-sided; he was the one who gave in their marriage. She never said that in so many words, but it was easy to tell because she was in the habit of saying a thing or two on occasions. She made up a lot of things, but I had learned to extract the actual truth from her jumbled talk. For a long time, he had tried to make her happy, but, I suppose, she had no desire to be happy with him. Instead of evolving or changing for the better, their relationship changed for the worse."

"What about her son? How did she feel about staying away from him?"

"She never talked about him. Any mention of him and Devika would just clam up. It was a taboo subject for her, you know, him having Down's Syndrome."

"Would she do anything for money?"

Sarita Joshi thought, and then said, "She might have if she was running short of it. Money was important to her. She had never seen much money before her marriage. Her father had decent-enough income from his junior stenographer's job in a government office to provide his family with three meals a day and a little extra on occasions. But he couldn't afford luxuries. After her marriage, she had gotten used to all the extravagances that money could buy."

"Could there be another man behind her decision to leave her husband?" asked Sharma.

"As far as I know, there was no other man in her life but her husband. But she flirted copiously, though it was harmless flirting on her part. I don't think she was interested in men. She loved admiration. It was essential to her ego. She resented her husband's lack of interest in her after their son's birth. She told me once how she had hated being pregnant and hated her enormous body. After her son's birth, she couldn't look in the mirror for weeks. Her body was sore and slack, she said, but her husband couldn't see anything other than their newborn son. She resented that. The birth of her son had given her a new distorted perspective on her married life—what it had done to her and her carefree life. She couldn't stand being tied down. She loved her independence too much. It never came as a surprise when I heard about her leaving her husband and son."

"Did you see her again after you both left college?"

"I met her once in Khandi by chance, and then for the last time when she came to visit me specifically."

"When was that?"

"A little over eight months ago. Devika came to see me at the hospital. It was unexpected. She had been to a nearby town and came to visit me as well. She seemed excited." Sarita Joshi's voice faltered. "She even hugged me when we parted, something she had never done before. I had never known her to display physical affection. She might have had a premonition that it was her last meeting."

"Did she tell you which town she had visited or why she had gone there?"

"No, knowing the way she guarded her emotions and her privacy, I dared not ask."

"Do you know if she had someone close to her living there, whom she might have gone to visit? A friend, a relative, or someone else?"

"No idea. But yes, Devika had worked in this part of the state for some time though, right after finishing her training. I assumed she had gone to visit someone who was known to her from her days there."

"Did you stay in touch any other way, write to each other maybe?"

"For some time, yes. I started working full-time. Devika accepted a private nursing job somewhere in this part of the state. I suspected she wanted to get as far away as she could from her family. It involved at-home care for an elderly paralyzed patient. The job, she said, was exhausting, but the money was good. They offered free lodging and food. She stayed there for a little more than a year until the patient's death. We stayed in touch during that time but stopped writing afterwards. I was the one who wrote all the time. She occasionally would reply. After I got married, I barely had time for anyone but family."

Sharma looked at her. "And those letters? Do you still have them?"

Sarita Joshi said, "That was years ago. I discarded them."

"What about her address there or the name of people for whom she worked? Do you remember anything at all?"

She smiled at him and said, "I should have it. Let me check."

She got up and left the room, closing the door behind her, and came back shortly after with a small pocket-sized black diary. After turning a few pages, she handed it to Sharma.

"Thankfully, I still keep the same old address book from my college days."

The address was neatly written with Devika's name. Sharma passed the diary to Rawat, who stared at it incredulously. He looked at his boss's face: it was impassive. Taking a cue from his boss, Rawat scrawled a few words and handed the diary back.

"You have been very helpful, madam."

She asked awkwardly, "Was her body . . . her face intact?" Then said, "You would think a beautiful woman like Devika would be self-assured, confident of herself. But that's not how it was with her. She was incapable of passing a mirror without scrutinizing herself for any flaw. She always worried about the transient state of her beauty. Once she bumped into a door and injured her forehead. It was just a superficial injury. She refused to leave the room for days because she couldn't bear to let people see her scar. No one had loved her for who she was except for her father. People could not look beyond her beauty. It was hard for her."

· "She was strangulated, and her face and body were intact. She died quickly, if it gives you any relief, madam," Sharma said.

Every person so far seemed to dislike Devika. Although each one of them resented her for a different reason, the reason they all disliked her was common: her calculated and devious nature. The picture of Devika, built from statements, testimonies, impressions, judgments, and rumors showed a scheming, manipulative, and selfish woman who was cold and heartless. During their investigation so far, the general impression they had formed about her was that she lacked the grace and class of a well-bred woman; mean-spirited as she was, she would go to any lengths to achieve her goals. Sarita Joshi was the first person, other than her sister, who had mourned Devika's death.

Chapter 34

"Take nothing on its looks; take everything on evidence. There's no better rule."

—*Great Expectations*, Charles Dickens

She was a good-looking woman in her mid-thirties. Her face was pale but she, Sharma noticed, had taken trouble in dressing herself. She was wearing a plain yellow *saree* with a bold printed blouse, and light lipstick. Her straight, shiny hair reached her waist and was worn loose with a middle parting. Rawat ushered her in and introduced her as Miss Neelam, Virat Chaudhry's fiancée.

Ignoring Rawat's obvious meaningful glance, Sharma asked her to sit down to which she refused and said instead: "I've wanted to talk to you for many days, sir. There's something important I would like you to know. But, I would rather not tell you in any official capacity. I hope you won't object to that. Can we go outside somewhere? I spotted a small tea stall just around the corner from here. We can sit there and talk," she said with a clear urgency.

Sharma had no objection, and together they walked outside to the tea stall.

Sharma and everyone else from the police station frequented the tea stall almost every day. It was a twelve by fifteen-foot, rectangular structure of wood and stone with a sloped roof. It had been there for the last few years and the owner, Dhani Ram, was a pot-bellied, cheerful man in his late fifties with grey hairs and a small moustache. He made one of the best spicy, *masala chai*. He opened his stall every morning before dawn and closed it only after sunset in any weather. The place had changed little in all those years except for the new seating arrangements—square plastic tables with four chairs around each one, in horizontal rows.

A few customers sat on the chairs arranged haphazardly outside the tea stall. Sharma asked Dhani Ram for two cups of *chai* and led Neelam inside the place. Dhani Ram, who usually liked to converse with Sharma, gave a quick, curious glance at Sharma's company, nodded his head, and started to make tea. They settled themselves on one of the empty tables. No one talked. They sat there watching him boiling tea leaves in a sturdy copper pot on a kerosene stove. Once the water started boiling, Dhani Ram poured milk from the milk jug and waited for it to come to a boil, and then spun their *chai* expertly through the air—the hot frothy liquid flowed from one jug to another.

Within minutes, their tea arrived in small glasses. It was steaming hot, sweet, and frothy. They wrapped their fingers around the warm glasses.

Neelam sipped her *chai* and said, "It's been on my mind for so many days, sir. Virat doesn't know about my visit. Otherwise, he wouldn't have let me come here. It was important for me to talk to you, but I couldn't muster the courage to come and visit you at the police station earlier."

"That's understandable."

Her voice was awkward when she spoke again, "It's about Virat's whereabouts on the night of the killing."

Sharma replied, "That's what I thought it to be."

"I know how Virat said he was at the cinema that night. He couldn't give any alibi though. His divorce proceedings were still in court at the time of Devika's murder. That must have put him under suspicion, I suppose." She looked at Sharma inquiringly but he kept quiet. She spoke with an urgent neediness then. "I wanted to come to you at once, but Virat was apprehensive. I would rather tell you about his whereabouts on the night in question now, than wait for you to take a harsh step, and then come forward."

"His reluctance to reveal his whereabouts under the circumstances could get him into trouble in the coming days. You took the right decision, madam," said Sharma sincerely.

"Virat didn't go to the Basant Cinema in Dongri. He went to the cinema, but he wasn't alone." She looked at Sharma and said without embarrassment, "We were in Shimla that day. Veena came to visit from Lucknow, and as she was home to take care of Sahil, we planned this outing, just the two of us. We went to the Regal Theatre in Shimla for the evening show. I still have the torn tickets with me from that night." She hesitated for a brief moment and then said, "After the picture was over, we strolled down the Ridge and ate at one of the small eateries at the Mall Road. By half past eleven, we were back in our hotel room. Next morning, we went to the Lakkar Bazaar adjoining the Ridge. I wanted to buy a few souvenirs. We left from Shimla at around noon and were back home by the evening of 13 August."

"But why didn't Mr. Virat Chaudhry disclose it to us? It could have saved you from all the trouble," remarked Sharma.

"As you know, his divorce proceedings were still in the court. Despite having zero intention to reconcile, Devika refused to go through with the divorce. After Virat's mother's death, it had been difficult for Virat and *Babu Ji* to take care of Sahil. Virat's divorce case was already in court, and hence our families planned our wedding. A simple *roka* was done, and we exchanged rings. But we couldn't get married because Devika, who wanted to get the divorce in the first place, suddenly refused to give Virat his freedom. But by that time, Virat and I had fallen in love. There wasn't any moral dilemma as our families desired the same for us. Virat and I were happy together, and Sahil was comfortable with me. We did not want to get out of that relationship at that point. Virat submitted another appeal in the court. We married in a temple then in the presence of family, and Virat bought the house next door in my name so we could be closer. That way I could take care of everyone. Legally, it was still okay as we weren't officially married or even living in the same house. People in the town knew. We were as good as married in their eyes."

"Did Devika know?"

"She suspected, but she couldn't do anything about it. She didn't have any supporters in Dongri. Knowing her callousness, the townspeople deemed it right, I daresay."

"It must have been difficult for you to accept things like that."

"Life is hardly ever perfect, sir. I was married before, but my husband divorced me because I was barren," she said easily, without pain, without regret. "Now I have Sahil and the whole family. Sometimes, I forget that I haven't given birth to him, that he isn't my flesh and blood. He considers me his mother," she said smiling. It was a genuine smile, of happiness, of bliss. She had the candour of an honest person. Sharma liked her. She took a sip of *chai* and continued, "I know it all seems so extraordinary, to live like that. But we were happy together. There were times when one of us would break down and think it couldn't go on. But then, moments like that are temporary. They don't last for long. They pass."

Sharma listened quietly. She said in a reflective tone, "It was awkward for all of us every time Devika came to stay, but it was even harder for her. She could barely stand living there for a few days. We would send Sahil to Lucknow to stay with Veena. He needed the stability of everyday routine. *Babu Ji* and Virat would stay at the shops all day. The indifference that everyone treated her with got on her nerves. She, it seemed, was getting tired of her own game. And then, knowing her obstinacy, we both accepted that life would never be perfect, and we were lucky to find each other. So, we stopped caring."

"All of you must have been worried about the consequences if the truth of your relationship came to light. That's why Mr. Virat Chaudhry refrained from telling us about his actual relationship with you."

"It all seemed complicated, sir. We did not know how the police would perceive our relationship, and what kind of conclusions they would draw from it. Legally, he was married to Devika. We knew officially the police couldn't do much about it; they wouldn't get any witness. Most of the people don't like to get involved in any kind of police matter. But we were scared. The police might perceive it as a strong motive in light of Devika's refusal to give a divorce."

"What made you come to me today?"

"It was hard to live under a shadow of constant fear. I found torn tickets from the cinema in my coat pocket two days ago. That's when I decided to come to you. I hope it would clear all the doubts."

"That would do perfectly. I want you to accompany me to the police station now and give your statement in writing. I hope you understand it's necessary for getting Mr. Virat Chaudhry in the clear. Without your official statement, he would stay on our list of suspects until we find the real killer."

"Certainly," she answered, her voice relieved of strain now.

Chapter 35

"It is easier to perceive error than to find truth, for the former lies on the surface and is easily seen, while the latter lies in the depth, where few are willing to search for it."

— Johann Wolfgang Von Goethe

Sharma spent the rest of his walk to the police station mulling over the current development. All the jumbled bits and pieces in the case seemed to be coming together now. He knew he only had to find one or two missing pieces and then everything would fall into place.

It was seven in the evening when he arrived at the police station. Rawat had left for home. His nine-month-old son had developed a rash and a fever, and he had to take him to the doctor. Sharma stayed in his office for another hour mulling over the case, tidying a few scattered thoughts up in his mind. He knew the end was near. He just needed to confirm something, and then he could close the file. It was Wednesday, 10 September, almost a month since the murder; about time he closed the case.

The dawn promised a hectic day ahead for everyone at the police station. Three thefts had occurred during the night in upper Kolahari and were reported at the first light of the morning sun. Instructing Rawat to deal with the thefts, Sharma left for Panchpula after a hearty breakfast of three *aaloo parathas* with *dahi*, butter, and mango pickle.

The drive to Panchpula was hassle-free. The day had started with a positive note. The sun had risen clear and bright. The sky was brilliant blue without any hint of yesterday's dark clouds.

Devika's mother opened the door and stared impassively at him at first and fidgeted nervously on her feet when Sharma explained that he wanted to talk about her last meeting with Devika. She led him inside reluctantly and sat squirming in her chair, which was a worn-out affair of metal and plastic.

"When was the last time you saw Devika?" Sharma got straight to the point, after they were seated.

"I don't remember exactly, Sahib," she said evasively. "But what has it got to do with her murder?"

"You can answer my questions here or accompany me to the police station. The choice is all yours, madam." The words were polite, but the tone conveyed firm authority.

She, Sharma thought, was shrewd enough to grasp the underlying warning, as she immediately started talking.

"I remember it now," she said, suddenly quick to recall when it was. "It must have been four months ago, four and a half months to be precise, Sahib."

That made it in the middle of April, calculated Sharma—three and a half months after their meeting in January when Devika came looking for something, searched the attic, and went to Lakshmi's house afterwards.

"Was there any particular reason for seeing her?"

Snehprabha said in a hesitant tone, "You see, Sahib, Vinay *Babu,* Lakshmi's husband, had had an accident and stayed in the hospital for a fortnight. It was expensive. I suggested we ask Devika for the money. So, we went to the hospital in Sanover where she worked and met her. She was furious at me for bringing Lakshmi there. When Lakshmi told her about Vinay *Babu's* accident she said she had no money to spare on a worthless fellow like him. But then she asked us to wait after Lakshmi started to cry. Lakshmi was in a bad state. Devika probably didn't want anyone from the hospital to witness Lakshmi's meltdown. Lakshmi would tell you otherwise, though. She believed her sister cared for her and that's why she agreed to help. But my Lakshmi is naive, Sahib. I know how Devika's brain worked. She loved herself and no one else."

Sharma stated, "So, she gave Lakshmi money."

"Yes, she did. She told us to go outside and eat something, said it would take a little time to arrange for the money. When we went back, she asked us to go with her to the porter's room. She took her purse from the locker there and handed it to Lakshmi saying it had more than enough for her needs."

"How much money did she give her?"

Snehprabha fidgeted in her chair, clasped and unclasped her hands, opened her mouth to speak but thought better of it and closed it again. Sharma waited in silence. Finally, she said in a hesitant tone, "There was no cash."

Sensing she was hesitant to reveal whatever secret she was keeping, Sharma asked, "Was it gold jewellery, madam?"

"Yes, that's what she gave us," Snehprabha said hesitantly. "It was a gold set; a necklace, *jhumke, tikka* and a bangle set with twelve bangles and four *kangan*. We don't want to get in any trouble, Sahib. We are illiterate people. How would we know if the set was her own or someone else's? Lakshmi was in dire need of money, so she took it without a second thought."

She knew it wasn't Devika's. She might have been worried about it being stolen, but why would she think like that, wondered Sharma? Only if the set was very expensive, something ridiculously pricey that she thought Devika couldn't afford. Also, it couldn't be an average gold set. An average gold set wouldn't have covered the hospital expenses. Sharma knew that jewellers usually cut twenty to twenty-five percent from the original price when they bought used jewellery.

"Don't worry. It won't get you in any trouble," said Sharma in a soothing tone. "Has Lakshmi sold all the pieces or is there something left from the set?"

"She sold everything, Sahib. The jeweller wanted to buy the full set."

"Was it a new set?"

"It wasn't bought from a jeweller's recently. It was old, well kept, worn many times. Devika couldn't have bought it for herself. She was too young to have that jewellery."

"You mean it was old-style?"

"Of course, no one wears that style nowadays. I might not be that young, but I know what's in fashion nowadays. I watch all the pictures. As soon as I saw it, I knew Devika hadn't bought it from any jeweller, that someone must have given it to her. It needed to be polished. I had seen magistrate Sahib's wife and daughter-in-law wearing sets like that. They were affluent people. I told Lakshmi what I thought of her *lado* sister. She was cross with me for questioning Devika's character, as if she herself wasn't aware of what her dear sister was up to living alone in the city."

Sensing she was wavering from the original topic once again, Sharma prompted her to tell him about magistrate Sahib. He looked at her expectantly while she settled herself comfortably against the worn-out chair cushion. Her fear was gone now. She was relaxed and seemed to enjoy the conversation.

"That was before my marriage, Sahib. Magistrate Sahib lived in Bombay with his family, but they used to come to the village on *Janamashtami* every year. They would keep *bhandara* for the whole village. They had their *pushtaini haveli* there, a huge mansion. They had old money and, on top of that, all the men in the family were government officers. *Badi bahu* and *choti bahu*, Magistrate Sahib's mother-in-law and daughter-in-law, used to wear that kind of jewellery in the *Janamashtami* celebrations."

The woman knew what she was talking about, thought Sharma.

"Could it be from Devika's in-laws?" he probed.

"Her *sasural wale* gave her a lot, but they couldn't afford that kind of jewellery. They were wealthy, but not like magistrate Sahib's family. And moreover, I would've recognized their set with my eyes closed; their sets were all light, delicate designs. I was hoping Devika would give me one or two sets of her jewellery," she said in a wistful tone. "For Lakshmi's marriage, of course—I had no use of her jewellery—but she flatly refused."

"We would like to have the address of the jeweller who bought it from your daughter."

She was nervous once again. She said, "Do you think it was stolen, Sahib? My Lakshmi had nothing to do with it. She took it from Devika, believing it was Devika's set. And whatever money she got, she spent it on Vinay *babu's* treatment. They can't return a single *paisa* now. There's nothing left."

She looked at Sharma pleadingly.

"We just want the jeweller's address. No one will trouble your daughter about the jewellery."

Reassured, she sighed heavily and said, "First we considered going to our local jeweller, but then thought better of it. Why stir his curiosity? He would've asked tens of probing questions. Of course, he knew our Devika had money, but at the same time, the whole town was aware that she had no contact with us. Lakshmi was too tense about her husband's health to worry about these things, but I made her see reason. Joginder had his taxi and he drove to Chandigarh often. So, Lakshmi went with him to Chandigarh to sell the jewellery."

Before Sharma could ask who Joginder was, she said, "Joginder is Lakshmi's younger brother-in-law, you know,

Vinay *babu's* brother. Both brothers run their own taxi service."

Sharma's next stop was Niligarh. He drove straight to Lakshmi's place and got the jeweller's address in Chandigarh. He passed it to Diwakar and asked him to make inquiries.

Diwakar didn't get any useful information from the jeweller, who was a heavyset, pleasantly spoken, shrewd man in his fifties and claimed that he had fashioned a new set from the old one owing to its old style and purity of gold. There was nothing left of the old design. The information failed to hamper Sharma's spirits as another idea had already taken shape in his mind. He knew he was getting closer to solving the case now.

Chapter 36

*"Truly it is reasonable to make a great
distinction between the faults that
come from our weakness and those
that come from our wickedness."*

—Michel de Montaigne

Even the chill in the air failed to dampen her spirits today. She walked swiftly, crossed the narrow, cobbled street, went up Shakti Avenue, and climbed the long twisting road toward the Upper Hill. Finally, the town was behind, and the noise—the deafening noise of the town; the footsteps of hundreds of pedestrians; the screeching of vendors and rickshaw wheels on the cobbled streets; the blowing horns of scooters, motorcycles, and buses; the chimes of temple bells; the shrieking laughter of the children playing *gulli danda* in the streets—was left behind. It was silent, peaceful finally. She stood there and gazed at the town below. Although it had not rained all day, the sun had stayed hidden behind gloomy-looking clouds until the afternoon. Now, in the late evening, the clouds had lifted to reveal a feeble sun behind. The sunlight, although meager, was resilient enough to smear the slated roofs of white-washed narrow houses with a fierce coral. Coral—every shade of coral—she had loved since she was a little girl. A few more days of this vast loneliness and then her colourless life would be filled with a fierce coral. She took a deep breath and smelled the evening breeze.

She thought about Rudra. She had spent many nights over the past few days lying in her narrow bed in almost a dreamy stupor. Thinking about him filled most of her solitary hours. She had thought about him for so long. With no expectation. With no hope. She didn't know what she had imagined, but it was not his declaration of love. He had not cared about her widowhood. He had asked her not to dwell on her past. It was of no concern to him.

She had shared her lunch once with him in the beginning when he was new in the hospital. At the time, there was no one to cook for him. Later, when he had found an old woman who kept the house for him, Vasudha continued to bring food for him. He never said anything. It had become a sort of ritual for Vasudha to get up early in the morning and cook for both of them. No one at home asked her anything.

The memory flooded back in her mind. That day, she had taken a home-cooked lunch for him as she did every day. He was in his office. He had unexpectedly talked about his childhood, his struggles, and his aspirations. She sat there listening to him speak, mesmerized by his deep voice, her eyes on his handsome face, and her heart happy knowing he considered her a friend. She was so engrossed in hearing him talk that she neither heard any footsteps in the gallery, nor hear Devika open the door. Only when she had heard her mocking words, "Having a good time, both of you?" was she stupefied.

Devika had noticed something on her face.

She had ignored her sneering comment and got up to leave. When she tried to open the door, Devika had placed her body right in front of her and said jeeringly, "I never knew an ugly cow like you could entice a man. It looks like you're flying too high. Usually, I never give advice for free. But I feel pity for you. Do you think he gives a damn about you? He doesn't, darling. Stop dreaming. It'll save you from bigger heartache later."

Vasudha had then told Devika to mind her own business which hadn't gone down well with the woman. She had then spat the ugly words at her, "It is not my business! Really? Have you ever seen yourself in the mirror? Even if you walked naked past any man, he wouldn't look at you twice." She had come closer then and almost whispered the words, "Seriously, it is so funny I could laugh all day." Devika had then patted her arm and left the office.

Dr. Rudra had sat looking at Devika. Vasudha stood there on shaking legs trying to control her mounting anger and then had finally opened the door and run out of Rudra's office. She had taken a half day off and walked to this place. Not even the rigorous walk could calm her down. She had sat there for hours and cried her heart out. Later, when the anger was gone, she felt hatred for Devika with an intensity she didn't know existed in her heart. She could kill her with her bare hands. She imagined her dead, and lying lifeless somewhere—her body stiff and robbed of decency. The thought comforted her mind. She had left for home at the end of her usual shift and stayed in her room all evening. But a blind hatred had crept inside her heart and settled there. She had realized she relished this hatred so much more than love itself.

All that was a thing of the past now. Rudra's love had given her courage. The woman was dead now; she was gone forever. In her mind's eye, she could see a new life for herself. And that meant a lot to her, everything in fact. Yes, God! Everything that was dignity. There was no longer any need to count the days, to wait for another proposal and yet dread it, wonder whether a prospective groom's family would say yes, and dread everyone's contemptuous gaze after another rejection. There was no need to carry a tea tray with meek obedience—with bowed head and lowered eyes while resentment and anger threatened to break her heart apart and she ached to throw its shattered pieces into the haughty faces of her prospective grooms' family. No more humiliating rejections by those fortyish and fiftyish grooms. No more enduring *Bhabhi*'s taunts after each consecutive rejection. No more looking into *Bhaiya's* worried eyes and wondering whether she was a burden on his shoulders after their father's sudden accidental death. No more seeing the looks of concern mixed with contempt for her plain looks, the *manglik dosha* in her horoscope, and her early widowhood in Mummy's eyes.

Rudra had asked her to wait and not talk to anyone in the hospital about them. He wanted to talk to his mother first. Vasudha could keep her job in the hospital after the wedding. They would buy a small house. They could even move to a different city—far away from everything—and start afresh. She wanted to forget Devika's smug smile, her mocking eyes that had laughed at her. She did not want to remember that conceited woman.

Thinking all that, she felt a tinge of anxiety. Rudra was there that night, at Devika's flat. They could not arrest him, not for being seen there. He had done nothing. He was innocent. She knew he couldn't have done it. The thought that she could lose Rudra was unbearable. The fear came back once again—the fear which occasionally would linger at the back of her mind. She felt the same desperation once again; the unbearable, irrevocable feeling of absolute loss which she had felt days ago and which had made her do what she had never imagined herself capable of doing. The mere memory made her shudder. She was afraid not for him but for herself now.

Chapter 37

"Oh, what a tangled web we weave,
when first we practice to deceive."

—*Marmion*, Sir Walter Scott

Kamla Devi opened door herself and wasn't surprised to see Sharma again after his last visit. Urvashi had gone to attend her friend's sister's *godh bharai* and would be back any minute, she informed him promptly and led him along the sizable panelled hall of their impressive bungalow, down three steps, then through another hallway. To their right, it opened into a formal drawing room where Sharma and Rawat had sat on their last visit. A door to the left opened into what looked like an informal drawing room. It was comparatively smaller and brighter. The curtains were drawn, and the curved window gave a view of the garden outside. Unlike the formal drawing room, this room wasn't arranged to impress. There was no blazing display of splendour, no rare antique objects, no knickknacks to impress, or a conscious striving for grandeur. The furniture, which consisted of a tufted leather wingbacked sofa and two chairs with all over nail-head trim, although opulent, was, no doubt, picked for comfort. The only other piece of furniture was a huge, impressive-looking, oak-and-walnut bureau bookcase set against the whole length of the back wall. Three pairs of doors with transparent panels and carved beading opened to shelves laden with books, and the bureau which formed one-third of its lower portion had three pairs of drawers with brass bale handles. The bookcase stood on engraved ogee bracket feet.

Sharma went through the business of explaining the purpose of his second visit. Kamla Devi seemed nonchalant listening to the circumstances of Devika's death.

"Coincidently, she, as I have come to understand, had worked as a private nurse at your house for a time between 1965—1966. Do you remember her?"

Only after he had taken out a picture of Devika and handed it down to her, she seemed to recall her.

She took the picture and glanced at it briefly. "Oh, of course, how could I forget her name? I remember her alright, difficult to forget that face. She was an immaculate beauty. Murdered? She must be barely thirty now; she was very young then. That's unbelievable. What happened? I can't imagine she rubbed someone the wrong way; she was rather a clever girl, worldly and vigilant."

It was the first time Sharma had heard someone saying nothing negative about Devika.

"We are still investigating. Nothing concrete can be said at this point. She had been here at the beginning of this year, sometime during January?"

"I wouldn't know that. I went to visit my late husband's niece. She had her first child, and I went to stay with her in January for a little more than two months. I only came back a few days before *Holi*. That would make it the second week of March. Urvashi must know."

Before Sharma could say something else, the maid arrived and informed Kamla Devi she had an urgent telephone call. Kamla Devi excused herself and went to attend the call.

After Kamla Devi had left, Sharma took the opportunity to observe the wall-to-wall bookcase full of what seemed like a mixture of Hindi and English volumes. There were many major English classics, literary criticisms, rare volumes, but the collection was mainly Indian literature, in English as well as in Hindi.

Most of the books seemed worn out, well read. They weren't acquired to be a part of any simulated display of intellectual advancement. It was the collection of a reader. They had, he thought, been bought because someone in this house liked reading them. They weren't obtained out of a customary obligation to add to the impressive collection of literary material.

There were names like Nirad C. Chaudhuri's *The Autobiography of an Unknown Indian*, and Rabindranath Tagore's *Gitanjali*, that he could recognize from Nandini's collection at home. Then there were authors like V. S. Naipaul, R. K. Narayan, Sarat Chandra Chattopadhyay, who no doubt ranked highly on the list of early modern Indian literary figures, which, nevertheless, had bored him out of his mind during his brief stint as a student of Hindi literature. Other than Tagore's *Gitanjali*, he spotted the work of Suryakant Tripathi Nirala, Jaishankar Prasad, Sumitranandan Pant, and Mahadevi Verma, major Hindi poets whose names were routinely mentioned on the radio. He hadn't seen Nandini reading the work of any Hindi poet though. She wasn't an aficionado of Hindi poetry. She loved poetic works of Punjabi poets like Shiv Kumar Batalvi, Amrita Pritam, and the Hindi translations of a few Urdu poets including Ghalib. But then, every Punjabi who loved books loved Batalvi and Pritam, and almost every Indian reader loved Ghalib's poetry. He himself could never understand people's love for books though. He disliked fiction. His newspaper reading was limited to the editorial sections and political news.

Nandini was of the opinion that his reluctance to read anything which constituted more than two hundred words could be blamed on his unwillingness to rack his brains to find deeper themes and ambiguity in just words. He knew she was right. Because he liked his comfort zone, he couldn't stand to put himself in the shoes of so many different people who were mere fictional characters in books. It made him horribly confused. That was the reason he couldn't complete his literature degree.

He had decided to do his master's in Hindi literature to fulfill his mother's dream of seeing her son teaching in a college or university. Within three months, he had started regretting his decision, and in another five months, after realizing the absurdity of his decision and to her mother's silent disappointment, he had left his master's and decided to join the police force instead. It had worked out well for him. He understood simple as well as complex criminology. He was good at analyzing. In his profession, he could make his observations while staying aloof. It was all business, his other comfort zone, where he wasn't required to reciprocate personal emotions. That was part of the reason for his success as an investigator.

His stupor was interrupted by the arrival of Urvashi, who was still in her festive attire: a plain light golden *saree* in net with delicate zari work on the border, a pair of small intricate-looking antique gold earrings and a matching necklace.

"I haven't read all of these, but I have a plan to read them someday. The problem is, I buy a book whenever and wherever I find one which looks interesting. Every time I come here to get something to read, the unread books scowl at me from their shelves." She traced her right hand on the glass door. "I can read all of them only if I stop accumulating new ones. I guess, I'm equally in love with reading books as well as acquiring them. Do you read a lot?"

"Oh, no. Not me. Reading isn't for me. But I know a lot about books. My wife is a voracious reader. I recognized many from your collection because of her. There are times when, despite my vehement reluctance, she likes to read a verse or prose to me which she comes across while reading and finds it interesting. She says she cannot move forward in her book, until and unless, I hear her read it to me."

"I know the feeling," she said, laughing. "There are times when I come across a thought, a feeling, while reading and I feel this absolute need to share it with another human being." They walked over to the sofas together. She went on, "I hope you didn't have to wait for long. If you had informed me about your arrival in advance, I would have cancelled today's tedious outing quite happily."

"We tried to telephone, but somehow the call couldn't get through. We have been having an on-and-off downpour for the last few days. The thunderstorm knocked out the telephone cables in many places. Instead of waiting, I decided to pay you a visit."

Sharma chose the wingbacked chair again while she settled herself on the sofa. She said, "It must be something important, I believe?"

"Do you remember Devika Singh Chaudhry? She worked as a private nurse for your father before his demise."

"Devika, of course, I remember her." The imposing figure of Kamla Devi emerged from the door. She walked over to the sofa and sat beside her niece. Urvashi went on talking. "She stayed with us for over a year to take care of Daddy. He had a major heart attack and hemiplegia . . . paralysis of the right side of his body. Devika was just fresh from college at that time. We found her most suitable as she didn't care about taking Sundays off. We needed a nurse every day of the week and she was happy to stay full-time. She was terribly sweet."

Just like her *bua*, Urvashi had only words of praise for the dead woman.

"She is the same woman whose murder we are investigating at Lifeline Hospital, the place where Mr. Rudra Bhardwaj works as well."

Urvashi couldn't speak for some time. She was dumbfounded. Then she said, "You cannot mean the same Devika though." She turned to Kamla Devi and said, "*Bua*, do you remember her? She took good care of Daddy. She was pained to leave us after Daddy's death." Her face was pale.

She went on, "She was full of life, so beautiful. Poor sweet girl!"

"It's such a strange thing, death, in itself. We know that we have only limited time in this world, and some day we have to leave this world forever," Kamla Devi remarked in a pensive tone. "And yet, it never fails to surprise us when we hear about the death of someone we know. But then, murder is bizarre. What a ghastly way to meet one's end!"

"How extraordinary! I can't believe she's no more," Urvashi remarked sadly.

"Did she visit you in January?" asked Sharma.

"She did. Her visit was unexpected. It had been almost ten years since she left. She looked the same, beautiful as ever."

"It must have been the end of January, Urvashi. Remember, I had gone for Nanda's delivery," said Kamla Devi.

"Yes, around that time. You had just left as far as I remember. I was astonished to see Devika after all those years. She said she had work in Tehlong, and hence she thought of visiting us as well. She didn't stay for long though. But wait . . ." she paused momentarily as if something unfathomable had occurred to her, and then continued. "Do you think he . . . Rudra has something to do with her death?" Sharma noticed her reluctance to utter her ex-husband's name.

"Although it could be a mere coincidence, their working together at the same place seems to point out a sinister possibility."

"I wouldn't put it past him, though. He didn't care about his family. The man is capable of doing anything if you ask me," Kamla Devi pronounced in a curt tone.

"I tend to agree with you, *Bua*," said Urvashi. She turned to Sharma then and continued. "So, you must be looking at him closely, I believe."

"In a way, yes. He seems very much involved in all the muck at this point," said Sharma. "Was there any particular reason for Devika's visit? Did she say anything?"

"She didn't mention anything specific. We talked about old times. She was sorry that she couldn't meet *Bua* and the children."

"How did she seem? Did you get the impression she was excited or apprehensive about something?"

"She was her usual self, happy to see me. But yes, I got the impression that she had something on her mind, and she wanted to share it with me. I didn't press her though, thinking it would come in time. She didn't say anything. Clearly, she had changed her mind."

"Was there anything that she did or said which you thought was unusual?"

"Now that you ask about it, I found her sudden departure weird. I had gone to attend a telephone call, and when I came back, she was in the outside drawing room. You know, we had been sitting in this very room. I have an indispensable fondness for this place. I like the quiet and warmth of the books here. Anyways, when I came back, she wasn't here. I went outside and found her in the drawing room. She was, all of a sudden, in a hurry to leave. I asked her to stay for lunch, but she refused. She had a necessary chore to take care of at the earliest possible opportunity. That's what she told me."

"During her stay as a home carer for your father, did she have any friends in the town? Was she close to anyone?"

"No one, as far as we know. Right, *Bua*?"

Urvashi looked at Kamla Devi who nodded and said, "She was living away from her husband, we knew, but there was no friend. She usually went out with Urvashi or sometimes alone as well."

So, he was right so far. Devika had indeed come to confirm the identity of Rudra Bhardwaj as Urvashi's ex-husband. A month after Rudra Bhardwaj joined Lifeline Hospital, Devika must have started suspecting him. She had seen his photo at Urvashi's house. But his picture had garland around it. And Devika knew no one put garland around living people's pictures. To clear her doubt, Devika went to her mother's house to collect some old pictures, probably, of her own taken at Urvashi's place. Rudra's photo with garland around it on the wall must be visible in the background. That's how she made the connection. It must be blurred though. Otherwise she wouldn't have had to visit Urvashi to clear her doubts.

Sharma changed the track of his questions.

"Mr. Rudra Bhardwaj, when he left, stole cash and valuables from the safe at home. There must be jewellery among all the valuables, I believe?"

"Yes, I had jewellery and bonds there. Luckily, I didn't have all of my jewellery in there. There were only a few individual pieces as well as a few sets in the locker."

"Were there any items from the full sets that hadn't been in the safe at that time, perhaps in some other place that he couldn't steal from?"

Kamla Devi, who had dropped inconspicuously out of their conversation, spoke before Urvashi could say anything. "There were two sets. I remember each and every piece that Rudra stole. I didn't mind that he took the other valuables except for those two sets. They were my mother's, and she had given them to Urvashi's *ma* at her wedding," she said. She pointed to Urvashi. "The earrings that she's wearing now are actually from one of the sets Rudra stole. My mother had gotten them so fondly for her daughter-in-law. Now, all we've left is this pair."

Sharma looked at the tiny beads of gold clustered together with sparkling diamonds to form a half-moon.

"What about the other set?"

"We have a *kamarbandh* left from the other set. I assume you would like to see it?" She looked at him inquiringly.

"That would be great."

"Let me fetch it for you then. It has just been to the jeweller for polishing. He only returned it yesterday. Luckily, Urvashi didn't get time to put it in the bank. You would have had to wait until Monday then."

There was nothing subtle about the majestic *kamarbandh* when Kamla Devi handed it to Sharma. The multiple gold chains with tasselled gold beads were gathered together at intervals with a single blue sapphire surrounded with tiny brilliant diamonds. It was exquisite.

"I might need to collect it as evidence later. That will be temporary though," said Sharma.

"That means Urvashi might have to become a witness. I warned you earlier, SP Sahib. There's no way I can let you drag Urvashi's name into this matter."

"That's the worst-case scenario, madam. Even then, I'm sure things could be handled discreetly." He turned to Urvashi and said, "Your evidence, if the need arises, which I highly doubt it will, can be submitted to the court in written format as well." He looked her straight in the eyes and went on, "I'm sure, you would agree with me that Rudra should be punished for taking a life and, if it comes to that, then you wouldn't hesitate to get involved."

Urvashi nodded quietly. Sharma was right: Urvashi had the strength and courage necessary to fight the social ridicule.

Chapter 38

"How often things occur by mere chance which we dared not even hope for."

—Terence

It was evening of Monday, 15 September when Diwakar informed Sharma who had just arrived in the police station that Dr. Namita had rung to talk about something important related to their murder inquiry. She had refused to leave a message and left her telephone number instead.

"Call her immediately," said Sharma.

"There was also a telephone call from Hari Prasad, the clerk at the district court, sir. He didn't leave a message but said it was an urgent matter," Diwakar said, and dialled Dr. Namita's number before handing the phone to Sharma.

"I will talk to him later." Sharma extended his hand and put the receiver to his ear.

"Was there anything important that you wanted to share, madam?" Sharma asked, when Dr. Namita picked up the telephone on the fourth ring.

Her voice sounded different on the telephone.

"You asked me to remember anything else that could be important. I've been thinking a lot, and just today it came to me." She was silent for a few seconds.

Sharma prompted her further, "Yes?"

There was a momentary pause and when she spoke, Sharma could detect hesitancy in her tone. "After Devika's death, Vasudha . . . Nurse Vasudha Haldar asked if Devika's body was displayed rather . . . improperly when the police found her." She was silent once again.

A quiver of anticipation ran through Sharma's veins. He recognized the sensation very well, for he had felt it countless times in his career when he knew he was about to hear something crucial related to the case.

He pressed his ear close to the receiver and asked, "What did she say exactly?"

There was a deep intake of breath. It seemed she had decided to say whatever was troubling her. Her voice came brusque and clear now.

"She asked about Devika's torn clothes and the crude display of her body. I had heard nothing like that, and I told her so."

Sharma felt his anger rising. He couldn't help but reprimand Dr. Namita.

"And you are telling me this now? You should have informed me when she first asked these questions."

Dr. Namita had, clearly, detected anger in Sharma's tone as she replied in a cross voice, "I could've mentioned it to you earlier if she hadn't been so vague in her query the last time she came to me with it. That was almost a week after Devika's death. She wasn't very specific at the time." And after a momentary pause, she added, her tone sarcastic now, "And for your kind information, I'm a doctor and not a police officer who has been trained specifically to suspect ordinary people's intentions. I'm not in the habit of analyzing each and every conversation I have with others."

Before Sharma could say anything else, he heard the concluding click of the receiver being placed back in its cradle. Dr. Namita had hung up.

Sharma, who was unaware of his own unfairness, couldn't fathom the reason behind Dr. Namita's sudden irritability. He shrugged and asked Rawat to tell Diwakar to get a team ready and wait for his next order. They left for Vasudha Haldar's house at once.

Fortunately, as Rawat steered the jeep onto MG Marg, the traffic was light, as was expected at this time of the evening. They were almost at Lifeline Hospital. Sharma felt a sense of ominous premonition.

Dr. Namita's conversation had made him concerned. Although it was merely speculative, the possibility of Vasudha Haldar gaining this knowledge about how Devika's body was displayed from Rudra Bhardwaj couldn't be discounted. It was a weeks old matter but after getting recent information about Rudra Bhardwaj, Sharma was confident that Vasudha Haldar hadn't shared her concerns with him so far. The man was dangerous: he wouldn't have stayed quiet knowing Vasudha possessed incriminating information about him.

A visit to Vasudha's home filled Sharma with further dread. Vasudha Haldar was supposedly off duty, but hadn't returned home. Her mother wasn't concerned though. According to her, it wasn't unusual for Vasudha to stay behind for another emergency shift if there was a staff shortage at the hospital. Now, sitting in the front seat, with Rawat behind the steering wheel, Sharma couldn't help but wonder about the impending danger hovering above Vasudha's head.

Despite his uneasiness, Sharma remarked in a casual tone, "Dr. Rudra has got away with it for long enough and avoided getting caught, only because Vasudha kept her apprehensions to herself. He had been counting on this marriage proposal to stop her from sharing her concerns with us. The way she kept her mouth sealed so far, he knew what he was doing."

"Even then, he wouldn't have gotten away with it for long, sir," said Rawat. "He must know that, sooner or later, some other witness would come forward. He isn't invincible and he must know it. And now, we already have Urvashi's testimony."

"He knows."

"Sir, Vasudha might have already talked to him about his intimate knowledge of the way the victim was found in her bed. She didn't seem like a clever sort of woman. During her interview, I had the impression that she was not very adept at keeping her inner feelings hidden."

"That's what is worrying me. Dr. Rudra wouldn't have taken a chance if she had shared this particular concern with him. He would have recognized her as a threat then. Let's hope she hasn't decided to clear the air, after all, and ask Dr. Rudra about his in-depth knowledge of the murder scene."

Chapter 39

*"La plus belle des ruses du diable est de
vous persuader qu'il n'existe pas."*

*("The devil's finest trick is to persuade
you that he does not exist.")*

—*Paris Spleen*, Charles Baudelaire

The front-desk staff confirmed that Vasudha Haldar's shift had ended at seven in the evening but she had agreed to fill a colleague's shift who, because of some family matter, could not finish her shift that night. The colleague was supposed to be staying until morning, but she had to leave at midnight. Vasudha had left at ten past seven to go home and take a rest so she could be back before midnight and fill in her colleague's shift. They did not know where else she could have gone. She hadn't informed them.

Concerned, Sharma and Rawat were about to leave, when a nursing orderly came and told them about Vasudha's return to the clinic at around half past eight. He had met her in the eastern wing on her way to find a place to rest. She had dinner outside. She had not gone home. Intending to spare her brother the trouble of dropping her off at the hospital at midnight, she had decided to stay in the hospital. She had mentioned something about getting sleep in one of the spare patient rooms in the eastern wing, but the orderly seemed perplexed when asked about the exact location of the room.

The sluggish, overweight receptionist who was in her twenties couldn't be bothered to check how many rooms were empty in the east wing. Only after Sharma used the characteristic harsh police voice, which he held in reserve for difficult witnesses and crooks, she told Sharma, in a sullen and almost tearful voice, that there were four extra rooms there. Tight-lipped and cross, she agreed to go with Sharma and Rawat to the eastern wing.

The search proved nothing. They couldn't find Vasudha in any of the spare rooms. Fortunately, on their way to one of the rooms, Rawat had a fleeting memory of seeing Dr. Rudra Bhardwaj's name tag outside a door. He asked the receptionist about it who, in light of their frantic search for Vasudha, had forgotten her earlier sullenness by that time. She confirmed the room was Dr. Rudra Bhardwaj's office. Sharma and Rawat exchanged a quick apprehensive glance and dashed to what seemed to be a locked but occupied room at the end of a somewhat darkened corridor, with the receptionist at their heels. A narrow stream of light from inside was visible underneath the door.

Rawat tried to push the door, but it was bolted from the inside. There were consecutive cracking sounds of splintering wood and then a loud crash as they forced the door open with kicks and thrusts of their shoulders.

She was sitting in the chair; her head slumped on the table in front of her. They simultaneously crouched over the girl's body while Sharma tried to lift her head. She fell backward against the chair like a rag doll. Sharma felt for her pulse and shouted at the receptionist to get the medical staff. She obliged at once and ran outside to get help. The girl was still breathing. Rawat lifted the girl's unconscious body in his arms and hurried to one of the patient rooms at the end of the hallway. Then Dr. Namita arrived with other staff and took command.

A shrill screech of a whistle announced Diwakar's arrival with the police party. Sharma heard a flood of confusing noises and running feet in the corridor. Rawat directed them to Dr. Rajinder Bhardwaj's house, in case Dr. Rudra had chosen to spend the night there. One constable was asked to stay put in the hospital and telephone the police station as soon as there was a new development in Vasudha's condition. Sharma asked Rawat and constable Prasad to accompany him, and together, they headed to Rudra's rented house in Kailash Colony.

When they got there, they could see a faint glow of light in one of the upper rooms. Rawat pounded the door with his fist. They stood and waited for a few uncomfortable moments that seemed to last for an eternity. Rawat was about to break down the door with a kick of his right foot when Dr. Rudra opened it.

"Getting ready for bed, Doctor Sahib?" said Rawat. "That will not be possible now. You must accompany us to the police station."

A shadow seemed to cloud Dr. Rudra's face, but only for a fleeting moment. The hand holding the door shook a little. Sharma noticed tiny drops of sweat dripping on Dr. Rudra's forehead. But he was too smart to give himself away. Although he had regained his composure by the time he opened his mouth to speak, the carefully constructed nonchalance in his voice wasn't lost on either one of them.

He asked in a tone too casual, "May I ask, what for?"

"Under Section 418 IPC for fraud. Remember Urvashi?" said Sharma.

Rawat looked at his boss. They were supposed to arrest Dr. Rudra for Devika Singh's murder and Vasudha Haldar's attempted murder. He opened his mouth to speak but thought better of asking anything at present.

The doubt, the uncertainty that Rudra had felt minutes ago, was gone. The calmness returned. They were talking about

Urvashi, he thought. They hadn't known about Vasudha, of course.

Rudra shrugged and didn't resist when Rawat put handcuffs on him and lead him to the jeep. He sat impassively next to Rawat in the back seat. Later, at the police station, Rudra asked for his uncle, Dr. Rajinder Bhardwaj. Sharma who had clearly decided to ignore Dr. Rudra's request asked Rawat to put the accused in one of the staff offices. Rawat was curious about his boss's decision of not locking Dr. Rudra behind bars for the attempted murder of Vasudha Haldar. As he opened his mouth to inquire further into the matter, Diwakar walked in.

"Sir, there's a telephone call from the court clerk."

Sharma had forgotten about the call from Hari Prasad. He strode to his office taking long steps.

Fifteen minutes later he came out of his office and barked his orders.

"Get Diwakar and two constables. We're leaving for Dr. Rudra's house to conduct a search."

"We won't be able to get any magistrate to sign the search warrant at this time, sir," Rawat replied.

"Don't worry about that. I've put everything on the record. Get someone to send a copy of the record to the magistrate. I want to finish the search before he gets out on bail."

"What is it we are looking for, sir?" asked Rawat as Diwakar steered the jeep toward Kailash Colony.

"Remember the doctor's Philips tape recorder? We have to find the cassette, the one he was playing when we visited him the first time."

The jeep ride was quicker than the last time. He asked Diwakar to park at the end of the street, then walked to Dr. Rudra's house with Rawat and the others at his heels. He was struck by the street's desolation, the almost eerie calm which hung over these old wooden terraces. As he stood in front of Rudra's house, tall, determined, he hoped they would find the proof easily.

As he had hoped, it didn't take long for them to find the cassette in the locker of the Godrej *almirah* in the bedroom. Rawat, who had no clue about the contents of the tape, was left speechless after Sharma played the confession of Devika's murderer which had been recorded on it.

Chapter 40

*"We are never deceived; we deceive
ourselves."*

—Johann Wolfgang Von

Tears started sliding down her cheeks and onto her folded hands in her lap. She made no effort to wipe them off for a while. Instead, she hid her face with her hands. Her body shook with silent sobs. Sharma sat there quietly waiting for her grief to subside. Finally, she lifted her face and wiped it several times.

She took a deep breath and said in a flat, unemotional voice, "As you already know, I didn't try to kill myself. One suicide of a girl is enough in Sanover. But whatever happened last night, I blame myself. It's perfectly reasonable that Rudra should try to kill me. He is skilled in treachery, after all. I was a fool to trust him. I should have seen through him long time ago." She sighed deeply and continued, "He knew that I suspected his involvement in Devika's death. That's why he approached my family with a marriage proposal. His sudden interest in me was a sham so he could keep me quiet, and I foolishly believed it to be his genuine liking for me."

"What caused your suspicions?"

"Devika came upon us alone in his office. I was there for some work. It was nothing. We were just talking, but Devika, who had known about my . . . fondness for Rudra, humiliated me." It was obviously difficult for her to utter those words, but she hesitated only for a brief second. "Now that I come to think of it, she had tried to warn me about him. She hadn't been kind though, when she uttered those warnings. Her words were painful and nasty. If only I'd had enough sense and humility not to be bothered by her spite, I could have understood the actual warning behind her rancorous words," she said with a rueful smile. "I had chosen to see only the good in Rudra. I disregarded her warnings as spite. After Devika's death, Rudra mentioned how her body was found displayed in an obscene fashion, and how it served her right. I had heard no one say that. It stayed at the back of my mind and started bothering me."

"No wonder you were enquiring about the circumstances in which Devika's body was found!" remarked Sharma.

She said in a soft voice, "I had asked Dr. Namita about it. She must have told you. I was not much subtle in my queries, although it wouldn't have helped me with Dr. Namita. She is sharp and adept at perceiving others' behaviour. She must have sensed something was wrong."

"What made you suspect Dr. Rudra?"

"On the night of murder, Rudra was on duty. I couldn't find him anywhere in the hospital at around quarter past nine when a patient asked for him. I saw him come from the main door an hour and forty-five minutes later, at eleven. He was wearing a different shirt when he came back. No one noticed it because it looked the same except for its collar."

Sharma marvelled at the women's inherent ability to see negligible things like shirt-collar designs. Why then, he wondered, had she consciously chosen to overlook his shifty personality?

She said, "Earlier, Rudra had this plain faded green shirt on, with a butterfly collar. But when he came back, he was wearing the same colour shirt with a slightly different collar: double lined on the inside, in a shade paler than the shirt's plain faded green. I made a slight remark about it, but he didn't say anything. I thought little of it at the time. I forgot all about it after he declared his love for me. It stayed in my subconscious mind though. Later, when he remarked about the circumstances in which Devika's body was found, I realized the connection. I was too stupid to question him about his absence, his change of clothing."

"What did he say then?"

"He made a feeble excuse about spilling medicine on his clothes."

"But you didn't question him about his intimate knowledge about the positioning of Devika's body."

"No, the way he reacted to my question about his change of clothes, I didn't have the courage to ask anything else. He was stunned that I suspected him. He asked me to share my apprehensions with you. He even offered to disclose this information to you. I was ridden with guilt."

That's when he must have approached her family with the marriage proposal, thought Sharma. Sharma looked at her face. Although it was passive, he could see the eclipse of grief clouding her eyes. She was hurting. But she would soon realize how lucky she was to have escaped unhurt except for a broken heart. She was young. Little by little, her heart would mend itself. She needed to give herself some time, and if she were lucky to gain the sense and maturity that comes with learning from bad experiences, she could turn her hurt into wisdom.

"That must have made him suspicious of my intentions because immediately afterwards, he approached my brother and expressed his wish to marry me. Although I was a bit apprehensive, his feigned interest calmed my fears. Putting aside my suspicions, I went ahead and accepted his proposal," she said ruefully.

"But you couldn't shake the apprehension completely from your mind. That was the reason you went to see Urvashi in Sambhalpura. How did you get to know about her?"

"Despite Rudra's explanation of his absence and the change of clothes, I had this nagging feeling of uneasiness at the back of my mind. I had failed earlier to confirm his story of the discovery of Devika's body. I didn't have the courage to raise the matter once again, recalling his reaction to my earlier queries. But then, I remembered his argument with Devika in his office," she said hesitantly.

"When was that?"

"That must have been two months ago. I certainly didn't try to listen, but I was right outside in the corridor. I couldn't help hearing some of their conversation. They were arguing about someone named Urvashi. Well, it was Devika who was talking about Urvashi. Rudra said he was tired and was doing as much as he could. He wanted Devika to accept whatever he could do or else wait for the right time. Devika started to quarrel then. Without wasting time, she wanted to plan a trip to Sumbhalpore to see Urvashi. It made no sense at the time. But I couldn't shake this nagging feeling about the essence of the whole conversation. It stayed on my mind. The more I thought about it, the more I recognized it as something disturbing. There was only one way to clear my doubts, and that was to see Urvashi."

She must have been oblivious to Rudra's faults, thought Sharma. She loved him. He couldn't have done anything wrong in her eyes. But later, when she became suspicious of him, she saw his conversation with Devika in a new light.

They had wasted much time trying to trace Urvashi in Sambhalpura. There were many villages and towns with the same name, and Sambhalpura was one of them. But the Sambhalpura in the northern part of the state had stayed Sambhalpura, whereas the one in the far west had been respelled Sumbhalpore to suit the local dialectic a few years ago. No wonder everyone kept recalling it as Sambhalpura during their investigation.

"But you left without meeting Urvashi. Why didn't you wait?"

"Roshani, one of my childhood friends, lived in Lohit. I had heard her mentioning Sumbhalpore a couple of times. I coaxed Mummy into visiting Roshni on the pretext of shopping for my wedding. From there it was easy to go to Sumbhalpore. I took Roshni into my confidence and we went to Sumbhalpore. The maid informed us that Urvashi wasn't home, had gone out of town for a week with her children and her *bua*. I asked her about Rudra, but she denied knowing anyone with that name."

"What happened then?"

"I felt guilty and doubtful about my decision to see Urvashi. I had heard only a part of Rudra and Devika's conversation that day. Even Roshni thought I was being too cynical and acting on a whim. Moreover, it was hard to extend my stay for another week at Roshni's house. Mummy wouldn't have agreed. Roshni promised me she would go to Sumbhalpore after a week and meet Urvashi in person if I still had some doubts about Rudra. After returning from Lohit, I decided to put my suspicions at rest."

Sharma did not know if she knew about Urvashi or not. He saw no reason to reveal Urvashi's real relationship to Rudra. That could wait.

Unaware of Sharma's thoughts she went on, "I am not good at appearing opaque to others. I was troubled and feeling guilty after returning from Lohit. Rudra must have noticed my stress and become suspicious of my earlier absence from the hospital. Yesterday evening, after my shift was over, he was already waiting for me outside. He asked me to go with him to dinner. He had an inkling about my suspicions and asked me to clear my doubts before the wedding. I decided to question him there and then about the discovery of Devika's body. I was tired of my suspicions and decided to clear up any misunderstandings, once and for all, and then face the truth. Moreover, Rudra was so downright sweet about the whole thing, about my suspicions, my insecurity, that I felt guilty. I confessed my visit to Sumbhalpore and asked him about his knowledge of the intimate details of Devika's body. He admitted he had gone to her flat to talk about Dr. Rajinder on the night of the murder and had found her body instead. He said he was scared to reveal this information to anyone for fear of getting arrested for her murder. He accepted it was a mistake on his part. But the cruel thing was, he made it feel like the mistake was mine, for doubting him. He must have put something in my coffee. We had it after dinner. It tasted weird and very bitter."

"But why did you write this suicide note? Did he ask you?" Sharma took the note from Rawat, and handed it to Vasudha. "We found it in your purse."

Sharma watched her reaction. Her face had gone ashen. But she didn't cry.

"After I told him about my visit to Sumbhalpore and shared my doubts, he suggested we part our ways. He had tears in his eyes when he said that. He seemed utterly shattered. Seeing him devastated made me forget my suspicions about him. I cursed myself for doubting him. I promised never to doubt him again. He suggested we both scribble a few lines that we weren't worthy of each other's love and were tired of everything; he was so devastated, he didn't want to live. He wrote his first and asked me to copy his note." Her compliancy might have even sounded absurd to her ears, as she added further, "I was so ashamed of myself for suspecting him I apologized for everything. I wrote the note and we made up. I forgot all about those dreadful papers. He must have slipped the note in my purse, later, on our way back."

"Was he the one who suggested you get sleep in one of the spare patient rooms?"

"He did, but not in the patient rooms though. After dinner, he asked me to rest in his office. There was a pull-out sleeping cot there. I could put the alarm on and get a few hours' proper sleep. He said no one would disturb me there. He handed me the keys and instructed me to bolt the door from the inside. I wanted to go home, but he saw no point in troubling Bhaiya at midnight. I complied foolishly."

He had left her outside the back door of the east wing. He arranged it well. No one would have known about Vasudha until Rudra himself opened the door the next morning. That was enough time for the pills to put her to endless sleep. And conveniently, she had that suicide note in her purse. No one would have suspected anything. Her family would have assumed that she took her life for fear of harming Rudra because of her *manglik dosha*. It was a perfect plan, if only she hadn't met the nursing orderly on her way there, marvelled Sharma.

Sharma asked for the sapphire ring she wore. Puzzled, she took it off and handed it down to him. He didn't have to look at the photographs of the *kamarbandh* to confirm that it was part of the same set that Dr. Rudra had stolen from Urvashi. He knew the design by heart, a single blue sapphire surrounded with tiny brilliant diamonds.

Sharma informed her she had to deposit the ring at the police station as evidence in the case. Vasudha didn't ask him the reason. She didn't speak, merely nodded her head in affirmation.

As Sharma stood up to leave, Constable Rane walked in and whispered something in Sharma's ears. When Sharma left the hospital with Rawat and Constable Rane, his face was grim.

Chapter 41

"Secret griefs are more cruel than
public calamities."

—Candide, Voltaire

Gayatri Bhardwaj was in her drawing room sitting in the chair where her husband had sat the last time Sharma and Rawat came to visit him. Her face gave nothing away. Only the way she sat rigid in her chair pointed to the strain she was going through. Leela kaki was sitting next to her mistress's chair on the floor, her face weary. There was an air of accusation in her eyes, the way she looked at Sharma, as if she held him responsible for the tragedy that had befallen her mistress. As Leela kaki started to get up, Gayatri Bhardwaj placed a firm hand on her shoulder and spoke to Sharma: "I would appreciate it if you could leave right away. There are no police formalities to carry out in my house. If you hurry to the police station, you will be able to reach it in time to take an important call from the honourable joint secretary in the state ministry."

Her voice was stony, the words straightforward. For Sharma the message was clear—As Mrs. Bhardwaj, she had high contacts in bureaucracy. Should he make her husband's suicide public knowledge, he will be sure to risk his police job.

He thought of her unhappy history, her childlessness, her unfaithful husband. He felt pity for her.

"Very well, madam," he answered ignoring Gayatri Bhardwaj's threat. "Now, if you would be kind enough to show me where Doctor Sahib's body is at present? I can find my way around the house myself if you don't mind."

Gayatri Bhardwaj looked at him icily. "It could cost you dearly, SP Sharma. You don't want to get transferred to some godforsaken place away from your family."

"I'm aware of the consequences, madam. But duty always comes first. And I have to do my duty now." He bowed his head slightly.

"As you wish," she said in a calm voice, then nodded to Leela kaki and, while resting her head against the back of the chair, closed her eyes.

Sharma turned to Rawat who opened his mouth to say something but closed it immediately. Knowing how his boss's mind worked, Rawat knew it was futile to press him further about the matter. Nothing fuelled Sharma's resolution to carry on a task more than someone trying to obstruct him. Rawat knew Gayatri Bhardwaj's threat would only encourage Sharma to investigate Dr. Rajinder Bhardwaj's suicide. Sharma asked Rawat to check if the ambulance had arrived and followed Leela kaki to Dr. Bhardwaj's study to look at the body.

Dr. Rajinder Bhardwaj, unable to cope with the prospect of facing the rest of his life under the humiliating scrutiny of people's accusing eyes, had decided to end his life. He had hanged himself from the ceiling fan with a rope after hearing about Dr. Rudra's arrest.

Dr. Rajinder Bhardwaj knew his nephew had his confession on the tape and would waste no time getting him arrested for Devika's murder. His death was quick.

He knew people's reproachful eyes would follow his wife for weeks after his suicide. The scandal would die down within a few months leaving her to cope with the dreadful sympathy of the townspeople—the sympathy which would no doubt replace their earlier accusations and which Gayatri would find difficult to cope with. But he also knew she was a woman of great resolution. She would cope.

After the ambulance left with Dr. Rajinder Bhardwaj's body, Sharma came to see Gayatri Bhardwaj who was still sitting in the same chair in the drawing room. Her eyes were closed.

"You will have Doctor Sahib's body back in the morning, madam."

She opened her eyes, looked straight at Sharma and said, "You are not afraid of anything, SP Sharma."

"I feel afraid all the time, madam. But fear . . . it never gets a chance to get to me because I never have enough time to give it a chance." He paused. "And I'm very sorry for your loss."

Without waiting for Gayatri Bhardwaj's reply, Sharma turned and left with Rawat at his heels.

Cowards are the first ones to abandon courage when they're faced with any horror that threatens to befall them. They never shy away from inflicting misery on others, but hardly ever prepare themselves for the time when they're expected to pay for the consequences of their own doings.

Dr. Rudra stayed unfazed when Sharma told him about the charges against him for destroying the evidence in the murder of Mrs. Devika Singh Chaudhry. He stayed unconcerned when he was told about the discovery of the tape at his house and his uncle's suicide. But he looked at Sharma in disbelief when Sharma told him about Vasudha Haldar's close encounter with death and her narrow escape.

He must have been so used to just carrying on, oblivious to his wrongdoings, he must not have expected to get caught. Rudra's overconfidence wasn't unexpected though, Sharma knew from his years of experience in the police force. He had dealt with many criminals and knew they usually overestimate their own qualities and abilities. Rudra must have thought himself to be much cleverer than the police were; all criminals liked to think that.

When Sharma informed him about the other FIR registered against him in the police station for the attempted murder of Miss Vasudha Haldar under Section 307 IPC, he lost his composure. Tears flowed down his face in a constant stream which, Sharma thought with repulsion, were probably those of self-pity.

He took no time to confess everything. He was in Devika's flat when Dr. Bhardwaj came with the money. When Dr. Bhardwaj knocked, he hid behind the heavy curtains in the bedroom. Devika, who was reluctant at first to let Dr. Bhardwaj come inside, suddenly decided to amuse herself with the chance of getting uncle and nephew face to face. She asked Dr. Bhardwaj to come to her bedroom so she could count the money at leisure. But she never got a chance to call Rudra. Dr. Bhardwaj had come prepared and he wasted no time in strangulating her. It was a quick death. Rudra decided to come out of his hiding place immediately. It was his golden chance to get his uncle under his control. He suggested they arrange things a certain way to make it look like the work of a disturbed mind, to which his uncle agreed.

"But there was no entry for you in the entry register?" asked Rawat.

"There was no one at the front desk when I went to Devika's flat with her. I was on night call but Devika telephoned me earlier to say she had changed her mind and had no intention of splitting fifteen *lakhs* between us. She wanted to keep all the money for herself. She was getting greedier. I asked her to meet me outside the hospital. I tried to reason with her, but she just kept laughing. She asked me to accompany her to her flat to sort things out with her. She was in a strange mood, vicious as always but exultant. I had already done my rounds at the patient ward and knew I could get away with being absent for a couple of hours. No one would dare to ask me except for Rajinder *chacha ji* and he was already stressed at the time. Devika was blackmailing me; she knew about Urvashi, my wife and she had a photo from Urvashi's house where there was a garland of dried flowers around my picture; she knew everyone in Sumbhalpore including Urvashi thought I died in a car accident. I agreed to pay her to keep her quiet, but she was getting greedier and I had limited income. I asked her to get involved with Rajinder *chacha ji* so we could blackmail him. I sent anonymous letters to Gayatri *chachi*. I asked her for the keys to New Kanauji villa. I knew she would rather go there than give it to me; she had always hated me. To make sure she went to the villa that same evening, I left another anonymous letter in the mail box on my way back. That's how Devika and I had planned it. But Devika had her own agenda. She went too far ahead and informed Rajinder *chacha ji* and Gayatri *chachi* about her pregnancy. Obviously, she didn't know *Chacha ji* well enough. The honourable Dr. Rajinder Bhardwaj couldn't let her give birth to his child."

Clearly, he didn't know about Devika's fake pregnancy report, thought Sharma. He felt no need to disclose this information to the accused though.

"And later you decided to blackmail your uncle!" stated Rawat.

"I wanted everything that was my uncle's. It was my inheritance and rightfully so. I was the only son in the Bhardwaj family. But I knew of Gayatri *chachi's* hatred for me. I knew she wouldn't let *Chacha ji* name me as his official heir. I wanted money to open my own hospital in Shimla. So, I decided it was time for me to act. I was well prepared when I met *Chacha ji* later. I hid the tape recorder in my clothes. It wasn't difficult for me to talk about the murder and led our conversation a certain way to get *Chacha ji's* confession on the tape."

"What about the note we received at the police station with Devika's pregnancy report?" Rawat asked.

"I sent the note to the police station because I wanted you to look closely at him. He had already made a new will but refused to give me more money for the hospital. I had fifteen *lakhs* and he said I wouldn't get anything else until he decided to retire. I wanted him to get arrested for the murder so I could run Lifeline Hospital."

The man made a fine criminal and a finer coward, thought Sharma.

Chapter 42

"When you have eliminated all which is impossible, then whatever remains, however improbable, must be the truth."

—*The Case-Book of Sherlock Holmes*, Arthur Conan Doyle

Sharma reflected once more, angry with himself, how he had talked about the possibility of Dr. Rajinder Bhardwaj being the murderer with Rawat a few days after the murder.

"We discussed it, Rawat. We discussed it at the start, right after we came to know about Devika's affair with Dr. Bhardwaj. But we ignored it. We got embroiled in the complexities of Devika's past while Dr. Rajinder Bhardwaj's motive, obvious and straightforward, lay before us."

"She had offended many people, sir. We couldn't zero in on Dr. Bhardwaj."

"But we were right."

"It was done to make her quiet then?" Rawat asked.

"He probably wouldn't have done it if Devika hadn't lied about her pregnancy. He knew people would pounce on the scandal if she gave birth to his illegitimate child."

"But, he knew she wasn't pregnant. He told us so."

"He must have known about it, but not immediately. He must have learned from Dr. Kalpana's clinic. Or he might've bribed someone in the mortuary to get the information. You know, it happens."

"That means, he went to her flat well prepared!"

"It was a simple enough plan. Dr. Bhardwaj probably knew about Devika's divorce case. He knew of her tendency to hurt others. Any person could have killed her as far as the police were concerned. He took out fifteen *lakhs* from the bank and carried it in a briefcase to her flat. He signed the register and talked to the watchman on duty as planned. Everything went smoothly until Dr. Rudra, who was already there to see Devika, came out of his hiding place after his uncle had strangulated Devika. That's when Dr. Bhardwaj lost control of things. Dr. Rudra suggested they arrange things a certain way to make it look like the work of a disturbed mind. Dr. Bhardwaj couldn't say no. He meekly followed Rudra's instructions."

"But there was no entry of Dr. Rudra in the register, sir. He visited Devika a few times and we didn't find his name in the register."

"He was always careful to enter the building unnoticed. He was cautious by nature."

"He didn't know Devika was lying about her pregnancy. That's why he sent us Devika's pregnancy report. She lied about her pregnancy when she told him about Mrs. Bhardwaj's arrival at the villa and the discovery of Dr. Bhardwaj's affair," said Sharma. "Devika showed him the false pregnancy report just for amusement. Remember, no one was her confidant; the deepest secrets she kept to herself. Nothing she did or said was spontaneous. Everything she told others had been deliberate, to achieve something or to amuse herself."

"But why did Dr. Rajinder Bhardwaj leave from the back door, if he had pre-planned his arrival witnessed by the watchman? That made us suspect him."

"My guess is as good as yours. I believe Dr. Bhardwaj saw Gayatri Bhardwaj walk to the building, and he left from the back door, or it could be just Dr. Rudra's idea. Dr. Rudra didn't leave immediately. He searched for the album that Devika had with his picture and left only after finding it."

"But sir, according to Dr. Sidhu, the killer was left-handed; her findings are never wrong. We know Dr. Bhardwaj is right-handed."

"Dr. Bhardwaj was ambidextrous, a person who could use both his hands with equal ease. He went to Devika's flat with the intention to kill, and he had thought out everything in advance. He knew we would be looking for a left-handed assassin. He was not a forensic pathologist, but he was a doctor and a highly intelligent man."

"What made you suspect Dr. Rajinder Bhardwaj, sir, when things were looking bleak for Dr. Rudra? We had zeroed in on him."

"After I visited Devika's mother and learned about the jewellery, I was sure that Devika had been extorting money from someone who worked in the hospital. Why would she carry pricey jewellery in her purse otherwise? Nurse Vasudha Haldar talked about how Dr, Rudra couldn't stand Devika, but Dr. Namita and Mrs. Sarveen Tomar saw them talking cosily. We checked Devika's passbooks. We knew during the last eight months, she had a fixed amount of money deposited in her account on the fifth of every month. The thought that it was Dr. Rudra Bhardwaj from whom Devika had been extorting money came to my mind, and this was confirmed after I visited Urvashi. But Dr. Rudra doesn't earn much money, not the kind that he could afford to deposit such a significant amount every month in her account."

"We checked Dr. Rajinder Bhardwaj's finances. He had taken out fifteen *lakhs* before Devika's murder but we couldn't find any fixed monthly transactions from his account. But there was so much going on, sir, we almost forgot that angle," said Rawat.

"Yes, with all the difficulties that we had to face to first trace Devika's family and later Urvashi, we almost forgot about the mysterious source of the monthly deposits in Devika's account. Dr. Rudra, with his murky past, had become our main suspect. I remembered the first time we visited him at his house, he was confident about being the sole heir of his uncle's wealth. But he was not close to his uncle. I could see Dr. Rajinder Bhardwaj bequeathing all his wealth to his only nephew but not Mrs. Gayatri Bhardwaj. She has her own nephews and nieces and she would definitely be interested in letting them get some part of her husband's wealth. I asked Hari Prasad, the district court clerk, to make inquiries in the matter. He knows people and is good at getting this sort of information.

A week after the murder, Dr. Bhardwaj had instructed his family lawyer to draw up a will and name Rudra Bhardwaj as his sole heir with the exception of the Bhardwaj house and a small tea estate reserved for his wife, Gayatri Bhardwaj. Hari Prasad telephoned me immediately after he got hold of that information, but we were busy with Vasudha Haldar at the time. He called me again in the evening and passed on the information. Dr. Bhardwaj is only fifty-five, still young. Why would he make a sudden will, and at a time when things were stressful for him and his wife? Only if he was forced into it. Dr. Bhardwaj was too intelligent to yield to any threat without substantial proof. I knew Rudra must have something in his possession that forced his uncle to draw up a will. Finding the tape at his house was not entirely a hunch. I remembered how he was in a hurry to put away the tape recorder and cassettes when we visited him at his house. I just made a connection and it paid off."

"The woman had it coming, sir. If Dr. Bhardwaj hadn't killed her, she could have died at the hands of Dr. Rudra some day. I wonder what stopped him from doing so? He is the sort of person who would kill even his own flesh and blood for money."

"He probably had thought about that, but he is devious and sly. Cowards always are. They stay in the shadows, hide and wait for the opportunity to strike."

"Dr. Rudra will inherit the Bhardwaj wealth now, sir. Even if he goes behind bars, he will come out in a few years," said Rawat.

"Dr. Bhardwaj annulled it yesterday," replied Sharma.

Dr. Bhardwaj must have made up his mind to end his life, thought Sharma. Otherwise he wouldn't have nullified his will and put everything back in Mrs. Bhardwaj's name.

"Sir. . . Gayatri Bhardwaj didn't want the matter of her husband's suicide to get out, but the town is buzzing with the news as it became a police matter." Rawat said hesitantly.

"Yes?"

"Sir. . . the telephone call from the state ministry, the one Gayatri Bhardwaj mentioned?" Rawat was still a little unsure of his boss's mood. "Do you think you will get another transfer order from headquarters?"

Rawat was used to Sharma's difficulty with those in the bureaucracy at top but still he was very pained. It seemed entirely unreasonable to him, a sad sign of the times, that a man should be made to suffer because he had high principles.

"I haven't received any such notice yet, Rawat. Usually they are fairly quick to issue the transfer order." Sharma looked at Rawat's relieved face. "Maybe they are getting tired of moving me around all the time."

Rawat grinned happily at Sharma.

The doorbell rang. Leela kaki came to find Gayatri Bhardwaj who still hadn't moved from her chair in the drawing room.

"I have asked Rani to get your clothes ready, *choti bahu*. People have started to arrive."

"You used to call me *choti bahu* when I came as a new bride to this house, *kaki.* Why did you stop saying that? It has been years since you called me *choti bahu.*"

"Twenty-two years!" Leela kaki pointed to the outside door, handed her a tall glass of apple juice, and said in a firm tone, "Now, take this juice to your room and get ready, *choti bahu.*"

She watched her mistress gravely as she climbed the stairs to her upstairs bedroom.

What a strange thing to have happened, thought Gayatri as she looked at her reflection in the mirror in her bedroom, the room she had shared with her husband for more than two decades.

The more she thought about all the events, the more she felt afraid of the consequences of her husband's careless digressions.

She thought of her arrival outside Devika's apartment building on the day of her murder, her husband, ashen-white, getting in his car and driving away, and her own reluctance to see Devika afterwards, fearing the worst. Her fears had been confirmed the next morning.

She heard a clatter of familiar voices outside. Her brother and *Bhabhi* had arrived.

She covered her head with the *pallu* of her white *saree.* She thought about that dark-eyed nurse whom she had seen flaunting the same peacock-blue *saree* her husband had gifted her on their fifteenth wedding anniversary. She thought about the women in her husband's life whom she had never met but knew about their existence. She also realized how lonely she had felt all those years.

She thought of her husband's handsome face, his illicit liaisons with Devika, her own arrival at the villa, and wondered if his encounter with her that day had been stained with half the sorrow that she herself felt now.

She thought of the initial years of their marriage and hoped she would be able to forgive him some day.

She thought about how they both had become strangers after the years of his betrayals, and her reluctance to ask questions for fear of hearing lies, and how—for the same reason—she hadn't questioned him about the night of the murder. Instead, she had kept a watch over him, followed him to their family lawyer's office, and learned about his new will. She had hated him then. She had hated him more than ever for letting her down once again and leaving everything to Rudra.

She had decided it was time to break her silence then, years of stoic silence. She had thrown the legal papers at his face and demanded he set things right. And he had obeyed. He had obeyed. For the first time in decades, she had asked for something and he had felt no qualms in giving it to her.

If only she had asked much earlier. . .for something else: his loyalty, his love. He might have given it to her. But she had never asked. And now it was too late. She would never know.

Glossary

A

Almirah: Wardrobe

Aloo gobhi: Vegatarian dish made with potatoes, cauliflower and Indian spices

Aloo matar: A Punjabi dish from the Indian subcontinent which is made from potatoes and peas in a spiced creamy tomato-based sauce.

B

Babu ji: Father

Badi bahu: Older daughter-in-law

Bali: Earrings

Baraat: Groom's wedding procession

Beta: affectionate term for son or daughter

Bhabhi: Sister-in-law (Brother's wife)

Bhai saab: Brother

Bhandara: Devotees prepare food on large scale as a religious offering to gods.

Bhayia's: Brother's

Bindi: A decorative mark worn in the middle of the forehead by Indian women. (Source Wikipedia)

Bua: Paternal aunt (Father's sister)

C

Chacha: Uncle (Father's younger brother)
Chacheri behen: First cousin
Chachi: Aunt (Father's younger brother's wife)
Chandan: Sandlawood
Chole: Chick-peas curry.
Choti bahu: Younger daughter-in-law
Chowkidar: Security guard

D

Dada: Paternal grandfather
Dahi: Yogurt
Dal makhni: A vegetarian dish of whole black lentil, red kidney beans, butter and cream.
Dal tadka: Yellow lentil cooked with turmeric and spices.
Damad: Son-in-law
Deodar: Cedar tree
Devrani: Sister-in-law (Husband's younger brother's wife)
Dhabha: Roadside restaurant
Diwali: Festival of lights

G

Ghod bharai: Baby shower.
Greh Pravesh: Bride's first-time entry into the house

H

Haveli: House
Holi: Festival of colours

J

Jagrata: A Hindu ritual: all-night vigil in honor of various goddesses

Janamashtmi: An annual Hindu festival that celebrates the birth of Krishna.

Jhumke: Earrings

Jija ji: Brother-in-law (Sister's husband)

K

Kaki: Aunt

Kamarband: A piece of jewelry women wear around the waist, a waist band

Kangan: Bracelet

Kulfi: Ice-cream

Kundli: Astrology chart

L

Lado: Darling, dear

Langot: Cloth diapers

Lassi: Yogurt based drink; blend of yogurt, water, spices

M

Ma: Mother

Mama: Maternal uncle.

Manglik dosha: In Hindu astrology, an astrological combination that occurs if Mars is in the 1st, 2nd, 4th, 7th, 8th, or 12th house of the ascendent chart. A person born in the presence of this condition is termed a manglik. (Source Wikipedia)

Mausi: Maternal aunt

MBBS: Bachelor of Medicine, Bachelor of Surgery

Mayaka: Paternal place

N

Nana: Maternal grandfather
Nanad: Sister-in-law (Husband's sister)
Nimbu pani: Lemon water

P

Paisa: Money, a penny
Palak paneer: Indian cottage cheese in spinach gravy.
Pandal: Hall
Pushtaini: Inherited

R

Raita: An Indian side dish of yogurt containing chopped cucumber or other vegetables, and spices.
Raja: King
Rajmah chawal: Red kidney beans in a thick gravy with many Indian whole spices, served with rice.
Roka: Pre-engagement ceremony
Roti: Flatbread

S

Sadhna-cut: Front bangs that cover the forehead (A hairstyle made famous in India by actress Sadhna in 1960's.)
Saree pallu: The loose end of saree.
Sasural: In-laws family
Sati pratha: is an obsolete funeral custom where a widow immolates herself on her husband's pyre or take her own life in another fashion shortly after her husband's death.
Sugar: Common name for diabetes

T

Tandoori roti: Oven cooked flatbread.

Thali: Plates.

Thanda gola: Frozen slurpee

Tika: Jewelry to place on hairline with a drop pendant that sits on forehead.

V

Vishwamitra and Menka: In Hindu mythology, Menka is considered one of the most beautiful of the heavenly fairy. She was sent by Indra, the king of the gods, to break the severe meditation undertaken by Vishwamitra

Acknowledgments

First of all, I would like to thank my editors. A special thanks to excellent Janet Laurence for her generous time and brilliant insights. She helped me unravel many problems in my storyline and taught me so much about writing. Thanks to Eloise Wood for her professional guidance. My sincere gratitude to Claire Rushbrook for her time and expert advice.

Thanks to Jyoti Singhal and Prakash Baruri for answering my endless queries. I would like to thank Samantha Cooper and Chris Howell for their skilled technical assistance.

Thanks to the many people who saw me through this book: to all those who beta read, shared their insights, and provided feedback.

To my family: without you, this book would never find its way to the world. Thank you for being there for me and be a constant source of motivation. Thanks to my brother, sister-in-law, my beautiful nieces (who think the world of me), and my brother-in-law. A special thanks to my father and sister for their nonstop nagging that helped me to complete my book. I owe a huge thanks to my mom who taught me to take it easy.

To my beautiful, awesome children: thank you for being the best and teaching me the meaning of selfless love. Hugs. I love you.

Thanks to my third child, the 84 lbs furry pup, without whose they-can't-come-crazier-than-me personality, this book would have been finished in half the time.

And finally, to my husband: without you, this book may not have been written (I could have finished it a year earlier, though, if not for your inability to lift a finger around the house). There's so much to thank you: for your confidence in me that I could write: for all those hours spent on reading every single word of my manuscript despite your strong aversion to any sort of fiction: for your not-so-gentle-critiques that helped me to do better: for your constant insistence that the book was terrific, and I was terrific. I would never have come so far without you by my side.

About the author

Neena H. Brar lives in Edmonton, Canada with her husband, two children, a highly energetic German Shepherd, and a lifetime collection of her favorite books. A hermit at heart, she's a permissive mother, a reluctant housekeeper, a superb cook, and a hard-core reader. Tied to Deceit is her debut novel.

You can connect with Neena on Facebook at facebook.com/NeenaHBrar or on Instagram @bookaddictnwriter. You can also visit her website, neenabrar.com to get more information about her upcoming projects or to read her blog.

CPSIA information can be obtained
at www.ICGtesting.com
Printed in the USA
BVHW071343301018
531512BV00001B/3/P